Amethyst Saga Book 1

Amethyst: Rise to Piracy

K. L. Dimago

Butterfly Books Publishing

Want to Learn the Tale Behind Amethyst's Trusty First Mate?

As a thank you for getting your copy of *Amethyst*, I'm *giving you* this free novella.
Learn how the fae conquered the mages, enslaved Darien, and how he partnered with Amethyst.

Go to: *kldimago.com/darienstale* and download *free* today!

The Amethyst Saga

-*-

Book 1
Amethyst: Rise to Piracy

Book 2
Ametrine: Twists of Fate

Book 3
Iolite: A New Era

Book 4
Tourmaline: The Pirate's Daughter

Summary: Amethyst must overcome an abusive past while proving herself capable at sea. Finally, she takes control of her life, determined to not just be free, but be reputable and respected.

www.kldimago.com

Praise for Amethyst: Rise to Piracy:

"Rarely do you get a chance to work with a writer as dedicated to their creation as K.L Dimago. The world of Aseath is one of the most vivid I've encountered - a magical reimagining of 17th century life on the seas. K.L. knows every inch of it and those details are richly outlined in *Amethyst: Rise to Piracy*. Throw into that world a cast of terrifically flawed characters and the stage is set for a swashbuckling adventure! The blend of action, magic, and a hint of romance makes for a novel that stands superbly on its own, as well as being an illuminating first in the saga." - Jake Waller

"If you like Pirates of the Caribbean then you will love these books. This book is well written and thought out and leaves you guessing!" – Desi Ledesma

"Fantasy lovers will enjoy this book about a fae who chooses to become a pirate." – Amazon Reviewer

N
W E
S
Northern Realm
Northern Seas
Tysek
Port Bl
Vorda I
Bohai Isle
Aeidahs Isles
Port Drelle
Orlesee
Sout
Se
World of Aseath

Amiob Oiil
Ieta Iezril
Clozza
Fae Territories
aise
sle
Port Mirka
Braza Isles
hern
as
Adriac
Aeoumrese

Table of Contents

Acknowledgments...xi
Runaways 1
The Silver Lady 15
To Become a Pirate...35
The Raven's Call..51
Breaking the Mold..73
Taking a Stand..91
A Name is a Reputation..113
To Become a Captain..135
Commandeering..149
The Ship Is Mine..161
The Phoenix Lad...183
Sanctuary 199
The One Who Calms the Nightmares...213
The Pirate's Letter..235
Glossary..245
About the Author 247
More by This Author...249
Thank You! 251

Acknowledgments

To my children and all of their playful love of pirates and swordplay. I hope when they're old enough, they'll enjoy this story.

To my husband, who continues to put up with my relentless pursuit of my passion for writing and patiently encourages me.

To my dear friend, Matt, for all of his support, excitement, encouragement, and input. Without him, this book would not be what it is today.

To Jake Waller, for combing through the manuscript as many times as it took to hash out the story and take it from good to amazing.

And finally to the special friends that gathered around me to push this book to success and celebrate every moment with me: Desi Ledesma, Shawn Carroll Morris, Kathleen Foster, Lisa Ceizyk, Elizabeth Pomawski, Kathryn Rebernick, and JoAnn Jeffrey.

A sincere and heart-felt thank you.

Runaways

"*A*methyst..."

A gentle groan escaped her lips.

"Amethyst!" a soft male voice hissed. A hand tugged at her shoulder.

She slowly opened her eyes, instantly recognizing her personal servant's angular and familiar face. His silvery eyes, ever calm and penetrating, were fixed on her golden ones, his form seated on the bed next to her. The room was dark, though she was still able to make out the elegantly designed dresser on the far wall and the canopy draped over her bed frame.

"Hurry. We must leave now," he whispered, rising to his feet. Darien was dressed simply in britches and a loose off-white shirt covered by a dark cloak. He held another cloak toward her in his pale hand.

Amethyst nodded and moved out of the bed, her thick eggplant-colored ringlets tumbling over her pale shoulders and across her face. She groaned again softly as she commanded her muscles to move. She ached, her curved body sore from the most recent abuse she suffered at the hands of her husband.

Her soon to be ex-husband.

She pushed away images of his hands mercilessly grasping her body and focused on the present. Amethyst was grateful that she at least slept in a different room than the monster who called himself her spouse.

Kneeling down, she grasped a small sack she had prepared before she had gone to bed. She had slept in clothes like those Darien wore on purpose. Slowly, she stood, donning the cloak he had presented. She was significantly shorter than he was, but the cloak somehow made her feel even smaller, and safer, as if it hid her away from the world.

At last, Amethyst nodded once more, this time confirming she was ready.

They moved toward her window, the night air drifting in through the rippling curtains. With a soft whisper of a concealment spell from Darien's lips, his eyes began to glow. Magic, something that flowed through the world of Aseath. Only some of the races could use it, including herself as a fae and Darien as a mage.

She didn't trust using her magic at that point. She was afraid that her husband, Merrick, would sense it. They were connected, after all, even if she despised it. So instead, she was trusting in Darien's abilities, even if he was less powerful. It was up to him now.

Getting away from the house was the easy part. Merrick believed he had her completely under his thumb and that she would never betray him. Perhaps he believed she feared him too much to try anything, so a guard was never something he had posted. Or perhaps he'd merely wanted to lessen the number of people who knew the truth of his nature. Amethyst was not entirely sure of his thoughts, but he had underestimated her will.

They slipped out of a window on the far left side of the house and made the short drop to the grassy earth below. The mansion itself was brown, white and elegant. It featured high posts leading to a single balcony on the front and had a spacious interior with numerous unused rooms. It stood somewhat lonely surrounded by a cobblestone pathway expanding from the front into a small gated courtyard with a fountain in its center.

The lights from Clozaa, the largest city in the fae territories, glimmered in the distance as they made their way down the slope and onto the pathway leading away from the house. The large forest at the edges stretched from the mansion down the territory and almost to the shore and also expanded northward across the fae lands. It separated Clozaa and the palace from other fae provinces as well as conquered territories.

Amethyst tried to keep her breath controlled as they raced along the pathway and into the city. As they made their way past several houses and statues, Darien's spell became more evident. They couldn't completely mask the sound of their footfalls against the old cobblestones but with the dark cloaks and Darien's magic, their forms were mere shadows in the torchlights.

Whether hidden or not, Darien grasped her arm and led her away from the streets, seeking the safety of the grassy landscape and towering trees of the large forest. Even with magic, the streets were too risky.

The trees dotting the rolling hills and expanding beyond the city provided shadowy coverage, their branches intertwined high above like countless archways. As soon as they were beneath the trees, Amethyst's breaths became shorter, fog escaping in small puffs in front of her. Her feet barely made a sound over the grass as opposed to the streets. She couldn't stop, couldn't look back. She knew they had to make it to the harbor before sunrise, or else she'd never escape this dreadful place. Truly, Darien was her only reassurance; he was her loyal servant and now her only friend.

She spared him a glance. His gaze was focused on the landscape ahead, and he had the sack of goods draped over his left shoulder.

In the darkness, Amethyst was grateful for the time she had spent playing along this very pathway as a child. Though not often used by anything other than game and wild animals, the worn trail was her guide to freedom.

They broke free of the tree line and continued down the hills. Amethyst was now able to make out the port and the market by the shore. Just as they reached the torch-lit road, the whisper of their cloaks rippled as they pulled their hoods further down their faces. No one could know they were here. They couldn't afford witnesses.

They moved through the market silently. Amethyst was close enough to hear Darien's breath. Against the horizon, several dark forms of merchant ships lined the harbor.

Now was their chance.

They slipped through the shadows of the buildings toward the beach. Dark clouds shielded the moon and stars from illuminating the sea and more importantly, their figures. Amethyst's first instinct was to move toward the dock, but Darien's hand gripped hers, his other gesturing toward the water.

'*It will be cold, but I'd rather a chill than be caught,*' Amethyst thought. She nodded in response to Darien and silently followed him into the waves. She sucked in her breath as the coldness gripped her, but she pushed forward, the prospect of some level of comfort aboard a ship keeping her going.

Soon, they were nearing one of the ships. It had an amber hull, illuminated by moonlight. Its sails were raised, but she could tell they were pale in color. Rising from the bow, the figurehead of a siren gazing outward with mouth open in song was carved into the wood. Amethyst didn't waste time looking at other details.

She heard Darien mutter something in his native tongue and his eyes took on a soft glow. Immediately, a small orb of light appeared over the surface of the water in front of them. The light danced, floating along the hull of the ship.

Part of her had wanted to slip in through the gun deck, but there was a chance they would be noticed if someone were there. She scanned over the wood quickly until she spied a hatch on the side of the hull toward the stern.

A small smirk slipped over her lips. Amethyst motioned and she heard Darien whisper again, the light vanishing as quickly as it had come.

She moved as quickly as her body allowed toward the hatch and after climbing several feet, she slipped inside. Darien soon followed.

The hatch led to a rather tight but short tunnel in the frame of the ship and a trapdoor on the third deck, which opened to a long hall lined with doors for the sailors' cabins. She peeked out slowly, and seeing the coast was clear, lifted herself onto the deck and then moved aside so Darien could follow suit.

She took in the deck quickly. They didn't have time to explore it.

Amethyst was glad she and Darien had planned the entirety of their escape before leaving. Verbal communication was out. The slightest noise could alert someone to their presence before they were ready. Instead, they made their way toward the back of the hall to a small stairway that led to the bottom deck where the merchandise was stored. It was stock full with barrels and crates of various goods.

Amethyst smiled at Darien. They were in the clear, at least for now. They carefully made their way past the crates, doing their best not to disrupt anything. There was a decent space against the other end of the deck near the bow of the ship.

Darien whispered another spell to draw the water from their cloaks and return it to the sea. The cloaks became makeshift blankets, and using each other for warmth, they curled against the hull and went into a light sleep.

Amethyst awoke with a start, panicking at the grip of the hand against her mouth. She looked around frantically. *'Oh,'* she thought as she took in the crates and barrels, the wood of the ship and finally Darien's face. She shoved his hand from her. "Just because I gave you your freedom doesn't mean you can do with me as you please," she snapped. He didn't deserve it, but she still felt shaken.

He shook his head. "You were having a nightmare. I didn't want you to scream and give us away. Not until we're ready to be known."

"Oh," she said, out loud this time. Her gaze fell and she curled her knees to her chest, her long pointed ears drooping against her head.

"It's nearly morning. We'll be leaving port soon," Darien said.

Amethyst nodded, gazing intently forward. She was finally leaving behind the nightmare she had lived for so long, yet she couldn't help but wonder if she would ever truly be rid of it.

The ship rocked, the dull sound of waves crashing against the hull constant. They had gotten away. They'd planned their escape and gotten this far. But... now what?

Amethyst's mind wandered to her life over the last few years since her marriage.

She couldn't go back to the fae territories. Not ever. She wondered if she could make a life for herself at sea. If nothing else, she had to try. It was truly the first time she had made a decision that was entirely her own. All her life she had been told what to wear, what to eat, when to eat, even when to sleep. Her parents, the lord and lady of the fae people, had always instructed her life. Her purpose. What they expected from her. They had even chosen her husband.

Among the fae, men were hard to come by. The females outnumbered them, and thus the competition between fae women often caused violence. Once a female found a proper male to marry, she would become extremely territorial lest another woman try to steal him away. Polygamy was forbidden. There could only be one female for one male. Thus finding a spouse was even more important.

Amethyst had felt these same urges even toward her abusive husband, and she had hated it. She knew his true reason for desiring her: to use her for magic. For power and gain and control. And she would've been perfectly happy if he had gone for someone else. But he hadn't. He had, instead, saw it better to torment her and attempt to use her.

Given the smaller amount of males, her father had guaranteed her marriage, and she knew she would be expected to produce male heirs, or males in general, to help with the next war. There was always war.

Merrick had been a trusted advisor to her parents. Before their marriage, no one had any idea of his cruel nature. His smooth tongue and manipulative ways, as well as his supposed alignment with her father's desires, had given him both status and position.

Under her father, the fae kind had seen an era of peace, though fae history was riddled with battle and conquest. Even the main road to the palace was lined with great figures of fae history – many of them fallen warriors or great leaders of battle.

One race that had long been subdued was the mage. They were seen as lesser in their use of magic and the fae had forced them into slavery. Darien had been assigned to Amethyst as her personal servant when in the fae palace and had accompanied her into her marriage. He was the sole witness to her abuse. He had often tended to her afterward, and had helped greatly in planning her escape. In return, she had granted him his freedom. Freedom to do whatever he pleased. He had told her he would stay by her side for her protection until he was assured she would be completely safe and taken care of.

She hadn't protested.

She wondered if her parents had any idea of the hell Merrick had put her through. Merciless pain as he daily forced her to do whatever he pleased and used her for his own gain. She had always been a fiery sort. Rebellious, stubborn, and wanting to do things her own way. Despite the severe abuse she had suffered at the hands of her husband, her will had remained intact. She refused to be broken, but he had ensured her silence through his abuse. He had told her that should she ever whisper a word to anyone, she would find herself dead.

Well he was her ex-husband now.

Not ever again, she secretly promised herself, would she submit herself to such pain. She would be in control. She would make her own decisions. She would dictate her own life. Now the only question was how?

Amethyst silently prayed that her answer would come swiftly.

Darien pulled open the sack he had brought and began eating a piece of fruit. He offered her some, but she waved her hand. "I'll eat later. Right now, we need to focus. And plan our future."

"You should try to rest as much as you can," Darien responded, "And we can plan later."

Her gaze met his for a moment, and at last she gave in. He was right. She was exhausted, and they would have a while before reaching the next port.

Amethyst closed her eyes and drifted off.

For a long time even before her escape, nightmares had plagued her sleep. It seemed, despite her physical escape, that those nightmares had followed her. For several days, Amethyst slept when she could, though was constantly awoken by Darien trying to keep her from screaming in her sleep and alerting the sailors to their presence.

When she was awake, she tried not to replay the horrific events of her marriage in her mind. Instead, she kept herself occupied by talking with Darien.

They remained where they were, moving around only to stretch their legs and then returning to the space beyond the merchandise. They hoped to make another getaway once they reached the next port. Lying near the bow of the ship, they weren't spotted when the members of the crew went below deck to gather food for their meals each day. And, with all the merchandise, Darien and Amethyst had plenty to eat once the food they had brought ran out.

"Tell me about you, Darien," Amethyst said one day after she was certain no one else was on the same deck. It was something she had asked him on occasion before her escape. He had never really talked much about his past. Since she'd met him, he had always been reserved in general - soft spoken, kept to himself. During her marriage, she had been more focused on survival and had left him alone if he preferred. Now, she wanted to know about him, and she refused to let him simply brush it off as he always had.

At first, he merely smiled and shook his head.

"Come on... you must have something to share," she insisted.

After much persistence, Darien gave in. First, he reached into his shirt and removed an emerald pendant hanging from the silvery necklace about his neck. She had seen it a handful of times in the past, usually when it had accidentally slipped out from under his clothing when he had been tending to her after an episode from her ex-husband. It seemed he never parted with it.

"This was my brother's," Darien began, "It's all I have left of him. When I was a boy, my parents fought against the fae. My brother protected me and swore we'd always be together." A small, sad smile slipped across Darien's face. "In the end, we were torn apart. The fae conquered our territory, as you know. I have spent my life in servitude, first to the fae general that defeated our particular province, then eventually in the palace where I was assigned to you. I don't know if my brother lives, but I cling to this necklace in the hopes that someday, I'll be reunited with him. I used to use it to search for his magic print, but I have yet to find it. Besides, it's been decades. Perhaps I should let it go."

Amethyst remained silent. It was not unusual for such a long period of time to pass. Those races with access to magic in Aseath had long life spans with extremely slow age rates once they were fully grown. Darien appeared to be in his early twenties, by human standards, though clearly he was far older.

"You're free now," Amethyst said finally. "Perhaps now you can find him."

Darien shrugged. "Perhaps." Whatever he was thinking on the matter, he said nothing more. "I've never told anyone..." he trailed off.

"Your secret is safe with me," Amethyst said, assuring him with a smile.

"Rest," he instructed her, returning to their current situation more quickly than she would have liked.

She wasn't sure how much rest she would actually get, but she only nodded and closed her eyes.

"Oy, Cap'n! We got a couple o' rats!"

At the voice, Amethyst woke, peering upward through still somewhat groggy eyes. A large, burly man loomed over her, Darien restrained by two others behind him. Most of the merchandise that had been kept on this lower deck was gone. That must mean they were at the next port.

"We don' like stowaways," the burly man who had woken her said with a sneer.

Soon, the thud of boots resounded as the captain descended the steps. He was as burly as his men with a full beard and round features. He had a large brown hat and wore a large, tailored coat over his dark vest and britches. "Thieving the merchandise, are ye? Or perhaps seekin' free passage?" Pale brown eyes peered at Amethyst from under the brim of his hat.

Amethyst stood, thinking on her feet as she did so. She stared him straight in the face with a prominent frown, drawing from her days in the palace when she had tried to defy one of her parents' demands. "Neither. We seek to join you and your men and help around the ship. We can cook, clean..."

She stopped as the captain moved closer, his lips turning down and his rough hand grasped her chin.

Amethyst forced back the memories of her husband grasping her in just such a fashion. She had to keep it together if she wanted a fighting chance at her freedom.

The captain's brows furrowed. Perhaps he didn't believe her. After all, they had sneaked aboard in the midst of the night and hidden among the merchandise. His silence as he scrutinized her only tore at her nerves. Still, she kept her gaze as firm as she could.

"Alright," he said at last. "'m sure there be use 'round here for ye." There was a glimmer in his dark eyes and a slight smirk on the corner of his lip as he said the words.

"Both of us," Amethyst made a point of insisting.

"This scrawny lad?" the captain said with a laugh, stepping back slightly and gesturing toward Darien. He turned back to Amethyst, meeting her determined gaze. Perhaps he liked something about her, because he smirked and said, "Alright, but the momen' either of ye ain't pullin' yer weight ye'll walk tha plank!"

The other men laughed at this.

"Move it ye dogs," the captain said, pushing Amethyst toward the stairs at the opposite end of the deck.

The other men released Darien who moved quickly and up the steps behind Amethyst.

As soon as they reached the main deck, they blinked in the sunlight. Amethyst wondered exactly how long it had been since they had left Ieta Iezril, the main port off the coast of the fae territories. It had to have been at least weeks. She also wondered if her parents knew yet of her escape, if they had issued an order to find her. She wondered what Merrick's reaction had been.

The assumption Amethyst had made when awoken by the burly sailors below deck that they were at a new port proved correct. Where, she didn't know. The azure sea glistened, and the decks were alive with sailors moving merchandise – crates of food, commodities, clothing, and barrels of various alcohols.

"Darrell!" the captain bellowed as he summoned another man toward them. He had been on upper deck and leaped easily down to the main deck. He was not as stout as the others they had seen but had broad shoulders and toned muscles. He had hazel eyes and curled brown hair. "These two are the newest members of tha crew. Show 'em around, savvy?"

"Aye," Darrell said, moving past them, "Follow me then." He paused, moving toward the main mast. "Either of ye know anythin' 'bout a ship?"

Amethyst shook her head and Darien merely shrugged.

"Well ye better learn quick if ye want to last. What're ye names?"

"Thea," said Amethyst, terrified he would know her identity if she gave her real one.

"Ignatius," Darien said, following suit.

Darrell simply nodded and took them across the main deck. He showed them the lines, the rigs, and the second deck, also known as the gun deck. It had eighteen guns – nine on each side of the ship – which was enough to defend against an attack, but hardly a warship. Afterward Darrell showed them the cabins, the kitchen area, which he called the galley, and finally the last deck where they had stayed. "This is where we store the merchandise. As a merchant ship, we don't make our wages without it."

With each part, Darrell explained it briefly, its purpose and the duties involved. As he'd said, he expected them to learn quickly and didn't leave much room for question.

As they passed the cabins, Darrell showed them a spare cabin, "Ye can stay in this one."

There was no arguing about sharing the cabin. Darien had stayed with her before plenty of times as her servant. The cabin had a plain pair of bunks on one wall and a simple dresser on the other. The bunks each had a small pillow and a blanket. Amethyst climbed to the top one while Darien was content with the bottom. It wasn't much... but it was better than nothing.

The Silver Lady

Amethyst did not sleep much that night, tossing and turning and trying to avoid her nightmares. She rubbed at her puffy eyes as she heard the thud of boots outside the cabin door followed by a loud banging from someone's fist. Whoever it was moved on to the next cabin immediately after. She stood, ears drooped slightly against her head, and moved toward the dresser across from the bunks. Inside were a number of plain brown britches and pale seaman's shirts, all the same. She picked out a pair and donned them.

"Darien," Amethyst said, grasping his shoulder and shaking it lightly.

He stirred. How had he slept so well aboard the ship? She didn't ask. Darien got up and also donned the simple sailor's clothes from the dresser and afterwards, they made their way toward the main deck.

The sea was calm, glistening in the sunlight and a soft breeze caressed the hanging sails. Already, the deckhands were busy with their duties. Some sat in a small circle with sailor's palms - rounded tools like thimbles, sail needles and thread, and a large canvas over their laps mending the sail as they talked loudly and laughed.

Others were high above, checking the rigging and the masts as well as the other sails for tears and damage. The rest carefully worked with paint and paintbrushes in hand to prevent the wood of the ship from being directly exposed to the sea.

Amethyst had no previous knowledge of ships other than stories as a child and books she had read about them, but she found what she had read helped. She knew each of the duties were important daily needs to maintain the ship and keep it from rot or sinking in a storm.

Before she could ask, Darrell approached them, shoving simple mops and slosh buckets with scrub brushes into their hands. "Ye'll scrub tha deck and then ye'll find me fer yer next duties 'till ye learn a sailor's life," he said gruffly before turning sharply and walking away.

In Amethyst's life, she had done little hard work. But she was determined to do what it took to remain on the seas and never have to think of returning to her old life. She refused to be seen as unable to do her share. She moved toward the stern and after setting the mop in the bucket and removing the brush, she began to scrub the deck. Her ears twitched as some of the sailors laughed. She didn't know if they were talking about her, but she chose to ignore it.

The sun had risen significantly higher when she stopped, meeting Darien halfway across the deck. Without a word, they stood, dumping the contents of the buckets overboard and taking them in hand as they searched for Darrell. He was helping the men who had finished mending the sail to refasten it with the rigging.

Amethyst raised two fingers to her lips, preparing to whistle at them, but she stopped as Darien's hand rested on her arm. She glanced at him and he silently shook his head.

"Wait. Aboard the ship, we're no one yet. They'll beat you if they suspect disrespect," he warned. Amethyst frowned, but nodded.

Finally, Darrell descended the mast, and approached them, wiping sweat from his brow. "Blimey, the deck actually looks decent," he said with a nod as if to emphasize he meant the words. Had he been expecting less, Amethyst wondered?

"Thea, was it? Ye'll go below deck to tha galley. Ignatius, come with me," Darrell instructed.

Amethyst glanced toward Darien, and he offered her a reassuring smile. Amethyst had done very little cooking in her life. The offer she had initially made of cleaning she felt confident enough about. But the cooking... well she'd hoped Darien would have taken over in that area. She found a nervousness settling in her gut.

Whether she liked it or not, she had no choice now.

"Aye, aye," she said with a curt nod before turning and making her way below deck. She glanced back once to see Darien accompanying Darrell toward the bow where it seemed he would learn more of the rigging and repairs.

Below deck, the galley was positioned after all of the sailors' cabins against the bow of the ship. It was a small room consisting of an iron stove with bars about the top to prevent the pots from tumbling in a storm and a handful of cabinets with simple ceramic dishes for the crew. From the stove and running upward through the upper deck was a long pipe to prevent the stove fire from being a threat to the ship.

Amethyst took it in slowly, trying to collect her thoughts. It couldn't be *that* difficult, could it?

A large pot was already set on the top of the stove though it was empty. '*Stew! I can do that...*'

She grasped the pot, making her way to the bottom deck where she and Darien had stayed hidden. Amethyst placed the pot down and began rummaging through the barrels. Near the stern were fresh fruits and vegetables followed by bread, flour, salt, butter, cheese, dried beans, raisins, salted pork and beef, fresh water and finally more barrels than she could count of whiskey, rum, and wine. They had only just sailed from port, so it made sense the amount of provisions they carried. Yet she hardly knew what to do with all of it. How long did it need to last?

Instead of lingering, she grasped the pot once more and filled it with chunks of salted meat, some of the vegetables, and water from the barrels stored there. Finally, she returned to the kitchen and placed the pot on the stove. She started a fire beneath it, and sat back. Amethyst wasn't sure if she should find Darrell again, or merely wait, but she remained. If question arose, she determined she would claim she had to watch the food so it didn't boil over.

While she waited, she entertained herself exploring the small room she found herself in. Amethyst carefully studied the structure about the stove which seemed to prevent it from dipping and the pot's contents spilling repeatedly. She resisted the urge to touch it, and simply noted the curved iron rods fastened to the deck and the way the stove itself perpetually remained upright regardless of the ship's movements.

After several hours, she heard footsteps in the hall. She looked up, feeling her shoulders relax as she recognized Darien's familiar form and a reassuring smile on his lips.

"Thank goodness!" Amethyst said, turning sharply as if to suggest she wasn't as happy as her exclamation implied and crossing her arms.

Her ears twitched as she heard him chuckle softly, a sound she hadn't heard from him in a long time, and she turned toward him once more, quirking a brow.

"Do you need a hand?" he asked in his ever soft-spoken manner.

"It's only stew," Amethyst retorted, raising her chin. "Perhaps from now on you should do the cooking I offered, though," she added after a moment, letting her arms drop.

Darien moved forward, peering into the pot and gave her a sideways glance, a smirk tugging at the corner of his lip.

She stuck her tongue at him and sat back, huffing. "Darien, was this really such a good idea?"

"The crewmembers aren't as bad as they first seemed," he said softly, dipping a spoon into the stew and raising it to his lips. At first, he hesitated, and then gave a nodding approval.

Amethyst felt another wave of relief wash over her as he did so, "Oh really?"

"This is only a stop in our journey," Darien continued, not answering her question.

"Indeed," she said, moving toward him to peek into the stew.

"So... how is it you know so much about being on a ship?" she asked him. She sucked in her breath, wondering if he'd share or if he'd give her something cryptic. She hadn't failed to note the way he'd instructed her on proper behavior as the newest crewmembers, or the way he had nodded knowingly when Darrell had showed them around the day before.

He shrugged. "I spent a considerable amount of time as a cabin boy during my servitude to the fae general. He had gained his title through conquest both on land and sea and captained one of the strongest Fae Navy fleets. Perhaps his approval of me ultimately granted me the fortune of becoming your servant." Darien smiled at her again, and she released her breath slowly, giving him a nod. "Perhaps we should alert the crew it's dinner time?" she asked.

"Aye," he responded, gesturing toward the doorway.

Not long after, the crew sat in another room on the second deck at the mess table. The pot sat in the middle and the men helped themselves to the stew, eating it with the simple bowls and spoons. Some of their wooden mugs were filled with grog, as they called it, a mixture of rum and water while others simply drank whiskey.

Amethyst had filled her mug with rum alone, finding herself unwilling to drink the other options. If a life at sea was ahead of her, she determined she would at least drink as she pleased.

The following day, Amethyst and Darien once more had to scrub the deck. Afterward, instead of cooking, it was Amethyst that learned more of the lines, the rigging, and the mending of sails, while Darien was sent to the galley.

"Yer task is t' put up an' take down the sails," one of the burly men that had found them told her. He showed her how to climb the mast and complete her task, and then left her to her work.

Amethyst struggled, and she worked at it for hours. Sweat soaked her clothing and her muscles strained. By the evening, she swore she had completed the task enough times to be able to perform it in the worst of storms.

At the sound of, "Dinner!" Amethyst actually felt excited. *'Finally a break, at least,'* she thought. She began making her way toward the mess table when a firm hand grasped her arm. She looked up, gasping slightly at Darrell's face so near her own.

"Ye'll be dinin' with tha captain, Thea," he whispered, pushing her toward the captain's quarters.

Amethyst quivered at the physical contact, a knot finding its way into her stomach.

The door to the captain's cabin creaked as she slowly opened it and looked inside. It was dimly lit and much larger than the sailor's cabin she had slept in the past two nights.

"Ah, Thea," he said aloud, gesturing for her to sit at the table against the wall on the far side of the room.

Amethyst stepped forward, her fists clenching and her heart beginning to race.

"Tha crew tell me ye only drink the rum, eh?" he asked.

Amethyst nodded, taking her seat and grasping the mug already filled before her. She was satisfied as she tasted the familiar contents, though was somewhat surprised as she observed the meal before her. It was extravagant, with meats, fruits, vegetables, and breads. Clearly the captain dined well while his crew was left to manage. She wondered if this meal were prepared by Darien, or if the captain had someone in particular he trusted to prepare his meals. She also wondered if that even mattered.

Amethyst swallowed a lump in her throat, staring directly at the captain. "That's not a problem, is it?" she dared to ask.

The captain smirked, "No, lass, ye may drink it if ye please."

Amethyst began to eat, hoping the meal would settle her turning gut. "So, if you didn't summon me about the rum, what then?" she asked.

She watched the captain raise a brow and lean forward, leaning his cheek on his knuckles as he propped his elbow on the table. His gaze was plastered on her, but not making specific eye contact. "Tell me, lass... what exactly be the bond between ye and yer scrawny lad, eh?"

"Ignatius is a brother to me," she answered, though as soon as she said the words, she wondered if she shouldn't have said they were more than that. The knot in her stomach grew larger.

"Well that's a relief. Y' see... There aren't many a lass at sea, and we men grow lonely," he said after a moment.

Amethyst swallowed forcefully, the knot in her stomach only growing more violent. She recalled once more the interaction between them when the crew had first discovered herself and Darien below deck. It made sense.

"And what if I say no?" she asked, forcing herself to look at him defiantly.

"Well, ye'd no longer have a purpose aboard," he said. It was an unspoken threat, she knew. The captain's words were ringing in her ears: *"Alright, but the momen' either of ye ain't pullin' yer weight... ye'll walk tha plank!"* Had her escape been futile? Was this the sort of life she was destined for?

Amethyst shoved the thoughts aside. "Very well," she murmured, eating another bite from her plate and gulping at the rum.

"There's a good lass!" the captain bellowed, taking a swig of his own mug's contents and beginning to eat at his plate more heartily.

Amethyst no longer had an appetite, but she ate anyway, forcing it down her throat. It would be a long night, she already knew. Now, she understood why the captain had given so little resistance when accepting her to the crew.

After that night, Captain Rada began summoning Amethyst to his quarters on a frequent basis. She found that the rum was the only ease for her mind. With it, she began to fight back her trauma, or perhaps merely suppress it. She bit it back a little more each time and in doing so, secured herself and Darien's stay aboard the ship.

Nightmares continued to plague her sleep as well as growing fears of being caught and returned to the fae territories. Amethyst feared not only for herself but also for Darien. If he was caught he would not simply be returned to slavery. He would be executed as a runaway who had assisted in her escape.

They sailed from port to port, and Amethyst was glad their escape hadn't been riddled with more problems. They had yet to be found or even identified by those aboard other ships. She hadn't even seen the Fae Royal Navy.

As time passed, she and Darien settled into ship life and even picked up the way the sailors spoke, at least around the others. At first, Darien did much of the cooking Amethyst had promised on their discovery while she insisted on learning the maintenance and ship repairs and helped in sewing the crew's clothing as well when needed. Still, she learned quickly the cooking also as Darien taught her.

She also learned of the types of ships and how to recognize them. The ship on which they sailed was a bilander, a small merchant vessel with two masts, one square-rigged and the other lateen-rigged: a triangular shaped sail. It was called the *Silver Lady.*

Most importantly, Amethyst learned how to discern her location and where the various ports and land masses were across Aseath.

But despite everything she learned and the success of their escape, Amethyst felt unrest growing.

The wages were poor and the helpings to the merchandise small. She began to wonder if there would ever be more. Had their escape been foolish? Amethyst desired more strongly than ever a life of true freedom. A life where she could dictate her choices and live as she pleased without fear of an empty stomach or bedding those she didn't like.

Each night Rada called for her, she fought back the same knots in her stomach. Only the rum seemed to be any help at all.

In some ways, she did miss her life before, particularly bathing and certain more luxurious foods. Only the captain had such choices, and even then he was ruled by his merchandise and the laws of the governments he sailed under.

Perhaps she could leave this ship for another? There were plenty of merchantmen, what the sailors called the merchant ships, to choose from, and she had no doubt that after they had learned so much, they'd have little trouble being hired as a member of another crew.

But she knew life would be the same. Even their travel was dictated. Their journeys were mundane, moving and bargaining for merchandise.

Night had fallen and the sky was clear. They were sailing from the Braza island chain toward Adriac beyond the southeastern seas. At the moment, the seas were calm.

Amethyst lay in the cabin she and Darien usually shared. She was glad tonight hadn't been one where the captain had requested her.

She glanced toward the far wall which was the hull of the ship. This wasn't the life she had imagined... or desired. Surely she wouldn't be stuck like this now for eternity.

Boom! The distant sound of exploding cannon fire carried across the water.

Whoosh! The sound of the cannonball as it tore through the air and dove into the sea just near the hull was followed by a splash that slapped against it.

"Look out!" someone yelled above deck.

Amethyst jumped, sucking in her breath and sitting up. It was instinct... she stood and flung the cabin door open. Immediately she moved into the hall and raced up the steps to the main deck. The sailors were in a flurry and the captain's face was a brilliant red. "Lower the sails, lads! Turn tha ship into tha wind! We're goin' to outrun 'em," he snarled.

Amethyst rushed to the edge of the deck, peering outward. Sailing toward them was a dark brig. Its billowing flags had pale skulls and crossbones sewn into the tattered fabric and brilliant bursts of light glimmered and then faded in the darkness followed by thunderous booms of cannon fire.

Pirates.

Of course.

The merchant ship on which she sailed now was designed for speed and maneuverability regardless of wind direction. She wondered if it had been put to the test before her and Darien's arrival. She was about to find out.

She turned sharply and made her way toward the other sailors.

"Thea," one shouted, "Climb to tha crows' nest, lass! Ye can tell us how far we've gained on 'em."

She nodded and began to climb the mast to the basket which served as a lookout's post. As soon as she'd reached it, she waved her hand to the men below. "They can't follow," she shouted. "The wind's our aid," she added with a grin. Apparently the fact they could sail into it while most other ships couldn't had its advantages.

Yet Amethyst felt the blood drain from her face as she looked up once more. Just ahead, smoke was rising from the surface of the sea and it appeared as though the last light of what had been an enormous flame was being drowned out by the waters.

Had the men seen the flames on the horizon and been attempting to flee what they had known to be the cause of the wreckage? Or had they been approaching with goals to aid another ship and only then discovered the presence of the pirates? She reasoned to ask about it later.

There was no turning course now. They could only sail forward.

Would they find any survivors?

"Look out fer debris!" she called down, though she choked slightly, sucking in her breath as the wake of the wreckage first touched their ship.

Not much was left of the other vessel but pieces of wood and the tattered remains of whatever had been on board. She spied what appeared to be fine dresses, fabrics, and food that hadn't yet sunken or been devoured by fire. There were some vegetables and chunks of meat among a few other goods.

But that wasn't what concerned her. There didn't appear to be a single body floating in the ashen waters. Had they already fallen to ocean's bottom? Or were there no bodies to find in the first place?

Her curiosity to learn more prodded at her mind.

Amethyst climbed down to the deck once more. "Should we look for survivors?" she dared to ask.

"Nah," one of the other sailors said with a shrug. "It's the way of the seas, lass. And it's better ye learned it now than with yer heart attached t' someone. 'Specially wit' pirates. If there were survivors…" he paused a moment, "We'd o' seen 'em by now. Let's just get past these dark waters and be on our way."

Amethyst looked out toward the wreckage once more. Did the other sailors recognize the pirate ship they had met? Or was this what pirates did in general?

It somewhat reminded her of the nature of her people: to conquest and shed blood without concern for who might be caught in the midst of it.

Somehow, it rung true for a part of her. And yet… hadn't she desired to be free of that?

No.

It was simply her own freedom she cared for. Her own desires to live and do as she pleased without opposition. Or perhaps to simply know what it was to live as a woman without being dictated by those around her. That was her true goal. So she supposed ultimately, what she had seen didn't concern her.

She only nodded and returned to her cabin.

"Feast yer eyes, lads!" barked one of the crewmembers. It had been several days since their encounter with the pirates and the coast of Adriac was in sight. The white sands glimmered brilliantly in the sun, beckoning sailors closer with a seeming promise of potential wealth.

Adriac was known for its flat plains and expansive deserts. What mountains rose were quite bare, with mere shrubs and cacti to dot their rocky slopes with splashes of color. Some had argued the lack of green in the landscape lessened its beauty, though others believed its skies were unmatched in all of Aseath, and its true charm was merely different.

The ship rocked as it pulled in to the harbor of one of the ports. "Drop anchor!" was heard before the great chunk of iron was plunged into the sea.

Despite the fact it was one of the closer territories to the northern fae territories, Amethyst wasn't worried about being discovered. The fae had mostly left Adriac alone. The desert didn't suit their kind well at all. It was hot and dry and required great resources to traverse.

Still... as the crew made their way onto the docks, she couldn't deny the alluring beauty to the landscape that lay far beyond. It was almost a tempting challenge, for those who might dare to explore it, to see if they could conquer the desert.

Amethyst released her breath. Despite the notion of losing herself in the heart of this territory, she could feel in her gut that the seas were where she belonged. Even if she hadn't quite yet discovered where precisely on the seas, there was a stronger pull from the ocean than from the land. She had spent all her life ashore, and it had only brought her restriction and torment. There was something about the seas that promised true freedom. This land's promises were different. Perhaps there were those who would discover their bounty here. But she was not going to be among them.

Amethyst set to work helping the others with the task of moving barrels of goods off of the ship and toward the market, where they would be sold or traded, and then moving the new barrels of other goods onto the ship for the next port.

Captain Rada announced they'd spend the night at port and leave for their next destination in the morning. Amethyst didn't wait for him to summon her to his quarters. Instead, she and Darien explored the market near the shore. There was nothing she could afford to buy, but she enjoyed looking. She moved into one of the clothing shops, a light coming to her eyes as she traced her fingers along the various fabrics and selected a few dresses to try. There were two stalls at the back of the shop where she slipped one of the dresses on. For a moment, she stared at herself in the mirror. Would she ever be able to dress like a lady again, having chosen the sea?

Amethyst pushed the thought aside and returned the dresses to the shop keep. Afterward, she led Darien to one of the pubs. She didn't pay attention to its name. As she stepped inside, she noted a few round tables with wooden chairs and a handful of torches jutting out from the walls. There weren't many others present and she made her way toward the bar slowly. "Rum, please," she said softly, feeling uneasy about speaking louder in such an empty place. The barkeep only nodded and returned after a moment with a mug.

Darien shook his head when asked and simply sat beside her.

Neither of them spoke, each lost in their own thoughts. Their encounter with pirates continued to circle in Amethyst's mind. After she finished her drink, they returned to the *Silver Lady*. The moon was well on its way to its peak which meant Captain Rada would already be asleep, and Amethyst was eager for a night to sleep on her own.

The next morning, they set course westward toward Orlesce. She knew it would be months before they reached it. She wondered if they would cross paths with pirates again on the way there.

The first part of their journey was rather uneventful. Several weeks passed and Amethyst and Darien continued the daily hum drum of duties as merchant sailors. There wasn't even a storm to weather nor did they encounter any other ships. They passed the Braza island chain and another mass of land was coming in to view.

"Land ho, lads! We'll be makin' a brief stop." The lookout waved down at the others.

They were only halfway through the passage to Orlesce. Amethyst looked outward to what appeared to be an enormous island. "What is that?" she asked one of the sailors standing near her.

"Vorda Isle, lass. We'll stop on tha north side o' the isle and sail round that way."

She had heard of it in listening to others' conversations and had occasionally glimpsed it on the maps laid out on the captain's table. The island itself was mostly uninhabited despite being the largest island in Aseath. It was rumored to have ferocious creatures that guarded the center of the island, though it had two main ports: one to the north, and one to the southeast side.

The northern port, Blaise, was a merchant's port. Ordinary humans as well as various peace-seeking races had made somewhat of a home and living there from fishing and trades. The rumors and the land-barriers were said to keep them safe from the other port. Mirka. A pirate's port.

Mirka was avoided at all costs by merchants, army, and warships alike. At any given time, the nastiest of pirates could be within Mirka's harbor, and anyone caught could suffer a fate worse than death.

Amethyst silently wondered if the pirates left Blaise alone for reasons other than the supposed monsters. Perhaps they were content to allow the trades to continue in order to profit from them in other areas at sea.

As they neared the island, Amethyst grasped a spyglass and peered through it. If their bearings were correct, they were still on the eastern side. That meant that even if they were trying to avoid Mirka, she could still get a glimpse of it.

Through the glass, Amethyst spied several ships anchored in the bay. Some of the sails hung low and billowed gently while other sails were raised. Ashore were numerous bodies, mostly male. This didn't surprise her. What did was the way they were dressed. Their clothes were those of nobles with coats and vests and brilliant accessories. It was almost comical watching them lounge on the beach in such high-class clothing. What females there were had elegant dresses and their hair done up as if they were going to a ball.

Amethyst was a little baffled.

If she were a pirate... would she appear so amusing? Despite her desire to laugh, she couldn't help thinking they looked so free and that all of the things she desired would suddenly become attainable if she were a pirate.

As she shifted the glass across the beach, she noted the way they strutted proudly, laughing amongst themselves and carrying either bottles or fine glasses with them. It was almost as if they lived in a whole other world.

She closed the spyglass and put it away.

More questions rose in her mind. She compared the first experience she'd had when crossing paths with a pirate ship to the scene she'd just witnessed. And then she thought of the stories and tales. They were cutthroats. Bloodthirsty heartless barbarians who had their luxuries because they killed and slaughtered and took what they wanted with no thought or care to who they affected.

Was it possible that in order to achieve what she was looking for... she must become a pirate? It was laughable. She, who had once lived as royalty sinking to the lowest of criminals.

And yet...

If she managed to become a pirate, if she plundered and fought... would she gain everything she dreamed of? Of course, she'd have to also avoid being caught. But that was a whole other matter. She couldn't help a slight bemused smile to herself. Here she was fancying the idea of becoming one. It wasn't so far off, perhaps. The fae might be considered by those they had conquered to be just the same, though she had never desired to participate in any of the fae wars or conquests whatsoever. She had only ever desired a life of freedom and peace.

In the palace, and even worse with her ex-husband, she had had no freedom at all except that over her servants. And even then, they disobeyed her if her father had instructed something different than her will. Her parents had told her what they wanted from her. Her path in life. They had tried to force her to a destiny she never wanted.

As a pirate, she could do as she pleased, when she wanted to do it. They were barbarians. But they were free. In her mind, they could go where they wanted and though they plundered for goods, she determined if she ever did so, it wouldn't be out of greed but necessity. Rather than being forced to do ship maintenance to earn dinner or avoid the plank, it would be done to avoid boredom, and she couldn't help romanticizing it in her mind.

Perhaps as a pirate she'd have moments of excitement. But ultimately they would earn her the peace she longed for. Amethyst continued to think of her end goals. She knew she would not be content to merely take orders as a member of a pirate crew. If she did, she would still be longing for more control in her life. She thought of Captain Rada and how she was under his thumb.

What if she were a captain?

Her heart began to race at the thought. If she were, she decided she'd have a ship and crew like no other. She would require her crew have a certain level of respect and dignity. Perhaps she'd make a crew all her own that was both respected by others and also unique and unheard of as far as manners for a pirate. They would be proper, clean shaven, free of boisterous behavior and unnecessary flaunting of their drunken achievements through ruining others' lives.

'To become a pirate captain...'

Well to rule was also in her blood, she thought. But she had never had any desire for it, really. No. Instead of being a dictator, she'd build a crew that followed her out of that same trust and respect she would want them to have as beings. She would create a crew on a ship worthy of the fae people. She would be the royal maiden of her own ship.

But Amethyst was not so foolish as to think she could get there by merely wooing a few sailors. No. She must become a cutthroat as fierce as the worst of them to attain her goals. She must put her foot down and defeat anyone who would question her or think she couldn't handle her own. Otherwise she'd have nothing but mutiny and she'd find her ship and possibly even herself at the bottom of Davy Jone's Locker, as the sailors always said.

And she'd have to be careful that bloodlust didn't take hold. For the fae, bloodlust was a common problem. Any fae that partook in battle ran that risk. Human blood could replenish energy. Or rather anyone's blood could, though humans tended to have a particularly delicious appeal. And once a fae got a taste, they might begin to crave it. The fae weren't vampires. They didn't need blood. But they drank it as a sign of victory, power, and even during sexual encounters, though that was somewhat different.

Amethyst promised she wouldn't lose herself.

Surely, somehow, her ideal was possible.

The more she thought about it, the more she wanted it, dreamed of it.

But she must wait a little while longer, she knew. Next time they returned to Vorda Isle... by then, she'd be ready.

It would be several more days before they would reach the northern part of the island, though the mountain at the center of the isle remained visible, a constant dark shadow in the sky. Even from the distance, Amethyst could see the thick, dense forest stretching down the mountain to the beach.

She returned to her cabin. Before she could move forward, she must first tell Darien of her thoughts. Amethyst was hesitant, afraid he would suggest that piracy was not how she had romanticized it. But she had to try.

Darien lay casually on his bunk, his nose stuck in his current book. It was something he had picked up near the beginning of their sailor life, mostly on the nights he spent alone or the days the sailors were permitted off from their duties.

He looked up as she sat beside him on the small bed and his eyes met hers. Immediately, he closed the book, a soft thud as it closed resounding before he placed it down beside him. "What is it?" he asked.

Amethyst turned her gaze toward the opposite wall. "Do you feel happy with our current arrangements?" she asked. Throughout this time, Amethyst had insisted on retaining her proper speech around Darien, even if they spoke like the rest of the crew when they weren't alone.

"I'm content enough," he murmured. She felt his eyes on her face.

"Don't you desire more?" she pressed.

He was silent a moment. "Amethyst," he said simply, his tone almost firm with her.

She released her breath, "I think... we should leave this ship, Darien," she said, her words almost hurried. Now, she met his gaze once more, feeling determined. "Perhaps not at this exact moment. But we'll pool our wages, spar when we can for practice's sake, and we'll even practice using magic so we don't grow dull. And then we're joining a pirate crew."

At this, Darien raised a brow.

"Think of it, Darien! We won't be tied down by anything other than the whims of the sea and the ship we're a part of. And someday, I'm going to captain my own ship and live the way I please. I'll be captain, and you'll be my first mate," she said, unable to hold back the light in her eyes and the smile on her lips. "We'll have a ship feared, respected, and unlike any other at sea!" She paused, "And perhaps once we get there... we can find your brother," she offered.

Amethyst watched as his gaze turned to the bottom of the bunk above them and he nodded, meeting her eyes again. "The decision is yours. I will remain your protector, always," he said, offering her a smile. "I'll make sure you get there," he added. He seemed to disregard her last statement, but she wondered if perhaps he desired to think on it.

Amethyst's grin grew and her pointed ears perked higher as she threw her arms around him and planted a kiss on his cheek. "Okay," she said.

To Become a Pirate

everal years passed, and they pooled their wages. They sparred with each other, and also with the sailors who wanted not just in on the fun but to learn.

Growing up, though her parents had hardly condoned it, Amethyst had been privy to swordplay and had trained with many of the boys who were destined to be members of the army. By the time Amethyst was considered a teenager, she was as capable in a fight as any of the boys, and even better than some. As adults, the boys were destined to assist in war and conquest.

Back then, she had also taught Darien. In her mind, what use was he as her personal servant if he couldn't defend her? Her parents weren't fond of encouraging captured races to fight, so Darien's training had been more secretive. She had known that any suspicion of rebellion would have meant immediate execution for him. They had intended for her to rely on the palace guards, but that wasn't quite good enough.

Aboard the *Silver Lady,* Amethyst and Darien used their magic when they could to keep their skills sharp. They tried to be discreet, mostly only using enhancement spells for strengthening the lines and sails during storms or animation spells to make their duties faster and easier. They also used sleeping spells to help Amethyst. Even with the rum, she often found herself waking violently in cold sweat from relentless torment in her dreams. It was far worse on nights when Captain Rada called her to his quarters, but those were the nights they used magic. She feared the captain would dismiss her if she could not sleep peacefully.

As time went by, Amethyst and Darien grew closer to their goal of leaving the merchant ship and at last, they were ready.

The captain had determined to set course for Vorda Isle once again to meet with a comrade and to trade. It was late morning when the isle finally could be seen on the horizon.

"Land ho!" cried the lookout.

While the rest of the crew began preparing to make port and trade their goods, Amethyst and Darien slipped toward their cabin, readying their few belongings including a handful of weapons, some extra clothing, and some food they had slipped away during the previous day.

Amethyst felt briefly reminded of her initial escape from the fae territories, but she pushed the thought aside. She doubted the crew would truly care if they went off on their own and further, she doubted they would try to prevent it.

As soon as the ship made port, the crew began bustling with activity. It was not difficult for Amethyst and Darien to make their way toward the trapdoor from which they had first entered the ship and through the hatch to the sea.

Amethyst did not hesitate as she made the small leap downward, the resulting splash barely heard over the activities from the docks. Darien was quickly behind her, and they swam easily toward the beach.

As they made their way past the port and its markets, Amethyst took in the details of it. In contrast to what she had witnessed through her spyglass of Port Mirka to the south of the isle, the people here seemed both incredibly busy and incredibly dull at the same time. Their dress was nothing special, though that was no surprise. They probably had meager earnings except for when one ship might come through with exceptional trade. She imagined they lived peaceful lives and wanted nothing more.

The mountain rising skyward at the center of the isle loomed before them, but she knew beyond it was the destination she hoped for.

Amethyst moved swiftly toward the tree line, hoping their venture would prove free of hazards. She had no idea what to expect from the wild parts of the isle beyond the port, though she hoped that the supposed monsters were truly nothing more than mere rumors.

The forest grew thick and dense and the humidity caused sweat to form on her back and brow almost immediately. There was no discernable path through it, so instead, she focused on the mountain as a guide.

Amethyst remained quiet, and it seemed Darien was content to do the same. The thick underbrush clung to her boots and she wondered why there weren't even small trails made by game or other beasts. Were there any in the first place, she thought?

In the distance, she heard low growls and screeching. *'Perhaps that answers that...'* Yet their slow trek remained uneventful, albeit full of discomfort. As the light slowly fell, Amethyst paused. "Darien, we should make camp for the night. If we continue, we will have to summon a light and that could draw unwanted attention."

Darien nodded and lowered the sack he carried. Amethyst did the same. They ate some of the food they had taken from the *Silver Lady*, and afterward used their sacks as pillows for sleep.

Amethyst awoke at the first light creeping in through the trees around them. She was determined to keep moving forward. She turned to wake Darien only to discover that he was also awake, and she smiled at him.

They continued their trek through the dense forest, pausing only to eat or drink. The days began to blend together; they camped at night and moved when the sun was up. During the third day, they encountered a small herd of rhinos and later that day a group of bears. Amethyst imagined there was much other life on the island that they weren't seeing. Along the way, they passed several creeks, and Amethyst was grateful that fresh water wasn't a problem.

When the food they had brought ran out, they fished. They felt it would waste less time and they'd have better luck, since the other creatures of the island seemed both more sparse and well-hidden. They occasionally attempted to catch the fish, but mostly Amethyst felt entirely comfortable using a control spell to draw the fish out of the water. There was no one around to witness, other than Darien who she trusted more than any other.

It became clear to Amethyst after the second week that the reason the pirates from Mirka left Blaise alone was simply because the journey was tedious. She realized it was partially an assumption, but she imagined the pirates were more content to lounge on the beach and drink their ale than to labor through dense forest just for a bit of merchandise they could easily plunder on the seas.

After three weeks had passed, the trees were beginning to thin and the glimmer of the sea in the distance was vaguely discernable. Amethyst hurried her step, wiping a hand across her forehead for what felt like the hundredth time just that day. *'What I wouldn't give for a bath right now!'*

It was mid-afternoon when she felt sand beneath her boots again and they made their way past the village houses and toward the market built around the port. It was as busy, loud, and bustling as Port Blaise had been, though it was not difficult to distinguish that those before them were pirates.

Just as she had witnessed through the spyglass last time they'd visited the isle, many of them wore clothes that appeared almost outlandishly elaborate, though she did note some others wore simple loose shirts and britches. Many of them moved in the same pompous strut, their ears and hands glimmering in the sunlight from various pieces of jewelry.

Amethyst, closely followed by Darien, observed one particular pub that seemed especially popular called the *Goblin's Goblet.*

'*Surely here I'll have some luck,*' she thought as she stepped inside.

The pub was rowdy with various people crowded around long tables or at the bar. Goblets were in almost every hand.

"Oy, Cap'n! If I win, wha' do ye say I take o'er tha ship, eh?" one man was shouting from across the dimly-lit room.

Another man laughed and said, "Aye! An' if I win, ye walk tha plank!"

Jeers and roars followed and a group gathered around the two, goblets and fists pounding the table in rhythm with the contents sloshing.

"First one down loses!" shouted the first man with a glimmer in his dark eyes.

The two began chugging goblet after goblet of ale until after the seventh round, the challenger's face twisted and he spilled the contents of his stomach onto the floor. Groans and shouts followed. Immediately after, he fell backward onto the floor with a dull thud.

"Bloody bilge-rat," the winner mumbled, followed by a loud and unseemly belch.

Just as quickly, the group dispersed and many began leaving. The pub was soon half as full as when Amethyst and

Darien had first entered and she debated if she should simply take a seat and ask for information, or if they should find a table and observe for a while. Were all pirates so rough as the ones that had just left?

If they were, Amethyst's notion that her crew would be different was then and there decided. No way would she captain such a brood. Someday, somehow, she'd find a way to captain a ship as well-mannered as it was powerful.

Finally, Amethyst and Darien moved toward the bar. She would never get anywhere simply sitting back and waiting. It was best to make opportunities for herself and then take them. In no way was Amethyst ready to walk aboard a ship and take over it, but she was ready to become a pirate and begin to learn what that meant.

Amethyst took a seat, gesturing toward the bartender. "I'll have rum," she demanded confidently.

Darien shook his head when he was questioned. Amethyst assumed he desired a clear head.

The pub had fallen into a dull roar and there was a tall, lean man seated to her right. The insignia of a raven was tattooed onto his right arm, and she could have sworn he was trying to burn a hole through the opposite wall with his pale eyes. His dark hair was slicked back and his sharply angled face was almost fixed into a scowl. "Have ye heard of the creatures of the island?" Amethyst asked, watching for the man's reaction.

"They're only myth, lass," he responded, his gaze unmoving. Not even a flinch. "Made up stories t' keep the navy dogs away."

"So what keeps them from the bay?" she asked.

"What is it ye want, lass?" he asked, ignoring her question.

"To join a pirate's crew," she said just as confidently as when she had ordered her rum.

At this, his gaze finally shifted in her direction. She felt the iciness of his eyes taking in her figure and assessing her, before he resumed his hole-in-the-wall-burning stare.

"Ye should talk t' Captain Sedra," he said finally with a gesture of his mug toward one of the remaining groups.

Amethyst followed his motion, taking in the group.

"There aren't many a lad that'll take on a wench aboard," the man muttered before rising from his seat and moving away.

Amethyst ignored his words and shot back the rest of her rum before rising from her seat also. She had heard pirates weren't fond of women aboard, but she had also encountered several merchant ships in her time at sea that not only had women, but welcomed them. Some captains and sailors even had brought their families aboard and their wives helped with the sewing and cooking. There were some sailors that frowned at the prospect of a woman aboard, but not all of them.

These were pirates, but she would prove wrong anyone that would question her worth or capabilities.

Amethyst approached the group, a twist of her ears telling Darien to stay back and observe for now. She sat down in one of the wooden chairs as if she belonged there.

"Which one of ye lads is Captain Sedra?" she demanded.

The men looked at her, pausing in their conversation and some of them slowly moving to set their mugs on the table.

"An' who are ye?" one of them voiced, one dark brow rising. He had brilliant hazel eyes and tanned skin, and his muscles were well developed. His britches and simple sleeveless shirt were black, while a pale cloth was wrapped about his head with the Jolly Roger insignia stitched into it. '*This must be Captain Sedra,*' she thought.

"Amethyst," she said, "the newest member of the crew." It had been long enough since her escape from the fae lands that she was no longer afraid of using her real name. She doubted these pirates would know who she was, or care.

"An' what makes ye think we'd let the likes o' ye aboard, eh?" Sedra asked.

Amethyst smirked. "Perhaps ye'd like a demonstration?"

"Be that a challenge?" he retorted.

Amethyst shrugged, rising to her feet once more. "Meet me at the docks, if ye dare."

With that, she turned, flicking a few curls from her face and making her way out of the pub. Darien quickly followed.

Amethyst held her head up, her shoulders back. "Darien, I don't want your interference. I don't want any of these brutes claiming I can't handle sea-life without a man, and especially don't want them thinking I can't handle myself. Otherwise they'll take advantage of me left and right."

Darien sighed softly. "I suppose there isn't any arguing with you. But know that I will not stand by and let you—"

"I can handle myself, Darien," she said, cutting him off. She knew he only intended to remain her protector, always. He had seen enough done to her for him to feel that way. But she was determined to fight back anyone that would try. And she knew he would be there and wouldn't hesitate to help if she changed her mind. That alone was enough.

They moved toward the docks, the sun glistening off of the white sands. The cry of gulls and the crashing waves echoed with the shouts of men and rolling of barrels.

The pirates from the *Goblin's Goblet* had followed after finishing their mugs of ale, Sedra leading the group. They were not far behind as Amethyst reached the docks.

"Gather round, gents!" he bellowed. Many of those working on the docks paused, looking in their direction. "This lass thinks she has what it takes to join me crew and has dared to challenge Captain Sedra." Jeers resounded and more gathered, forming a ring around them.

Now that they were in the sunlight, Amethyst sized up her opponent. He was average in height, but his size was not a concern for her as much as the question of his swordsmanship. Perhaps he thought she would be no match because she was a woman.

He drew his sword, which was broad and single-edged with a simple leather-bound hilt. It contrasted with her sabre – a double-edged curved blade with a golden hand guard to protect her thumb. It was one of the few things she had brought with her from the fae territories.

He lunged first, cheers resounding from the gathered crowd and she rose her sword in defense, blocking his attack as a brilliant zing sounded from the clashing of metal. She ducked, stepping to the side and then lunged at him.

He blocked. He was fast, she noticed, but she still hoped to use his weight against him. The sounds of the crowd around them were already drowned out as she focused on her duel.

She leaped backward and lunged again, though only blocked his attack, and she stepped to the side once more. He faltered for a moment, then lunged after her this time, and she blocked.

Amethyst coughed as his fist landed a blow to her gut. He brought down his hilt. She caught his wrist in her hand, raising her knee and landed a blow to his stomach, pushing him backward.

Their fight was a dance around the ring the crowd had formed, and Amethyst grimaced as sweat droplets ran down the side of her face. Sedra's brow gleamed also. The clashing of blades was a constant resounding echo around them and they each landed several more strikes.

Amethyst dove sideward as Sedra lunged for her, his momentum causing him to stumble forward and she rolled, pushing herself upward and kicking a boot into his behind. He fell into the sand, though caught himself with his hand, attempting to roll.

As he did, Amethyst lunged for him, kicking his sword from his hand and stepping onto his wrist. He attempted to grasp her leg with his free hand, but she placed her other boot into his gut and pointed her sword at his throat, a smirk forming on her lips.

He scowled up at her. Silence hung in the air like the calm before a storm and then the gathered crowd burst into shouts and hollers.

"Well, ye scalawags, it seems this lass has what it takes, eh?" Amethyst shouted, almost mocking the words Sedra had uttered at the beginning of the battle.

She stepped back, offering a hand though Sedra only shook his head and rose on his own, collecting his sword from the sand. "Very well, lass." He paused, turning his gaze to the others. "Scatter, ye dogs! There be nothin' left t' see," he barked, his eyes sharply moving about the gathered crowd.

The other pirates only laughed as they resumed their work on the docks, and Sedra focused his gaze on her. "Amethyst, welcome to me crew," he paused. "Come to th' edge o' th' sea near th' docks at sundown and I'll show ye aboard, savvy?" he said. With that, Sedra turned and made his way to his crew and they headed back toward the *Goblin's Goblet.*

Amethyst returned her sword to her scabbard, grinning at Darien. "Perhaps we could kill some time," she said.

The sun was setting over the horizon and the sea had turned from azure blue to brilliant golds and reds. Amethyst stood on the beach, one hand gripping the hilt of her sabre. The sea breeze rippled through her curls, though they were tied back with a pale strip of cloth.

She assumed Sedra would find her, but she had asked Darien to wait on the docks in case the pirate captain had decided to leave port without her. She was determined to leave aboard a pirate ship whatever it took.

She barely heard the sound of boots treading sand behind her. "So, lass, ye wish to join a pirate's crew do ye?"

Amethyst nodded, her gaze still fixed on the sea. "Aye," she responded. At last she turned, frowning as her gaze met Sedra's. There was something in those eyes that sent a pit right to her stomach.

"Did anyone ever tell ye that a wench aboard a ship is only good for one thing?" he asked, a glimmer in his hazel eyes. He moved closer.

Would she never rid herself of this fate?

She knew that women at sea were fewer than men, but that, to her, was hardly an excuse. "I know my way 'round a ship," she responded, attempting to remain calm and collected. "I can do any of the duties the men can."

Sedra grinned, his eyes almost dancing. Did he believe her, she wondered? Or did her abilities even matter? He lunged toward her, grasping her body with his hands and pushing her down into the sand. "Did ye really think ye could make a fool o' me without consequences, wench?" he said, grasping at her arms.

Amethyst felt tears burning, and then fury rose from her chest. She hadn't spent the last few years aboard the *Silver Lady*, giving herself and training herself for nothing! She would give herself to whom she pleased and never again to someone who wanted to use her only for his own gain. She was stronger now than when she had been with her ex-husband and more hardened by the sea.

She let the rage flow through her body, her nails and fangs growing longer and raising one knee, she shoved it between

Sedra's legs. She smirked as his face twisted and contorted in pain.

As he faltered, she raised her other knee, pushing both into his gut, and he rolled off of her onto his back in the sand. She quickly moved to her knees before he could regain himself, using her own weight to keep him down and pummeling at his face with her fists.

How dare this fool attempt to mock her or to belittle her! A snarl formed on her lips, her fangs bared and she instinctually bit into his neck. She could feel the scum's life slipping away.

It was the first time Amethyst had truly tasted blood. Part of her was disgusted and trembled at the thought she had taken a life. But the other part of her felt powerful. At last she stood victorious over Sedra's body.

No longer would she allow anyone else to ever intimidate her or make her do anything she didn't want. On the contrary, she would be the one making the orders and decisions. She would never give herself to another either from fear or for an agreement. She knew that the conquering nature of her people in her blood had been kindled. No one would stand in her way. And anyone who dared defy her, threaten her, or act against her would meet an unsightly end. She couldn't help a proud smirk at the thought.

Amethyst kicked at Sedra's body, and finally pushed it into the ocean. She muttered a spell that would cause the body to float long enough for it to get out to sea and then turned away. She didn't need his ship to get started anyway, she told herself. Surely there were plenty of other captains that would accept her – ones that had witnessed her defeat of Sedra in the duel earlier in the day.

Amethyst wiped the blood from her mouth and made her way toward the docks, waving at Darien. He quirked a brow and his eyes seemed full of questions as he approached.

"There's been a slight change of plans," Amethyst announced, "we'll no longer join Sedra's ship. Let's get a drink," she finished, turning briskly back toward the pub.

"Amethyst..." he paused, "What happened?" Darien asked.

Her ears twitched. She heard the concern in his tone. "Nothing I couldn't handle. The bastard tried to..." she paused, "Well he thought he could mess with me and he found out just what happens to anyone that tries." She glanced back at Darien, a slight smirk on her lips.

Darien nodded in response, and she could've sworn she caught a smile as well.

The *Goblin's Goblet* was bursting with sound as they approached. Amethyst slammed the door open, the last of the fading sunlight making her form appear a dark silhouette in the doorway.

A few heads turned in her direction, though many continued their drunken banter.

Well, if she couldn't get their attention that way...

Amethyst moved toward the bar, grasping one of the tall wooden chairs and climbing on top of it. She raised two fingers to her lips and a shrill whistle echoed around the room. At last, the banter quieted. Well she had their attention. "Which o' ye scalawags is brave enough to take me on?" she demanded, a glimmer in her eyes.

"An' be sword-whipped tha same way ye did, Sedra? Ye proved yerself already, lass, ye can handle a sword," one burly man said.

"Aye," echoed from several others.

"Then who be willin' to take me aboard?" she pressed, "I can do anything ye gents can do, and hold me own." She did her best to stare each of them down, her eyes moving slowly from one person to the next around the room.

"Blimey, lass, ye don't give up do ye?" hissed one man seated in the chair next to hers.

She looked down, and saw that it was the same man from earlier in the day who had suggested she talk to Sedra. She frowned. "No one has gotten anywhere by giving up," she retorted, irked.

His pale eyes met hers. "Git down, lass. I s'ppose ye've earned at least a chance."

Amethyst simply stared at him for a moment, and then finally leapt down from the chair. She didn't sit, but rather continued to watch the tall lean man that had spoken. Slowly, the banter resumed.

"It just so happens I be lookin' for crewmen, so I'll take ye aboard. I'm Captain Ehren of the *Raven's Call*. But tell me, lass, why do ye wish to become a pirate?"

"To live the life I choose," she replied, her gaze unwavering.

Ehren turned his eyes once more away from her and nodded. "I can drink to that," was his reply. He stood and wordlessly made his way out of the pub.

'Captain Ehren, what sort of man are you?' Amethyst thought as she followed him. What had been the point of sending her somewhere else if he was willing to accept her? Had he been trying to test her?

Amethyst followed him once more toward the docks. The moon had begun its rise and the sun was long gone. The sea was dark but reflected the pale light from the cloudless night sky. "My companion, Darien-"

"Aye, lass, he's welcome," Ehren said before she could finish, never once turning to look at her on their trek.

She couldn't help wondering why Ehren had so readily accepted Darien. Or perhaps he had already known she would not go without him.

Ehren did not hesitate once as he passed the docks and went straight to the water's edge. A rowboat rested there. Darien stepped forward, and he and Ehren pushed the boat into the sea. Ehren climbed in and gestured for Amethyst and Darien to follow.

As soon as they were settled, they each grasped a pair of oars and quickly moved seaward.

The *Raven's Call* was anchored nearly a mile off shore. It was a barque ship – one that featured three full decks and four masts. Three were square rigged while the aftmost mast was fore-and-aft rigged. Barque ships were known for their ability to sail both with and against the wind and they required small crews. The *Raven's* hull was a deep navy blue. It could almost have been mistaken for black. The dark sails were lowered and billowed gently, though hanging behind the figurehead – the neck and head of a raven, beak open in an eternal song and beady black eyes peering downward – it gave Amethyst the impression of an enormous beast swooping to its prey.

She found herself curious about the story behind Ehren becoming captain of this ship. She also wondered if he would even tell her.

They reached the ship and several men threw down ropes which were used to secure the rowboat. It was then pulled upward onto the main deck. As they boarded the ship, Amethyst did her best to take in the details – though they weren't entirely clear in the darkness.

Ehren was silent and only gestured for Amethyst and Darien to follow as he led them to the second deck where the cabins were. The other deckhands present only watched them, just as eerily silent as their captain.

The captain parted as soon as he showed Amethyst and Darien to one particular cabin near the stern of the ship.

The cabin was as simple as those aboard the merchant's ship they had lived on. She noted the pair of bunks on one side and a dresser on the other side. This dresser was far more elegant than she'd expected. She opened the large wooden doors, peeked inside to the empty closet space and traced her fingers over the curled designs etched into the drawers. It reminded her of some of the furniture she had possessed in the fae lands.

Her ears twitched at the sound of the waves. They were near and crisp as if right beside her. In the far wall of the cabin was a single-framed window. She moved toward it. It was small, only enough to peek out of. The sea beyond was both endless and magnificent as it met the darkened sky.

Finally, Amethyst sat on the lower bunk and her mind wandered to the days ahead. Once more she found herself thinking about what sort of man their captain was.

The Raven's Call

*T*he morning rays of sun had already made their way through the small window of Amethyst's and Darien's cabin. She stirred, realizing that no one had pounded the door to alert them it was time to get up.

The first thing she noticed was the emptiness of Darien's bed. She frowned as she looked at the tidied sheets. Why hadn't he woken her?

She rose, donning the simple clothing in the dresser, tied her ringlets back as she had so many times in the past and made her way toward the main deck.

The crewmen sat about, some with pipes in their mouths, and others with bottles of various drinks. They talked amongst each other softly. Only the whisper of the sea and the waves lapping at the hull of the ship resounded.

Amethyst looked up. The sails were raised. Wasn't there maintenance to be done?

Finally, she spotted Darien. The sea breeze toyed with his navy locks and he leaned over the railing of the deck. Beside him stood Captain Ehren, his pale eyes as fixated on the horizon as they had been on the wall of the *Goblin's Goblet.*

Was he always so serious?

She approached them. "Good morning," she said, trying to sound cheery.

Darien turned toward her with a smile. Ehren didn't move. "Morning," Darien responded. "The captain was telling me what to expect from the life of a pirate."

Amethyst raised a brow, glancing toward Ehren.

"What are our duties?" she asked, getting straight to the point.

"Well the care of the ship is the same. But with the size of the crew, the work is done quickly," Darien told her.

It was true. Amethyst had already noticed the crew was significantly larger than those she had seen aboard any merchant ship.

"If the crew can already handle it, why take us aboard, Captain?" Amethyst demanded.

"Me barque only needs between ten an' twen'y men t' sail. But t' raid another ship we need numbers and skill. Yer abilities with a sword be reason enough."

It infuriated her the way Ehren only stared into the distance as if she wasn't worth his full attention. He had only turned his head so that the sea wouldn't carry away his words and then had resumed his stare. She also noted that he seemed to have engaged Darien more than herself. Was there something about her specifically he wanted to avoid? And if so, then why take her on in the first place?

She pushed it aside for the moment.

Amethyst wondered how long it would be before they crossed another ship. She made her way toward the other deckhands. "Good morning," she offered.

They looked up at her with a mixture of expressions.

"I'm Amethyst."

"Have a drink, lass. What be ye choice?" one of them offered. He was average in size and had hair as dark as the captain's, though it was wavy and unkempt and hung over the greenest of eyes.

"Rum," she said, and accepted the bottle thrust toward her.

She tipped it to her lips. "Is the captain always like this?" she dared to ask.

"Nay, lass. We lost th' first mate in a storm afore we made port."

Amethyst nodded, glancing toward the captain once more.

Who had the first mate been? And more importantly... who to the captain?

"When we cross another ship, what then?" Amethyst asked.

"Whatever suits ye best, lass. Can ye ready tha cannons and hoist the sails?"

"Aye," she said.

"When we raid a ship, we board it, kill or capture the crew, and take the booty as quickly as we can. Our advantage is in numbers and speed. And we get away just as quickly as we take the ship. Ye must decide for yerself what part ye'll play."

He offered her a small dagger. "Ye'll want to make yerself a collection o' these."

"Thanks," Amethyst murmured, placing the dagger into her boot.

"Sail ho!" cried the lookout after three days of sailing with no disturbance. The men rushed to the edge of the deck, some with spyglasses. In the distance, the white sails of a merchant's fluyt glimmered. Immediately, those aboard the ship sprang into action. Some slipped below deck and began to ready the cannons while others hauled ropes and grabbed smaller guns and rifles. The sails aboard the *Raven's Call* were lowered as they made their way directly toward the other ship.

"Ready yerselves, gents!" cried the crewmember that had offered Amethyst the bottle of rum.

Amethyst wasn't sure how she felt about killing those aboard the other ship. Only a few days before, it could've been her on the receiving end of the raid. Then she remembered the nights with the captain of that ship and the body of Sedra on the beach, and she remembered her end goal.

She drew her sabre as the *Raven* drew broadside to the fluyt. The explosion of guns and ship debris resounded as did the shouting of the pirates. On impact, Amethyst joined many of the pirate crew in boarding the merchant vessel, barreling into the sailors.

Amethyst felt her instincts take over as she plunged into battle, the scent of blood only spurring her onward. She thrust her sword into one sailor's chest, rolling to avoid the sword of another oncoming sailor. As she rolled, she drew the dagger from her boot, plunging it into the next sailor's stomach.

She pushed up to her feet, making her way toward the main mast. Amethyst quivered as she began to climb it, hoping none of her fellow pirates would shoot it down at that moment. She made her way to the lookout's nest, gripping it with one hand while she slashed at the rigging with the other.

The whoosh of the sails and the creaking of the lines as they tumbled blended with the sounds of battle and Amethyst slid downward once more, raising her blade to block an oncoming attack. She shoved her boot into the sailor, kicking him backward to the deck.

As she looked up, she saw her fellow crewmen finishing their own skirmishes and the sailors that hadn't been killed were grouped together in surrender. The ship was theirs. After all, fluyts were merchant vessels designed for maximum cargo with minimum crew, and they were lightly armed.

Amethyst's ears twitched at the sound of Captain Ehren's voice. "No survivors, gents! Take it all!"

Jeers resounded from the pirates and Amethyst watched as one by one, they cut down the sailors that remained. She stood by silently. Was this the truth of a pirate's life? There wasn't any reason for their deaths; perhaps they merely had bad luck. She decided she was just glad it wasn't her. Before she could dwell on it any longer, the others were making their way to the merchandise.

Amethyst made her way below deck with them. There were countless barrels of goods. She peeked in one, noting spools of silk in various colors. Numerous other fabrics, foods, drinks, and building supplies were in the other barrels. Finally, she noted a wardrobe with different items of clothing and an ornate box with jewelry and accessories. As quickly as they could, the crew hauled them aboard the *Raven's Call*. At last, they were pulling in the plank and sailing away, leaving the wreckage of the fluyt for any passersby.

Was this what her life would be as a pirate? Killing and taking and otherwise spending long days doing whatever they pleased?

The days of leisure she didn't mind. It felt true to the freedom she had desired. Perhaps she would come to understand the rest of it in time.

The crewmembers waited once their booty was gathered for Captain Ehren to look through the barrels. "Suit yerselves, lads. There be plenty to fill our pockets and to take what we desire." With that, he moved away toward his quarters, leaving the crewmen to their spoils.

Amethyst hesitated. She was the newest member to the crew. Yet as she gazed over the goods, she missed her days before her marriage. In the fae palace, Amethyst had been privy to whatever luxuries she desired, so long as it agreed with her parents. She had had someone to serve her hand and foot at any time of day.

She turned away, intending to make her way toward the main deck.

"Amethyst!" Her ears twitched and she turned to see who had called.

It was the one with startling green eyes she had met on first arrival. "Ye earned as much as we did, lass. An' what we don' keep we'll trade for riches. We'll fill our pockets with the rarest of all tha commodities!" She knew he meant the precious stones used in trades. Ever since the fae conquests, gems had become more widespread and accepted as a means of trade. Various gems could be offered instead of coin; their value was determined by their rarity and their purity.

Had they taken the booty in order to spend their days freely for as long as they chose? Or had they taken it merely to prove they could? Would they plunder the next ship they encountered even if they didn't need its goods? Were they pirates merely for greed?

Amethyst gave in, allowing her fingers to trace over the fabrics she had seen. There was silk and cotton and lace and velvet as well as full-length dresses waiting to be worn. *'How long has it been since I've dressed as a woman? Should I even bother?'*

She removed one particular dress that fanned outward from the waist in a full skirt. Its white sleeves were short and puffy and the black corset beautifully contrasted the blue folds. She held it to her frame, noting it was too long. She glanced toward Darien, searching his face for his reaction.

He smiled at her with an approving nod.

She picked out a few other pieces of clothing and a new pair of dark leather boots. When she passed the jewelry and accessories, she stopped as the shimmer of silver caught her gaze. There were countless gold and silver hoops, woven and intricate designs, and even hair pins and elegant combs. Her ears already had two piercings in each lobe, though they hadn't seen even the hope of decoration since she had left the fae lands.

'Well, I suppose if I wish to live my life freely, it may as well start now.'

As soon as she had selected what she wanted, Amethyst made her way to her cabin.

She hung her clothes within the closet space in the dresser and carefully placed the jewelry and other items in one of the drawers. *'If only I had a mirror, even if it is entirely impractical.'* Amethyst recognized if she did have one it would probably shatter during a storm.

She pulled the pale cloth from her hair, letting her ringlets tumble about her frame. Then, she slipped into the dress she had chosen and poked two of the silvery hoops into her pointed ears. It was the most ladylike she had felt since before her marriage. Amethyst felt a smile form on her lips. She couldn't help the swell within her chest. As a merchant sailor, she never could have afforded to wear such adornment, or even attempt to show dignity, except perhaps with her eating habits.

She realized that in choosing the life of a pirate, she could be as terrible and at the same time as much of a woman as she desired to be. Of course, she had dreamed of it before joining the *Raven's Call*, but now it was a tangible reality.

In a flurry, Amethyst swept out of her cabin and toward the main deck. The others had sprawled across the deck with bottles and pipes in hand and were relishing in their victory.

"Blimey! We have a lady aboard, lads!" Boisterous laughter ensued and Amethyst felt her cheeks grow warm.

No one made even a budge toward her, however.

"Amethyst, lass, we began t' wonder if ye were truly feminine," one of the men hollered.

Amethyst frowned, feeling the warmness in her cheeks turn hot as her temper flared. In her mind, she was still just as much of a woman regardless of the tasks she did or the clothes she wore. The tasks were necessary and the clothes convenient.

"Aye! The way ye fight is like the bloodiest of cutthroats. Ye tore tha riggin' beyond mendin' an' those poor lads didn't stand a chance against ye."

She simply stood there, staring at the lot of them. She wasn't sure how to react to the last statement.

"Here, lass. Drink some o' tha rum," one offered her with a toothy grin. "Ye look as though ye want to cut someone in two!"

Amethyst grasped the bottle, tipping it to her lips.

Soon, the warmth that often came after drinking flowed through her system and she carried the bottle with her toward the side of the ship.

"Darien," she called.

He turned toward her, having been lost in his own thoughts on her first arrival, and his face twisted as his jaw slightly dropped before he composed himself. He raised a hand to his mouth and coughed softly. "Amethyst."

She smirked to herself. Darien hadn't seen her dressed so in as long as it had been since she'd done it. "So, how is it?" she asked.

She watched as his lips curved upward into an approving smile, "You're beautiful as ever."

"Well, thank you, lovely," she said somewhat giddy.

Darien's gaze shifted toward the captain's cabin. "Though it's not very ladylike to be drinking from the bottle."

Amethyst scoffed, waving a hand idly. "I'm not a lady. I'm a pirate!"

"Well you won't get very much accomplished aboard a ship all dressed up," Darien said.

Amethyst brushed his comment aside. If anyone knew her it was Darien, and she wondered if he were only trying to gauge her emotions. She couldn't lose her resolve at any point. She knew that. But there was no harm in enjoying herself a little, she thought.

"I'll be in britches again soon enough," she said. "But only the finest from now on for me."

Darien didn't respond.

They remained silent a moment. Amethyst enjoyed listening to the sound of the waves as they rocked the hull. The sea was so still.

"I'm going to pierce my ears again, Darien," Amethyst said. It was common practice, but for her it had meaning.

His eyes turned toward her and his dark brow rose upwards.

"It will signify our first successful raid as pirates and what we've gained. Perhaps I'll even get one for each raid in which I take something of value for myself until my ears are full."

Darien sighed softly. "Whatever you wish," was all that he said.

They continued to sail southwest toward Orlesce, and for several weeks they did not cross another ship. Amethyst and Darien both aided in duties and when she wasn't dressed in britches, Amethyst resorted to sorting through the barrels and picking out clothing she liked and wearing it.

Captain Ehren remained the same as he had, mostly lounging in his cabin or the upper deck.

Amethyst found his silence somewhat unnerving. It was not the reserved silence she was accustomed to with Darien. Rather it was a cold sort of silence. She felt as though at any moment he might suddenly burst into a fit of madness. Or maybe he was simply that way toward her.

Yet at the same time, his pale gaze held something that drew her curiosity. She had a desire to pry into his secrets.

Still, no matter what she tried in her brief attempts at conversation with him, he remained aloof. It both stoked the fires of her temper and yet only spurred her onward to try harder. His lack of response prodded her stubborn nature as if he was presenting her with a challenge. During her first days on the ship, the men had told her he wasn't always so grey, but she'd seen nothing to indicate its truth.

They were nearing the Orlesce coast, the furthest part of Aseath from the fae territories. Soon they'd be attempting to trade goods or perhaps lounging on the beach instead of the ship for a change.

Amethyst made her way from her cabin toward quarterdeck. Ehren lay on his back, eyes staring upward. His nearly black hair was sprawled around his head with several wisps contrasting against his pale forehead. She wondered if perhaps his skin was incapable of anything darker.

She didn't spend long taking in his angled features but rather chose to sit beside him. She was dressed in her tall leather boots and britches, in part because Ehren seemed to have no care about how she was dressed. *'Today will be the day,'* she told herself. *'I'm going to stay until something happens.'*

"We'll be making port soon," Amethyst said. *'As if there's anything better I could've said.'*

Ehren didn't respond, his expression unflinching.

She followed his gaze skyward and immediately felt the urge to either slap him or shake him. Instead, she pushed down her rising temper. "There's not a cloud in the sky. What's got yer attention, Captain?" She attempted to keep her voice even.

"There be nothin' holdin' me attention, lass, other than me own mind," he said.

This wasn't the first time they'd shared similar words. How would he react if she did attempt to physically grasp his attention? Again, she pushed down her aggressive urges. "Well then what's on yer mind?" she asked, determined.

"Ye've asked before, lass, an' the answer's tha same."

"Well, *Captain*, it does concern me as a member of yer crew. If ye keep loungin' about tha men might think ye've gone soft, or perhaps that ye should resign." She couldn't help the edge that started to slip into her voice.

At first, he didn't respond. After all, she knew there wasn't that much validity to her argument. The men had been with him through thick and thin before she'd arrived and they vouched for him every time she'd asked. They brushed her concern aside as a woman's fickle emotions and told her he'd come around eventually. At some point she had asked about the lost first mate. The men only told her it had been a woman and not to ask. They'd warned her not to bother the captain and that if he felt like telling her the details, it was up to him.

She found it irksome she couldn't learn more, though she felt she at least got a glimmer of understanding. Amethyst wondered if when she was a captain, such states of being would ever happen to her.

"Careful, lass. Ye might make me regret takin ye aboard."

Amethyst frowned, staring at his eyes. She wished he would meet her gaze just once long enough for her to attempt to read him. She took a deep breath and let it out slowly.

"Captain, perhaps ye fail to recognize I'm merely concerned."

"Yer pryin' into business not yer own, lass. If I wanted t' talk, I would. Be on yer way with yer rum now."

Amethyst felt a shiver run down her spine despite the warmth of the sea breeze around her. Would he lose his temper with her? Would he have any reaction at all if she disobeyed?

Amethyst remained seated and stared off. Images of her days in the fae palace flashed through her mind. Days long before her marriage to Merrick when she had toyed with suitors and tested her limits. When she had defied those above her and even tried different approaches with others to watch for varying responses. At times she had even learned what to do to elicit the exact reaction she desired.

Slowly, she reached a hand out and grasped Ehren's arm. It was the first time she had deliberately sought non-violent physical contact with another besides Darien since she'd run away. Part of her did it in stubborn rebellion to his instructions. And part of her was wildly curious for his reaction.

Ehren's pale eyes turned from the sky and toward her hand. Her cheeks grew warm with fury that he still refused to meet her gaze but resisted the urge to squeeze his arm in her grasp.

"What are ye doin'?" he asked, returning his focus skyward.

"I don't know... if anyone's said condolences is all..." she dared.

She watched as his mouth curved downward. As soon as the words escaped her lips his pale eyes met hers, though they flashed with the fury lying beneath the surface. Was he furious that the men had told her, or was he furious she had brought it up?

Just as soon, his wrinkled forehead eased and for a single moment, she saw something soft in his gaze, as if he wanted to tell her everything, or perhaps it was something else. Just as soon as it had come, his eyes turned from hers once more. "Be on yer way," he commanded more firmly than before.

Amethyst stood and whirled in frustration. He had almost shown *something* other than his perpetual darkness. Why did she care so much? Was she getting too emotionally involved, as the crew told her? No. She was here to make her way toward being a captain. However, she was getting nowhere! She had hoped Ehren would shed some light on what it took to be a captain and how to become one. But instead he wasted his days away *moping* and didn't relent to any amount of conversation whatsoever.

Amethyst silently wondered if perhaps she should attempt to find a new crew. But it wouldn't bode well she'd only joined the *Raven's Call* a few weeks before and further, she knew it would be a challenge in and of itself to find a ship willing to take her aboard.

"Land ho!" cried the lookout as she stormed onto the main deck.

If only it were a merchant's ship they were crossing instead of nearing the coast. A fight would help her blow off some steam. She sucked in her breath and released it slowly and forcefully.

"Amethyst, what's got ye in such a tizzy?" she heard one of the men ask.

She snapped her gaze to meet his and then glanced away. "Nothing," she said, brushing past. Amethyst made her way below deck to her cabin and flopped on her bed.

"Darien. How can I learn anything when Ehren spends all his time as if nothing matters to him? He won't answer my questions and he barely gives me the time of day!" she huffed.

She turned her gaze toward her companion. His eyes met hers only for a moment before he shrugged and glanced off once more. "Perhaps, Amethyst, you're being too forward. You'll become a captain one day. But for now, just learn from the crew and decide just exactly how you'll do everything you want to do, hmm?"

She sighed impatiently. But somewhere inside she knew he was right. He never steered her wrong, but she was still frustrated.

How much longer must her life be controlled by the whims of those around her? She supposed ultimately, she couldn't really control anyone else. She just wanted to, at the very least, be in control of her own life, her own direction. She felt that was endlessly not the case.

At that moment, images of Sedra's body lifeless beneath her flashed through her mind. It had felt good, taking over the situation and *doing* something about it. Perhaps it was high time she made it a practice for herself. Instead of letting herself get tossed about like the waves, she should be the one swaying those around her. Yes, Darien was right. She needed to change tactics. There were other ways to get what she wanted. She must do as he said. Be more patient. More... coy.

She licked her lips slowly and sat up. "You're right, Darien. As always," she said. "Perhaps I just need to enjoy myself a little and take things a step at a time."

He only smiled at her.

With that, she returned to the main deck where the crew was busy preparing to make port.

For the next few weeks, Amethyst did just as she'd promised. She left Ehren alone and spent her time with the other members of the crew, content to sip on rum and help them with the duties about the ship.

Yet, she continued observing her captain. She needed to find a way to gain his trust.

At first, she hadn't felt using her womanly charms would be a good idea, nor did she want to resort to it. That area of her life had always been abused and led to trouble.

But maybe, as long as she remained in control, it could be different.

She must find what advantages she had and use them. Once more the memories of toying with suitors had come to her mind. It was time to discover just what her abilities and limitations truly were. If anyone tried anything she didn't like, well, she'd be sure to give them terrible consequences.

It was early evening and they were somewhere in between Tysck and Orlesce. Amethyst was on lookout duty for the night, and she was content to lean against the edges of the crow's nest, gazing seaward. The sky was brilliantly lit by the sun with oranges, reds and yellows and the sea seemed to blend as one with it.

Truly, it was breathtaking.

She glanced down, noting that the captain was on quarterdeck, also gazing seaward. Once more, she found herself wondering what was on his mind, but she pushed it aside.

As her gaze shifted, she noticed a dark cloud on the horizon. They were headed straight for it. She frowned.

They were sailing northwest at the moment, and with their current path, if they tried to avoid the storm they'd sail straight into a small island between the two continents. However, if they set their course due east, they'd at least only encounter the edges of the storm.

She placed two fingers between her lips and whistled downward. The other members of the crew quickly noticed the storm and set to work. Amethyst slid down the mast, joining them.

It didn't take long to adjust their course; the storm came quickly. The sky turned dark, blotting out the setting sun and in moments the crewmembers were soaked through.

Now Amethyst knew why it had reached them so quickly. The wind gusts were enormous, thrashing at the ship. It quaked under the pressure as if the wind alone could tear it apart.

"Continue east!" Amethyst heard someone shouting, "We'll go 'round the storm!"

She looked up as thunder boomed and flashes of lightning briefly illuminated both the sky and the ship. For only a few seconds, she could make out the others around her and the captain climbing the mast to raise the sails so they, at least, wouldn't be torn apart.

There were a handful of other crewmembers doing the same.

Amethyst frowned and followed after the captain. There was a feeling of foreboding in her gut.

The wind and sea tossed the ship like a doll. Amethyst clung to the mast with elongated nails to prevent being thrown away from it. The others used daggers that they clung to like life-lines. She aided the captain to raise the lowest sails on the main mast, followed by the next ones.

As they reached the final sails, they waited for a break in the wind to set out to the spars. Ehren reached outward, making his way toward the first of the lines and he slipped, gripping the spar to catch his fall. The wind whipped his body about.

"Captain! Grasp me hand!" Amethyst called, her form wrapped about the mast and her arm extending toward him.

His gaze met hers and he reached for her.

His hand grasped hers and she pulled him toward the mast. Her hand slipped. "Captain!" she screamed as his body plummeted.

As swiftly as she could manage, Amethyst climbed downward.

The captain had gripped at each of the lower spars on his way down which had at least slowed his fall. As she reached the deck, Amethyst ran toward the others which had gathered around the captain's body, lying in a heap.

"Captain," she said again, kneeling beside him.

He groaned, his eyes opening and then shutting. Good. He was conscious.

The ship had made it to the edges of the storm and was nearing clearer waters, though it remained dark. The only indication was that the wind had slowed and the rain was lighter.

"Can you stand?" Amethyst asked Ehren.

He only nodded. She and one of the other crewmembers gripped his arms, pulling him upward. He winced and then gasped sharply, but she could feel as he tried to support himself. Immediately, she noticed one of his legs was bent awkwardly. Blood had already begun to pool.

"C'mon," she said, moving his arm around her shoulders and helping him to his cabin. The other crewmember took the captain's other arm and aided in his support. The others that had gathered followed them to his cabin where they helped him lie down.

"Someone get the doctor," Amethyst said, glancing to the others. She didn't want to leave his side, afraid she would get blamed for his fall. The other crewmembers had already accepted she was just as capable as the rest of them and on her words, some of those present left.

Amethyst knelt beside Ehren's bed, watching him. Soon, the doctor arrived. "Prepare some hot water and bring bandages and whiskey," he instructed the remaining crewmembers. Amethyst stayed put, the others bringing the things he had asked for.

As soon as they were gone, Ehren groaned. "Leave me," he said gruffly to Amethyst. "I'll be fine." He winced as he tried to adjust his leg.

"You're injured," she argued. "And I can help." She may not be a doctor herself, but she had witnessed other injuries aboard the *Silver Lady* and at times had helped the doctor with their care.

The doctor dipped one of the bandages in the water. "Hold still," he commanded. He gripped the fabric about the broken leg, starting a tear with the tip of a dagger, and ripping it away.

Ehren sucked in his breath sharply, his facing scrunching and his knuckles turned white as he gripped his bedframe.

"Good. It isn't so terrible that ye can't heal from it. I'll have to set your leg," the doctor said, glancing to the captain's face.

Amethyst grabbed another of the bandages, holding it toward him. "At least it won't have to be removed."

Ehren scowled at her, but took the bandage and put it in his mouth, gripping at the bedframe once more. He nodded to the doctor that he was ready.

It occurred to Amethyst that she could simply heal him with a little magic, but she wasn't sure she could really trust it or him right now. He may have accepted her to his crew, but they knew nothing about each other, and even if he knew she was fae, that didn't necessarily mean anything. Besides, she was determined to earn her way *without* magic.

"Amethyst," the doctor said.

She looked at him.

"I'll need yer help, lass. Ye'll need t' hold him so's I can straighten it."

Amethyst raised a brow, but nodded. She stood and stretched her arm over Ehren's middle, her chest also covering his stomach so she could adequately hold him down.

"If he moves tha wrong way, it could get worse or not set right," the doctor warned.

Amethyst only nodded once more, pushing her weight down.

The doctor set to work, and Ehren bit hard into the bandage in his mouth. His knuckles were white from his grip on the bedframe, and he grunted, his leg bone making a cracking noise as the doctor corrected it. Afterward, the doctor handed Ehren the whiskey while he grasped at the bandages, carefully wrapping them tightly about his leg to hold it exactly as it needed to be. Ehren drank heavily and gasped.

"Until it's healed, ye'll stay in bed," ordered the doctor when he was done. "No exceptions, unless ye want t' limp tha rest of yer life." With that, he nodded and abruptly left.

Amethyst once more returned to kneeling beside the bed and glanced toward Ehren.

"I don't need a nurse," Ehren said sourly.

"Ye do, and ye'll have one," Amethyst said stubbornly. "Now close yer eyes, and get some sleep."

He didn't argue with her, or even scold her for her addressing him in such a fashion. Instead, he seemed content to at least attempt to sleep.

Amethyst continued to sit by his bed, her mind drifting. She felt that the captain would be alright after the doctor's work. Ehren's reaction to her help proved he still wanted to remain reserved, but if she simply let him be, she would certainly miss out on a chance to get closer to him. This could prove to be an opportunity for her to learn his secrets. Her eyes began to droop and she rested her head on her arms, exhaustion overcoming her.

Amethyst awoke with a start, the images of a nightmare still vivid in her mind. How long had she slept? She looked at Ehren's face; he seemed undisturbed. She stood and moved out of his cabin.

As she stepped out, she blinked in the brilliant rays of sunlight. The rest of the crewmembers were busy with duties after the storm, carefully making small repairs to the hull and to the sails. She picked up a handful of tools and made her way toward them.

One of the men glanced her way. "How be tha cap'n?."

"He's asleep," she said.

The crewmember nodded and another said, "He'll need all tha help he can get. Doc says he'll be stuck fer four months. Perhaps ye can help 'im pass tha time, eh? Leave tha mendin' t' us, lass."

Amethyst only shrugged and replaced the tools. Instead of immediately returning to the captain's cabin, she moved to hers. She was alone and she changed her clothes and tidied herself a little. Then, she made her way to Ehren's quarters, pausing before the door, then knocked. She hoped he was awake.

"Leave me be, lass," she heard on the other side of the door.

She frowned. How'd he know for sure it was her? She stubbornly pushed the door open and stepped in.

The captain was sitting up, one hand to his forehead and the other on his leg. He was breathing heavily and it looked like he had been attempting to push his way out of bed and had paused to take a breath.

Her lip curled into a snarl of frustration. "Captain, what do ye think ye're doin'?" she demanded, closing the gap between them with ease. She grasped his arm, pulling it away from his leg.

"Ye'd have me waste away in here, eh?" he asked.

Amethyst scowled at him. "Well ye'll never get out if ye don't follow what tha doctor says. Ye'll probably only make it worse," she scolded him. "Besides, ye won't be all alone."

She moved across the cabin toward his windows, pushing the panes open. "There, see? Ye can still taste, hear, and smell tha sea from yer cabin." She watched as he met her gaze for a moment, and then seemed to give in.

She sighed and made her way toward the bed once again. The room fell silent, save for the call of the birds and the lapping of the waves against the ship.

"Why do ye care?" he asked.

Amethyst's ears twitched lightly and she glanced toward his face for a moment. His gaze was seaward, like so many times she had seen him before. "Well, it's partially my fault you fell," she said, forsaking the sailor's speech.

"I meant..." he paused.

Did he mean - the times she had spent questioning him before? Had his injury softened him a little? Perhaps this was why he wasn't offering more resistance toward her. "Because there's no use letting what you can't change control what you can. You just have to accept what's already happened and keep fighting for what's to come," she said, not quite giving him the chance to finish.

"Hmm..." she heard him murmur. "Perhaps," he said. "An' what of tha pain tha' comes with losing?" he asked her then.

"You just have to grow stronger," she whispered. She wondered if he'd even heard her. As she said the words, she almost felt as though she were trying to convince herself as much as him.

"Have ye done so?" he asked.

Amethyst frowned. Did he want her to share her story? She knew she wasn't exactly living what she was speaking of. She was fighting for her future, but she was still overcoming her past in many ways. Did he know it? Or was he only suspecting? Perhaps he knew that emotionally, she hadn't opened up to anyone other than Darien since even before her marriage, or at least that she still kept herself closely guarded.

"Love is a lie," she said after a moment of silence. She felt the bitterness in her tone. "Every man who's said they love me has only been after his own gain. How he can use me in some way. To be beaten, lied to, and tormented is all that *love* has ever brought me. But I refuse to be broken. Someday, I'll show them. They will pay for what they've done." She could feel the fire beneath the surface: all of the desires that lay in her heart for her ultimate goals.

"So ye finally answer me question..." he mused softly.

She glanced at him once more. "What?"

"Ye never told me why ye wanted to be a pirate," he said. "An' now I understand."

She folded her arms. "So what of you?" she asked.

"I've seen that love is pain..." he said softly, and then lay back.

Was that all he was willing to say?

She let her arms drop and only turned away.

Breaking the Mold

*T*he days began to blend together as the captain slowly recovered. Every so often, while he was asleep, Amethyst whispered a spell in her native tongue to hasten his healing. She was careful to avoid being caught.

Little by little, he seemed to grow more comfortable with her; his features softened and he even smiled at her. He learned some about her such as her natural way of speaking, as opposed to the common sailors' speech.

Yet he still refused to tell her what exactly had happened to change him from the captain his crew had described to the captain she saw now. And further, she still couldn't get much out of him about becoming a captain herself.

Still, she was certain she was slowly gaining his trust. He no longer avoided her gaze, but actually seemed to pay attention when she spoke, in part because at some point she'd told him how infuriating it was he rarely made eye contact. And at least being aboard the *Raven's Call* was better than her time as a sailor under constant orders.

Tending to the captain had its perks. She could pass instructions from him to his crew, or tell them to get something if he needed it. She also didn't have to worry about ship duties elsewhere and when he was sleeping, she could let her mind drift freely without disturbance.

Finally the captain was able to begin getting out of bed and using his leg. He needed her then to help him move about and adjust. After so much time in bed he had lost some strength. The secret spells she had whispered during his recovery had helped, and before too long he returned to full health.

It was afternoon, though the sun would soon be making its descent to the horizon. In the time of the captain's recovery, they had remained in the northwestern seas, preying on other ships for supplies or at times for a brief bout of excitement.

Amethyst hesitated before the door to the captain's cabin. He was fully recovered now and she had no reason to simply walk in without asking. She knocked and on hearing no response, opened the door slowly and peeked in. He was standing by one of the windows, his gaze distant. "Evening, Captain. I just wanted to be sure you're doing alright."

He turned toward her, leaning back against the windowsill. "Aye, lass. I be just fine," he said. His eyes held hers a moment.

She stepped in, closing the door behind her. "Well, I suppose you don't need me anymore, then. But, I do have one last question... before we resume normality."

He raised a brow. "What be that, lass?"

She wondered if things would be as they had been before his injury, if he would close himself away and become irked with her for trying to break apart his silence. "Will you have me for dinner tonight?" she asked.

His eyes widened, brows rising slightly, perplexed.

It was hardly courteous, inviting herself, but it was already done, so she waited his response.

"Aye," he said after a moment. "I should be thankin' ye somehow anyway," he said with a brief smile.

She nodded and left. He had failed to truly open up to her during all of his time under her care. Perhaps... perhaps tonight would be her final chance.

As soon as she was in her cabin, she began preparing herself.

She turned sharply as the door opened. "Darien," she breathed, turning once more and thumbing through the dresses in her simple wardrobe.

She heard his light footsteps as he moved toward his bed and sat. Amethyst glanced toward him, watching as he rubbed the back of his neck with his palm.

"Are you alright?" she asked him.

"Are you?" he asked.

She paused, frowning. "I asked first," she insisted.

His eyes met hers a moment. "I worry for you, Amethyst," he admitted finally.

"Well you shouldn't," she said. "I'm not helpless anymore. And everything I do is to reach our end goal. You still want to come with me, don't you?"

He moved toward her, grasping one of her hands. "Of course I do. But you should be careful and guard yourself. I can't always protect you, especially when you're on your own."

"I took your advice," she said. "I've decided to change my approach to things. I've realized that to pursue my desired future, I must first overcome a part of my past."

"What part is that?"

Couldn't he guess? "The part that continues to torment me," she said simply. Amethyst turned her gaze from his and toward her wardrobe once more.

He sighed softly and gently squeezed her hand a little tighter.

"Besides, I don't see why I can't explore a little and play with possibilities. Discover my own limitations. After all the things I've been forced to do and all the ways I've been explored and toyed with." She paused, "Well, it's only right. I should find out exactly what *I* like to do for a change."

She gasped slightly as he pulled her into an unexpected hug. "Darien?" she asked softly.

He was silent a moment, resting his chin on her head and simply holding her tightly.

She slowly grasped his arms, looking up at him with a mixture of shock and curiosity.

"I know," he said, "no one should ever go through what you've had to endure."

For a moment, he didn't need to say anything more. Silently, they both knew what the other was thinking and the words were both unspoken and understood. It was part of why he had stuck with her all this time. He had been the sole witness to the horrors of her marriage and had been powerless to do anything but care for her battered body after each delivery of abuse. And even once they'd escaped, she had been resigned to a similar fate. He had then also been powerless to keep her from it other than to aid in her sleep and provide a sense of familiarity, comfort, and encouragement.

She wasn't sure exactly of his feelings, but she also knew that his desire to protect her stemmed from what he had witnessed and walked with her through. His loyalty wasn't only because she had freed him from his servant status.

Darien released her and turned away, sighing softly. "Do what you feel is best for you, Amethyst. I will always be here for you." He paused.

She felt as though he was hesitant to tell her something. "What is it?" she asked him softly.

"I failed those I've loved in the past. You are my second chance. I won't fail you," he said, turning slightly to meet her gaze once more.

There was determination and care in his eyes. She smiled at him, and nodded. "I know."

Amethyst turned back to her wardrobe and finally selected the dress she wanted. It was one she'd taken from a particularly difficult plunder since she'd joined the *Raven's Call*. The merchant's ship had been better armed than they'd anticipated and some of the pirates had taken what goods they could while the others kept the sailors occupied in battle. The ship had sailed away without being entirely destroyed.

The dress was a stunning green with brilliant gold buttons about its collar and a golden sash at the waist. It cascaded gently about her figure, accentuating her curves, and as a finishing touch, Amethyst added a sinful slit in the skirt to just above her knees.

Darien raised a brow at her for a moment when he saw her do so.

"I haven't attempted anything remotely close to tempting a man since before I was married. Every bit helps," she said with a slight grin.

Darien shook his head slightly and laid back, picking up one of his books. She suspected he was still against her decision, but as she'd already told him: it was only right she face this area of life and take control of it.

She tied back only a portion of her hair, the rest of her curls tumbling down her back, and she painted her lips a gentle plum color. A soft touch of purple-red blend.

When she was ready, Amethyst made her way once more toward the captain's cabin. She wondered if any of the crewmembers suspected what she was up to. As she stepped in, her nose was hit with variant aromas. Near the opposite end of the cabin, the table was prepared with cooked pork in its center and a flourish of vegetables, some bread, and a handful of fruits.

Finally, her eyes settled on Ehren. It seemed he had also tidied himself up. His dark hair was slicked back and he wore a gentleman's coat.

"Well, isn't it a bit much, for just the two of us, I mean?" she asked, moving forward.

"This comin' from ye?" he asked, his eyes briefly traveling her figure and then settling on her eyes. She knew he meant the manner in which she'd come.

She smiled at him and took her seat. "Fair enough."

Silence fell as they started their meal. Amethyst noticed the way Ehren attempted more manners than she'd normally witnessed, but didn't ask.

"Amethyst, I do wish to say me gratitude fer yer aid these months," the captain began, breaking the silence. "I'd be a fool not to realize if it weren't fer ye, I might be dead or at leas' permanently crippled."

Amethyst smiled and dabbed at her mouth with her napkin. "It was no trouble, Captain. And besides, anyone could have helped. I only followed the doctor's orders."

Ehren smiled and closed his eyes a moment. "Ye pretend to be modest now, eh?" When his eyes opened, he looked her dead in the face. "I know ye did more than jus' that," he said.

She shrugged, taking another bite of food.

"Me recovery wouldn't have been so swift or complete without the aid o' magic. I'm no fool."

Amethyst hesitated. Had the show of the evening on his part only been to butter her up before he informed her he'd be dismissing her from the crew?

She finished her bite and took a dainty sip of rum before gently rising from her seat. "Well, Captain," she began, moving around the table's corner and toward him, "How could I possibly forgive myself if I didn't do everything possible to help?"

He frowned at that. "We've been over this, lass. It wasn't yer fault. All manner of things happen in a storm."

"Perhaps," she mused. "But even so, I did what I saw fit."

"Aye," he said softly, "and ye have me thanks."

She hesitated, placing her palm on the table and leaning against it slightly. "Ye won't tell anyone?" she asked.

"Nay, Amethyst," he said after a moment. "Though I don' see how it matters. That the fae use magic is common knowledge."

She shrugged, "Well I wouldn't want to be known for or suspected of gaining any advantage through magic," was all she said. "It's about merit."

He nodded, "Very well."

"But aside from that, Captain, I have my own reasons for requesting dinner with you," Amethyst said.

He leaned back, resting his cheek on his fist. "Oh?"

She stepped toward him once more, closing the gap between them. "Perhaps even reasons for aiding in your recovery," she murmured. She pushed against his chair until it turned away from the table and she bent toward him. "I'm curious," she said, "Have you ever thought of me as anything other than a mere member of your crew?"

His gaze briefly moved from her face down her jawline and neck to her bosom and returned once more to her eyes. "Nay..." he murmured.

"Not even once?" she pressed, her curls falling over her shoulders and about her arms and chest.

"Why?" he asked her in response. "Ye yerself have told me again and again how men only see ye as something to put their hands on. Can ye not accept that not all men are tha same?"

She shrugged, raising a finger and daring to gently push a few locks of hair from his face. "Aye, it's a little perplexing, but I can accept it, perhaps because those aboard the Raven aren't that way." She paused, "Ye make me feel... more comfortable. And a little daring." *Like a challenge.* Though she didn't speak that thought for fear he'd shut her away again within moments.

"Will you let me...?" she asked, wondering how his mind might finish the sentence.

Part of her wanted to know his thoughts. He stared into her eyes silently for what felt like forever, though it was seconds. Ehren raised a single hand and grasped hers, his thumb stroking her palm. "Aye," he murmured.

For a moment, a pit rose in her gut as it had so many times in the past. And then her conversation with Darien flashed through her mind. She could do this. She was in control. And this time it wasn't against her will as it always had been.

Amethyst stepped back, lacing her fingers with Ehren's and pulling him from his seat. She used his momentum to draw him toward her into a kiss. As he let her, she could sense his nervousness. Was it because of the secrets he had yet to reveal? Or was it just towards her?

She pulled him toward his bed, guiding his hands across her skin and eventually to the ties in her dress that once undone caused the thing to fall about her feet.

Not once did his desire overcome him. He let her do exactly as she wanted. Even when she pushed him down and removed his own clothes at her pace.

It was the first time the experience hadn't only brought her bitterness and some sort of pain.

In fact, for the first time, she began to see that it could be pleasurable. That it could be fun.

Hours later, Captain Ehren was asleep beside her. Yet she lay wide awake, her mind unable to be still. She couldn't help wondering if when he awoke, he would send her away. Or if perhaps he would begin requesting her to join him more often. Would anything change?

She closed her eyes, but the more she tried to sleep, the more she couldn't. She didn't want to leave lest he wake up from her movements. He wasn't a particularly deep sleeper, which she knew from her time caring for him.

Instead, she tried to think of something to pass the time. A memory of an old fae folk song drifted through her thoughts, and she focused on it, repeating the words and letting the tune flow through her mind. At least it put her worries at ease for the time being.

Sometime later, Ehren stirred, turning toward her. He was silent a moment.

"Did ye sleep, Amethyst?" he asked.

She smiled at him and shrugged.

"Perhaps ye'd like some rum?" he murmured.

Did he care so much if she slept or not? "Perhaps I'll make up for it later," she said. "I should return to duties with the crew."

"Very well," he replied, "If ye wish it."

Why was he being so complacent? Was it only since she had helped in his recovery? Would his compliance with her wishes change once he felt he'd repaid a debt to her?

She felt so uncertain.

Still, she supposed she'd enjoy it while it lasted.

That night she returned to the captain's cabin of her own will. She wanted to test herself. What did she like or not like? What were her true limits and expectations?

She began to grow more comfortable with her own body and her own will.

She returned again the next night, and the next, and time began to slip by once more.

All the while, Ehren seemed not only willing, but his eagerness steadily grew. It almost became expected for her to join him in the evenings, though if she chose not to go but rather to stay in her own cabin, she never heard complaints or questions. Yet for all of it, she found she couldn't grow attached emotionally. They seemed to have a mutual understanding. At least she felt so. They both remained somewhat guarded, never quite reaching that step of vulnerability.

Several more months passed and they decided to set course for the southeastern seas for a time. The night was particularly cool and Amethyst lay close to Ehren for warmth. He gently trailed a finger up and down her arm, causing her to shudder lightly from the touch.

"Do ye remember at the beginning my coldness toward ye?" he asked.

She looked up at his face, taken aback by his question. It was so... out of the blue. "Yes," she murmured, wondering where he was going.

"Do ye wish to know why?" he asked.

"I always have," she responded.

"Ye reminded me of me lost first mate. It's part of why I took ye aboard. But I didn't want to get too close. It was too soon, and I wanted to help ye. But, I was afraid if I got close I'd get hurt again, y'see," he said.

Amethyst was silent a moment. "I heard she was lost in a storm."

"Aye," he said, "One much like that where I was injured. But she wasn't as fortunate as I."

Amethyst wasn't sure how to respond. For as long as she had waned to pry into his heart and mind, she now almost felt worse off for knowing. Did he think she had been trying to take her place? No. Perhaps in a way, she had.

"I'm sorry," she offered simply.

He sighed slowly. "It's in the past. If there's one thing I've learned from ye it's to move on and let go, eh?"

Amethyst briefly though back to what she'd said during his recovery and nodded. In her own way, she'd been fighting against her past with what she'd done with Ehren, and he had helped her also. Perhaps they'd helped each other.

"Amethyst," he murmured, "I think I love you."

She was startled, looking up at him again. Immediately, her mind returned to a whirl of thoughts.

"Ehren..." she bit her lip, sitting up and turning away. Her heart was pounding. What was she so afraid of? It wasn't like he had asked her to marry him!

But if she reciprocated, she felt she'd be tied down. She wasn't ready for that yet.

"Ye don't have t' respond," he said when she hadn't spoken.

She sighed softly. "It's best if ye don't become attached to me, Captain," she said finally. "I have me own path. Thank ye for all ye've done to help me." Perhaps she returned to the sailor's way of speaking to put distance. It had only come out naturally. She turned back toward him with a smile.

He nodded slowly. "Aye," he said. "Just stay the night then." he finished.

She gave in. There was no harm in it.

"It's time for us to move on," Amethyst told Darien the next day during duties.

Darien raised a brow. "Is everything alright?" he asked.

"Of course. But it's time to find the next ship and crew."

Darien remained silent a moment.

"I'll share with you more later," Amethyst said finally. "For now, will you come with me? We should continue learning how other ships are run and who the other captains are to contend with."

"Aye, Amethyst," Darien said, offering her a smile.

She was glad he didn't question further.

"Do ye have a particular ship in mind?" he asked after another moment of silence.

"We'll see who we encounter," she said with a shrug.

At that Darien frowned, but didn't argue. It was common enough to cross paths with other pirates, though they each typically went on their way. It would be best to join a new crew while at a port where it was more subtle and less dramatic, but she wouldn't hesitate if another opportunity presented itself. Amethyst planned to either leave directly with a peaceful interaction, or spy another ship from a distance and take one of the row boats.

Several weeks passed and the only ship they encountered was a large merchantman with a bountiful plunder.

During that time, Amethyst visited Ehren's cabin only once.

"I'm moving on," she told him over dinner.

He watched her with gentle eyes and nodded. "I can't convince ye to stay, eh?" he asked, offering a smile.

She shook her head. "Thank you for what you've done for me. My place just isn't here."

Did he really understand?

He nodded once more. "Very well. So be it."

Silence resumed and they finished their meal.

In those weeks, she eventually told Darien what had happened with Ehren and why she so abruptly decided to move on to the next ship. The idea of commitment at the moment was terrifying for her.

Ehren left her alone. She suspected it was in part to make it easier for himself.

She found she began to miss the intimacy, though, and she began to crave the pleasure. She kept that bit to herself and turned her focus to consuming more rum. She hoped it would distract her.

"Sail ho!" cried the lookout one particularly crisp, clear morning.

Amethyst had been up early to busy herself and keep her mind off the captain. She rushed to the edge of the deck and grasped a spyglass. A smirk slowly crept onto her lips.

Brilliant red sails with white full moons sewn into the canvases billowed. It was the *Bloody Moon*, a ship with a crew known for being hardy and bloodthirsty, but who also loved to eat, drink, and be merry. Perhaps this was her next destination. Amethyst waved to the lookout and they raised a white flag to indicate their approach was peaceful for the other ship to see.

The two ships sailed toward each other until a bit later they were broadside. By that point, most of the *Raven's* crew had assembled, including its captain.

As soon as they were close, Amethyst quickly took in what she could from the *Bloody Moon*. It was a corvette - sometimes mistaken for a sloop-of-war – a ship with one full deck and several partial decks and three square-rigged masts. It was smaller than other ships, but hardly less formidable. The crewmembers above deck had paused in their work and were staring at those aboard the *Raven's Call*. They were men, and appeared both young and able-bodied.

The captain, who stood near the edge of the ship, was shorter than Ehren with dark brown hair and a mixture of green and blue eyes. He had a strong physique and his youthful face featured an angled jaw and handsome features. She also noticed he was elaborately adorned with jewels, accessories and various weapons. He clearly held great pride in his possessions.

Amethyst frowned. She could almost see him vainly viewing women as trophies for him to flaunt and use to his pleasing. Maybe he thought he had a way with wenches that swooned before him. Well, she decided to accept this one as a personal challenge. She'd wake him up from his delirium. She would introduce him to something different than the women she imagined groveling for his affection. And if he ever crossed a line with her, perhaps she'd show him to Sedra's fate and take his ship for herself. The thought was pleasing. Amethyst realized she had grown in confidence from her time aboard the *Raven's Call*.

"Permission to board?" she asked, stepping toward the plank that had been thrown from one ship to the other.

"Permission granted," the captain said.

She swore there was a glimmer in his eyes as he drank in her figure. She chose to ignore it, for now.

"What business do ye have with me?" he asked as soon as she'd made it across the plank.

Amethyst glanced toward Ehren a moment.

He only gave her a curt nod.

"I wish to join yer crew," she said frankly.

"Oh?" he mused. "Ye'd so readily abandon yer own, eh? Or perhaps ye've heard the tales of the Bloody Moon? Tell me, lass, why should I trust ye? That ye won't leave me crew as readily as this other one? What good can ye offer?"

At that she smirked with confidence. "I've heard yer ship's reputation is a bloody one. I can be of aid in yer plunders. As for yer crew verses the Raven's, we've simply had our differences." It wasn't uncommon for pirates to split ways over an argument. "Would ye like a demonstration?" she asked him.

He nodded after a moment and motioned with two fingers to a couple of his crewmembers. Two on one? She laughed inwardly and wondered if he thought she'd find it unfair. She drew her sabre.

Amethyst lunged toward the first sailor, not waiting for him to attack first. He made a grimace as she used her momentum and her body slammed into his. She leaped back, turning and landing a solid kick into the other pirate's gut.

The pirate grunted, but lunged toward her, bringing his sword down.

She met his blade, the zing of metal resounding, and then ducked to the side.

The first pirate had regained himself and she turned, striking upward with her fist and landing a solid blow to his jaw. He stumbled backward into the mast, his eyes dazed.

She immediately turned her focus toward her other opponent. From the corner of her eye, she saw his movement and she turned, kicking her boot outward and causing him to fall to the deck. She plunged her sword a mere inch from his neck into the wood below him, his eyes widening in shock.

The battle was over quickly.

She stepped back, keeping her focus on the two crewmembers but glanced toward the captain. "Not bad..." he mused.

Amethyst didn't like his arrogance, but she had already determined she'd have her fun and teach him a lesson, and to do so, she must join his crew. Besides, it had been settled she'd leave the *Raven.* This ship was merely the next step in her journey to becoming a captain herself. She had decided to continue to join other ships and toy with their captains: learn their strengths and weaknesses and then rise above them all.

"So ye can handle a sword, but can I trust me ship in yer hands?"

"Aye," she said both confidently and boldly. "I can get 'er through tha worst of storms and do anythin' the men can do."

"We shall see," said the captain.

Amethyst looked to the *Raven* and beckoned for Darien to join her.

"What's this? A package?" the captain said with a laugh.

Darien moved across the plank.

"If ye wish to join, ye must also prove yerself. Are yer skills tha same as yer companion?" he demanded.

Darien drew his sword. "Care to challenge me?" he asked, his voice calm.

The captain paused, assessing Darien closely.

Perhaps he was debating the wisdom of accepting the challenge, or how he might handle a loss. Amethyst dismissed that thought. This captain seemed the type to think a loss for himself impossible.

The captain drew his sword. "Aye," he responded to Darien with a grin. "Defeat me, and ye're welcome aboard."

Amethyst stepped back, as did the *Bloody Moon*'s crew. She noticed the way Darien's eyes flicked over the captain. She knew he was silently evaluating him, trying to see his potential weaknesses.

Darien didn't wait for the captain to attack. He stepped forward and the captain parried, a confident smirk finding its way onto his lips. Darien attacked once more, his footwork beginning a dance as he maintained balance and swung wide.

As the fight continued, the captain blocked Darien's strikes, not quite attacking his opponent. Was he trying to wear Darien down by not allowing him to land a blow?

Amethyst had sparred with Darien enough times to know he was only beginning. Sweat hadn't yet broken on his brow. She grinned to herself as Darien's eyes narrowed slightly and his attacks become more serious, swift, and steady. She knew he had learned the captain's pattern of movements. It was a part of Darien's experience and technique.

The captain's confident smirk vanished as he fought back, their blades colliding.

Darien narrowly avoided a blow to his shoulder and the captain in turn dodged one to his face.

The captain lunged in, and danced away, but Darien followed, thrusting his sword inward. The captain attempted to parry Darien's thrust, but his blade slipped, and Darien landed a cut in the captain's arm. However, the captain's sword plunged downward gashing Darien's thigh. The height of the battle seemed to have dulled their senses as neither of them showed their pain.

As the fight continued, both seemed equally matched. Their breathing became heavier, their skin beginning to glisten in the brilliant sunlight. Darien was pushing the captain backward, cornering him against the mainmast. The captain snarled, ducked and whirled, attempting to land a blow to Darien's side. Darien didn't falter, but rather lunged back, blocking the captain's blade. The captain moved in again, a flash of silver glimmering as a knife was produced from his person in combination with his sword's attack.

Darien blocked the captain's sword, and Amethyst couldn't help the wave of relief crashing over her as Darien moved to his right and the knife sliced through the air beside his neck. Darien grasped the captain's sword wrist, and his thumb pressed into the flesh, causing the captain's sword to clatter to the deck. The captain hissed, attempting to strike with his knife once more.

Darien gripped the captain's other arm, releasing the arm he had previously grabbed and landed a solid punch to his gut with his now free hand.

The captain grimaced but attempted to quickly regain his composure. He stepped back, reaching down to pick up his sword.

Amethyst smirked. Served him right for trying to fight dirty. She wondered if the captain had hoped no one would notice, or she had been right and he really was the type to think a loss for himself impossible. Perhaps he had realized the falsity of the notion and decided to change his tactic. As soon as the duel was over, she rushed toward Darien, partially in case they suddenly found themselves under attack for the captain's defeat.

The captain straightened himself, returning his sword to its sheath.

"Well fought," he said with a grin as though he had indeed won the challenge. He then turned his gaze toward the *Raven's Call* once more. "Captain Ehren! Ye let these go with such ease? Perhaps ye mean to cast away yer filth?"

"Nay, Captain Siilas!" Ehren called back. "Ye'll see fer yerself their worth and value. I let them go that they may follow their decided path."

At that Captain Siilas, as Ehren had called him, fell silent a moment, eyes scrutinizing Amethyst and Darien.

Finally, he spoke once more. "Very well. Welcome aboard!"

He turned then, waving a hand. "Set sail, ye dogs! We continue due east!"

"Aye, aye!" resounded from the crew.

Amethyst and Darien moved toward the rest of the crew and began to aid with their duties.

As they sailed away, Amethyst glanced back toward the *Raven's Call*. She couldn't think of regrets or what Ehren was thinking. She needed to move on for her own future, and with that, she pushed her thoughts aside.

Taking a Stand

$\mathcal{I}$t didn't take long for Amethyst and Darien to become accepted as one of the crewmembers aboard the *Bloody Moon*. Darien's cooking won over their bellies, and they quickly learned he was more than capable with the rest of the work.

At first, they were harsher toward Amethyst.

It was the day after they had joined the crew, the sun nearing its highest point. Darien was below deck in the galley and Amethyst was working with one of the other deckhands on inspecting the rigging.

"Oy, ye there, wench! Grab tha slosh buckets and swab tha deck!"

Amethyst's eyes snapped downward, searching for the one who had hollered at her. She had grown used to the idea that there weren't many women at sea, and that men thought women didn't belong or that their duties were rather specific. The *Raven* had been unique in that all of the crewmembers were seen as equals unless circumstances demanded the leadership of the captain. But she was no longer some sailor aboard a merchant's vessel bending beneath the rules of rank, and she refused to be treated with such disrespect. Her lip curled into a snarl, one of her fangs protruding. With a fluid motion, she swung down the mast.

"Care t' say that to me face?" she challenged.

One of the crewmembers stepped forward with a smirk on his lips. "Ye may have swayed tha cap'n, lass. But a wench is good fer a good time and a man's biddin'. Tha only wenches aboard the Bloody Moon are tha ones we desire fer ourselves. Ye're a pretty thing. Who knows, perhaps one of us'll deem ye worthy of our beds." He paused, the rest of the crew laughing. "Now, wench, see to the swabbing."

Amethyst reached for her sabre. "Come at me, then," she said, eyes flashing. "If ye want me to bend to yer will, ye'll have to *make me*."

"With pleasure, wench!" the man said, drawing his sword and lunging for her.

Fool, she thought. Hadn't he witnessed her skills when she'd first asked to become a member of the crew? She blocked his first attack, their blades resounding with a clash of metal before falling apart and coming together again.

Jeers from the crew began to grow louder.

She circled, watching his steps and his movements closely. Clearly, he was more skilled than those she had first fought.

He came at her again, feigning a downward slice and changing his angle.

She smirked, shoving her wrist upward and colliding with his before turning and shoving her elbow into his gut and jumping back. He grimaced and collected himself, stepping toward her once more.

Well, she gave him credit for persistence.

She caught his blade with hers, blocking his strike once more and then lunged in, landing a solid punch to his face.

He stumbled back, his eyes a mixture of shock and fury.

Perhaps he'd never been bested by a *woman* before.

Amethyst didn't merely jump back and wait for his next attack. Instead, she followed after him, shoving her boot into his stomach and pointing her sabre to his throat. Only then did she step back. Her muscles were tense, and she wondered if he would still come after her, or if any of the other crewmembers would jump in in his place.

She started as a voice boomed over the deck.

"Is this how fae women behave?" Captain Siilas asked her.

She turned her gaze sharply in his direction. He stood on the quarterdeck, his hands grasping the rails at its end and looking down to the main deck.

"I only fight when provoked, and I'll be treated tha same as any of ye! I'm no mere wench," she said, glaring toward the man who had first challenged her.

"Enough!" Captain Siilas' voice bellowed again. "Ye'll treat each other better aboard me ship. Ye're all members of the Bloody Moon!"

"Aye!" the crew responded.

Amethyst sheathed her sabre, returning to the mast and making her way upward to resume her work with the rigging. She glanced toward the captain, frowning. Had he meant to imply that a *woman* should behave better? And had his words to treat each other better meant to imply the others shouldn't treat her, as a woman, so violently?

She breathed slowly, pushing her temper down. Either way, she found the implications insulting. What did it matter if she were fae? Or a woman? Even if she'd grown used to much of the male sailors' mentality, that didn't mean their views didn't infuriate her. She was a member of the crew like the rest of them. *And* she was a *pirate.* From what she'd seen, that meant a certain amount of daring and violence automatically. The question of if her life would remain that way flitted through her mind. She shoved it aside, focusing on her work.

After the skirmish, the crew seemed to at least leave her be, yet the crewmember in particular that had challenged her didn't seem to be satisfied.

The next night, the crew had gathered in the mess hall. The duties for the ship had been done early in the day and the crew chose to spend their time with drinking games. Some of them had declared bets on who could kill and gather more on their next plunder.

Amethyst had joined them briefly, though she had no desire to participate in the drinking. However, when the bets began, she was all too eager to participate. "Ye all be fools!" she declared. "Our next plunder will leave me beatin' all of ye, and whatever each of ye bets I'll take for meself." She smirked as the crew laughed and jeered. Well, if they were all bloody cutthroats, then she'd prove herself by being the worst of them.

She moved out of the room and toward the main deck, a bottle of rum in her hand. She silently promised she would prove herself better than all of them.

"So, *wench,* ye think ye're better than the rest of us?"

Her ears twitched. It was the crewmember she'd fought the day before. She scoffed, sipping at her rum.

"Oh? Ye're too good to even answer me?" She ignored him as he moved closer. "Well ye're not better. Ye're just a mere lass."

Her gaze snapped to his as his fingers grasped her wrist. Well, she had half a mind to break the bottle she was holding over his head. But that would be such a waste of perfectly good rum.

"Get yer hand off me," she hissed, her voice low.

"Or what?" he teased. His tongue reminded her of a snake as it slicked over his lips. She recognized that look in his eyes. That desire to subdue her and overpower her.

The girl that wouldn't have fought back was long gone. And she was stronger than she looked. In a moment, her nails had lengthened as did her fangs. She put the rum in the hand he was restraining and used the other to slash at his cheek.

He cried out, stumbling back and grasping at his face. A slew of curses flew from his lips, his eyes flashing.

"Do ye want more?" she asked with a smirk. She moved toward him, swaying slightly, taunting. "Don't ye wish to push me beneath you?"

He lunged toward her with a dagger. It tore through her pirate's shirt and sliced a cut into her arm. "Well, I don't think tha cap'n would be too thrilled about this," she said with a slight pout. She stepped sideways and turned, kicking her boot upward and landing a solid blow to his groin. "Ye should know I'd like nothing better than to spill yer filthy blood all over tha deck. But I think I'd rather stay in the captain's good graces, savvy?"

He crumbled in a heap, groaning softly.

She smirked, walking away and once more sipping at her rum.

Perhaps now he'd at least leave her be. Amethyst silently wondered if the captain would've taken her side or this scumbag's, had he witnessed the whole thing.

No matter, she supposed.

First, she wanted to make good on her bet with the rest of the crew. The *Bloody Moon* hunted other ships, as opposed to the pirate ships that sailed with the hope of crossing another but didn't hunt specific ships down. It wouldn't be long before their next plunder, she knew.

Word got around quickly of what had happened between herself and the bilge rat that had tried to lay his hands on her. She didn't care to know his name, nor did he deserve for her to use it. The others seemed to respect her a little more, and also were wary of her.

Several days later, another ship was at last in sight.

The crew prepared themselves quickly, loudly reminding each other of their previous bets. Amethyst ignored them, silently preparing herself. She knew they remembered the words she'd spoken. As they got closer, she debated how to get a head start on the rest of them. She could be one of the first to leap to the other ship or to move across the plank. Another idea struck her, and her excitement grew.

Most pirate crews relied on their advantage in numbers during their plunders as opposed to trained skill, as she had learned when she'd first joined the *Raven's Call*. Ehren had told her their advantage was in numbers. However, having been trained from her youth the same skills of the fae army, Amethyst was someone who could overcome numbers with her skill, depending on how many she faced at once.

They were growing closer. The other ship would not be able to make it far ahead of them with their speed. Amethyst grasped one of the lines, climbing up until she stood on the edge of the ship. She waited, and once she knew she wouldn't be run over, she dove into the water.

The thunderous booms of the first round of cannon fire rippled through the water just as Amethyst reached the hull of the merchant ship. She had already lengthened her nails and fangs and she clawed at the wood, scaling the ship quickly. With a skilled leap, she pushed herself over the side of the ship.

The other pirates swarmed the deck with brute force and numbers, taking trinkets from each of their kills. It would be their proof for winning the bet after the battle. Many of the passengers ran for cover, though some of the brave ones reached for guns. The sailors fought back to defend themselves as much as the passengers.

Amethyst had begun her attack just before her fellow crewmembers. The sailors had been focused on the oncoming ship and hadn't noticed her coming from the side, which had given her a brief advantage. Amethyst didn't stop as she made her way across the deck using a combination of daggers and her fists. Her will to rise above the others on the *Bloody Moon* urged her onward.

Another blast from cannons rocked the ship. Amethyst wiped sweat from her brow and surged forward. With each kill, Amethyst ripped something from the body: cufflinks, jewelry, pieces of their clothing. She wondered if the other pirates had noticed the way she'd plunged toward the merchant ship, or that she'd made it before them. She saw one of the pirates swords locked with that of one of the sailors. She smirked, throwing a knife and plunging it through the sailor's back. The pirate looked her way sharply, a mixture of expressions in his eyes. She had taken the kill; she only laughed and continued her tirade.

"The ship is ours!" she heard Captain Siilas bellow above the roars of battle.

The merchant ship quaked and the wood groaned as the fighting slowed. The cannons had taken decent chunks from both ships.

Amethyst pulled her sword from a passenger's chest, his body falling with a dull thud. She reached down and tore a link from the cuff of his shirt. As she stood, Amethyst looked around. Fires licked at the sky and bodies lay strewn across the deck, staining the ocean red. The ship was in ruins. The pirates set about taking the merchandise aboard the *Bloody Moon* and Amethyst couldn't help taking mental note to the damage they had done. Siilas' ship and crew had certainly earned their reputation.

Cheers and song echoed from the *Bloody Moon* later that night. The men were well on their way to slumber after so much drink and stuffing their bellies. "So lads," one of them had shouted at the beginning of the party, "who won tha bet, eh?"

The men began shouting over each other their kills and gathered loot.

Amethyst waited, sipping at her rum from an ornate goblet and watching them. She had taken a jacket from one of the men she'd slain and now wore it over her shoulders. Such a broad of uncouth, unmannered brutes, she thought, though perhaps that was hypocritical of her after the massacre she had wrought from her own hands, let alone theirs.

She gulped back the last of her goblet's contents, setting it down with a thud on the table. Afterward, she stood on one of the bolted benches, placing one of her boots on the table. She threw the jacket back, stretching out her arms. An array of torn strips of cloth, pieces of jewelry, and even some other accessories dangled freely. Each one was a trinket of proof taken from each of the bodies she had cut down. They had laughed at her. Looked down on her. Would they now?

The men gawked, the room slowly falling to silence for but a moment. "Blimey, lads!" One sailor's laughter resounded, more joining in. "Alright, lass, ye've earned it," he said, tossing a small coin purse to her end of the table. The sound of clanking coins filled the room then as the others who had taken bets one by one tossed their purses.

For a moment, she had considered leaving the sacks on the table to make a point that she cared less for the coin and more about their respect of her. Instead, as she thought about it, she felt saving the coins for once she did become a pirate captain would be far wiser.

Amethyst gathered the coins, collecting the sum into a larger sack and tucking it into her belt. "Perhaps ye'll think twice before challenging me again, eh?" she said with a laugh. She leaped down from the bench and grasped the bottle of rum, taking it with her. "Enjoy yer evening, lads!" she shouted as she moved away and toward her cabin. She didn't trust they wouldn't try and take their coins back from her at some point.

She was somewhat glad to find the room empty, though she wondered what Darien was up to. Since her days as a merchant, Amethyst had chosen to share a cabin with him in part because she was used to it and in part for her own peace of mind. Her night terrors were worse when she slept elsewhere, and Darien was able to, at the least, provide sleeping spells to help her.

Her eyes scanned the cabin. There was nowhere she could truly hide anything if someone was looking. She sighed; she'd just have to use magic. She decided on a shock spell: anyone that tried to lay a finger on her coin would receive a jolt of electricity. That would do nicely. She closed her eyes, breathing slowly and whispered the spell in her native tongue. As soon as it was done, she placed the sack under her bed.

Having hidden her coin, she moved out of her cabin and toward the main deck. She breathed in deeply as soon as the smell of the sea and the feel of the wind hit her face. There was nothing like it... truly.

"Care t' join me, lass?"

Her ears twitched slightly and she turned, her eyes settling on the captain's form. She wondered what he wanted, and the last words he had directly spoken to her rang in her ears. He stood not too far from her, a goblet grasped by the rim in his fingers.

"Why not?" she said. Her boots clacked softly against the deck as she closed the distance between them.

Siilas tipped his goblet to his lips and set it down on the deck by his feet. "I'm curious..." he started, "why is it that ye wanted t' join me crew, eh? I've 'eard of a few lasses that be makin' names fer themselves on tha seas. An' I've seen tha way ye fight. Ye could probably have anythin'. Th' only wenches aboard me ship are the ones I invite t' give me a good time. So tell me lass, what is it that ye want?"

Amethyst shrugged. "For new experiences," she answered him. She took a sip from the bottle she'd brought, keeping it in her hand. "Isn't that reason enough?"

He chuckled softly. "I've 'eard tha crew talkin'. They say t' steer clear o' ye if ye know what's good fer ya. There isn't many a wench that turns me away."

Amethyst scoffed. "It's only the money, the reputation and the notion of glamor that draw the women, Captain," she told him. "I don't need any of that from you."

He met her gaze a moment, and she wasn't sure if she saw contempt or surprise in those eyes. Perhaps both.

He chuckled once more. "No matter, lass. If that's not what yer after, then what is it?"

So persistent. "I told ye, new experiences. That's all."

With that, she moved away from him.

At first, he remained where he was, but then she heard the soft sound of his goblet scrape the deck as he picked it up and his boots made dull thuds as he turned and followed her.

She stopped, frowning.

"Didn't ye learn manners, lass?" he asked as he got close.

"Ye mean as a *woman*?" she asked, feeling her temper flare.

He continued forward until he stood beside her, facing her. "Do ye believe me a threat?" he asked.

She sucked in her breath and glanced toward him. His eyes were softened and there was a charming sort of smile at the corners of his lips.

"Aye, lass, part o' me feels a woman should be treated to 'er 'earts' desires an' shown a good time. It's somewhat difficult to watch a lass sweatin' an' workin' as hard as us men, savvy? Is that so wrong?"

So his implications were that because she was a woman, she should be treated like royalty? Or was it that she should let a man care for her and then bend to his whims as well? She hated the way his implications could be entirely romantic or entirely piggish.

"Aye," she said simply. "Yer opinions leave no room for a woman's choice in tha matter. Some women take pride in standin' on their own two feet, *savvy?*" she said sarcastically.

Siilas' smile persisted and he nodded, shifting to stand beside her.

Was this the way he seduced the common wenches in the pubs, she wondered?

"Perhaps, lass. Though perhaps yer secrets 'ave damaged yer faith in men, eh?" he chuckled and moved on ahead, twirling his goblet in his hand once more.

She watched him, biting her tongue. He was right, and his perceptiveness was almost like a punch in the gut. He caused her temper to boil in a very different way than Ehren had.

Amethyst scowled and went her way, her enjoyment of the evening entirely ruined. She shouldn't let him get to her so, she thought. It would only spoil her fun and may even lead him to believe she was just like all the others who eventually succumbed to his seduction. She smirked. If that was how he saw women, she could use it against him.

They were sailing further southeast, which was uncharted territory. Because of its lack of discovery, it was not uncommon for merchants and pirates alike to venture there, pirates more often, in hopes of discovering something new and achieving fame.

Several days passed since Siilas' attempt to pry into Amethyst's secrets, claiming to be a man of chivalry and trust. Evening had long gone and the night was so dark that the deck had to be lit by torches. She was standing on the main deck, lost in her own thoughts.

"Evenin, lass," Siilas' voice drifted across the deck.

Amethyst ignored him, gazing into the ever darkness. She wished there were even a sliver of starlight on the horizon. Her ears twitched as he got closer, his face now illuminated in the torchlight and the shadows dancing across his features.

"Still without proper manners?" he asked with a chuckle.

She couldn't hold back the sharp glare as she met his gaze a moment, hoping he could see the fire in her eyes, before she turned back toward the sea. "If I wanted to behave like a lady, I would," she said stubbornly. "I'm a pirate. I can do as I please."

"Aye," Siilas responded. "But-" she sucked in her breath as he grasped her dangling hand in one of his and his other hand gently traced a finger up her cheek to tuck some stray ringlets of purple behind her ear. "It's so unbecoming."

Amethyst couldn't help the heat that rose in her cheeks but she tried to play it off and smirked, pulling her hand from his. "Is that meant to cause me heart to swoon?" she asked with a slight chuckle.

He lifted his arm and rested his elbow on the edge of the ship, using his fist as a prop for his head. That same simple smile found its way onto his lips. He really did think he was just the most charming thing, didn't he? She continued to stare into the distance, partially to make him see that whatever he tried made no difference.

"Well, perhaps I wouldn't try so hard if ye'd not play so hard to get," he mused.

She scoffed. "It's no play, I assure you," she muttered.

"Actually I find yer indifference intriguing. Ye've got me curiosity, Amethyst." The way he said her name would've made anyone blush.

She shook her head. "Well if ye can tell I don' care, leave me be," she said, ignoring his unspoken question of why she was refusing to cave to him. She knew he was still trying to pry into her secrets.

"Very well," he murmured with a shrug and went on his way.

She glanced toward his back a moment and then once more gazed seaward. Amethyst wondered if that was only surrender on his part for tonight. She doubted he would actually leave her alone.

Instead, he stayed true to his word.

As they continued south, he helped with ship duties or stayed in his cabin. Amethyst attempted to remain aloof. She dared not let him catch her looking his way. If she let him believe she was like other girls, desirous of him, she was certain she would be treated as them also. She would never truly get close enough to discover his weaknesses. She must remain true to her purpose: learn as much as she could, including where each captain she encountered fell short, and then rise above them all.

Weeks passed without another close interaction between Amethyst and Siilas. She began to wonder if he would seek her out again. Then another thought crossed her mind. She should see it as her opportunity to hook his attention and turn the tables. Make him play her game.

They had turned their direction northeast, having discovered nothing on their voyage of interest. Any further south and their direction would change toward the north and the fae territories.

Amethyst waited until the crew had retired for the night and filled the mess halls with their drunken song before she made her way toward the captain's cabin.

How scandalous, she thought, if one of the crewmembers caught her venturing in on her own. She brushed it aside. What business was it of theirs?

Firelight glimmered from Siilas' cabin and she knocked.

"Come in," she heard on the other side of the door.

Amethyst stepped in, closing the door behind her.

He met her gaze a moment and resumed whatever it was he was doing. There were papers arrayed across a simple wooden table on the far side of the room and his finger traced over the one in front of him slowly, his brows furrowed.

"Evening, Captain," she said softly.

He looked up once more. Perhaps in part for the way she said it.

"What is it, lass?" he asked.

"Well, Captain, I've changed me mind," she started, making her way casually across the room. She traced one finger along the edge of the wooden table when she reached it and slowly stepped around it until she was nearly beside him.

"Why be that?" he asked her, his eyes drifting from her finger up her arm and to her face.

"Well, perhaps I've decided to entertain ye," she said, tilting her head slightly until some of her curls cascaded about her shoulder.

That same simple smile she had seen on their last encounter caused his lips to curve at the edges ever so slightly "Very well," he said, tracing her cheek in the same manner as he had before. "I'll have ye join me tomorrow for dinner."

Perhaps he was trying to shift things toward his terms instead of hers. Amethyst sucked her tongue and shrugged. "Till then, Captain," she said, turning and exiting. Perhaps he thought he'd won, or that she was giving in to his suggestion. She smirked as she made her way back to her cabin. Very soon, he would learn he was nothing more than a part to play in her game.

The next evening, she arrived a few minutes after he'd told her to. Amethyst partially intended to spark his temper, and wanted to assert her control over the situation. She knocked.

"C'me in," she heard before she stepped in and closed the door behind her, smoothing out her skirt.

He was sitting as though he were a king on his throne, leaning back into his chair and sipping on a goblet. She breathed slowly as his eyes traveled over her figure. She wore a long flowing skirt that gently twirled about her legs when she moved and a pale blouse that complemented her figure. Her clothing was hardly elaborate other than a shimmering comb she had tucked into her curls.

Amethyst moved toward the table, taking her seat. He gestured toward the meal. "As you please," he said simply.

She knew it. He professed to have chivalry, and yet coyly sat as though she were his new prize.

Conversation was idle chatter, all surface for his true intent. And hers for that matter.

He stood once they were finished eating, setting his goblet on the table, and made his way toward her. She looked up as he extended a hand. "May I?" he asked.

She was a little confused, but placed her hand in his.

He smiled and pulled her toward him from her seat, brushing his fingers across her cheek. "Do ye want t' know what I really want?" he murmured, swaying into a simple dance.

She followed step, "Aye," she played along.

"Beautiful wenches draped across me left an' me right at me beck n' call. To do as I please and follow me each request. To please me an' treat me as the lord I am," he said with a chuckle.

"Is that so?" she said, prodding him further.

"Aye," he said, "Which is why I find ye so intriguing, lass. Ye'd never view me as anythin' so grand as tha wenches at port do. I wish to have ye especially succumbed to me."

At least he was honest, she thought. "Well, Captain," she said, her voice soft, "Ye have me now, don't ye?"

Would he believe she was really giving such a shameless offer?

He smiled at her, "Aye," he whispered, sitting back once again. "Pour me more rum, lass," he told her, gesturing toward his goblet.

She grasped the rum, and smirked coyly before tipping it to her lips. "And what would ye do with a stubborn one like me, eh?" she asked, stepping back and gently swaying the bottle in her hand as if taunting him just out of his reach.

He stood, moving toward her. She stepped back.

"Do ye wish to light a fire?" he said. She knew he meant his temper. Oh, so he really wasn't used to being refused.

She smirked, moving toward him. Instead of giving in to his request, she grasped his shirt and pulled him into a scorching kiss, pushing the bottle into his hand and tracing a finger along his skin until he gasped.

She stepped back, licking her lip softly and then turned and left his cabin.

The next morning, she was slightly surprised to find the captain knocking on her cabin. She heard his voice before the knocking began. "Be on yer way, gents. Me business is me own," he barked and then knocked on her door.

Amethyst stood, ignoring Darien as he shot her a look that warned her to watch her actions.

She flung the door open, smiling at the captain. "Good mornin', Captain," she said as if the night before had never happened.

He brushed past her and closed the door. He glanced toward Darien a moment, his mouth curving downward and brows furrowed before he rolled his eyes and folded his arms over his chest. He must have decided Darien was no concern. "Explain yerself, lass. I'm not a man t' be toyed with or led along like a dog on its master's leash, savvy?"

Amethyst shrugged. "Oh, like the women ye like to toy with?" she asked.

He frowned and didn't respond. She knew he was still awaiting an explanation.

"Perhaps me actions are simply from me own desires, eh? If I want to, I will. An' if I don't, I won't." She knew he'd know what she meant. If she'd wanted to stay and entertain him the night before, she would have. She'd seen no reason to play into his requests.

"Very well," he murmured, "But ye'll visit me cabin again tonight," he instructed before he left.

Amethyst laughed, leaning back against her bed. "Did you see his face, Darien? He's in such a tizzy!"

Darien heaved a sigh. "Amethyst, perhaps you shouldn't ignite his temper."

"Darien, I'm not a poor little damsel willing to throw myself at his feet for a bit of money and attention. And he needs to learn that *women* aren't to be treated as playthings, either. Perhaps I'll teach him a bit of respect. And if he's incapable of learning it, well, perhaps he may end up walking his own plank."

"Amethyst, you're getting ahead of yourself. The moment the captain no longer desires you, the moment the rest of the crew attack you like filthy dogs."

Amethyst scoffed. "Then they'll all suffer their fate at my hands."

"Even with my help, you can't take all of them on, especially at once."

"Darien, I've already decided what path I'll take. And part of that is making my own choices including with my own body. I'm nobody's play thing. And if I need to teach every man I cross that lesson - that no woman is a play thing, especially me - then I will."

"I just hope we don't end up dead in the process," Darien muttered. He picked up a handful of small throwing knives, twirling them in his fingers and then practiced throwing them against the opposite wall.

Amethyst returned to the captain's cabin that night. This time, she dressed in her simple britches and pirate's shirt.

Rather than eating, he was standing behind the door and as soon as she stepped inside, he closed it behind her.

She glanced back at him. His arms were folded over his chest and a soft smirk was on his lips. He dropped his arms and grasped one of her hands, pulling her toward him in a kiss like they'd shared the night before. He put his free hand in the small of her back, pulling her against his frame. She could sense his will wasn't the same as the ones she had encountered that only wanted to dominate and control her. It was a confident seduction to draw her into willing compliance.

She played along, curling her fingers into his hair and gently squeezing the hand that had grasped hers. He pushed against her slightly and she stepped back with him.

His hand on her back slid downward. He continued to kiss her until they stopped moving and she sat back in one of the chairs at his table. His lips traced her jawline and down her neck, his hands growing gentler as they danced about her skin.

She could feel his desire, his anxiety to taste and feel her. It was almost amusing, how much she could sense his hunger. She grasped his head with her fingers curled through his hair, pushing him downward. He slid his hands up her arms, pulling them down in kind and stood, pulling her toward him until she slipped from the chair onto her knees. She was looking up at him then, and she knew what he wanted.

She smirked, grasping his sides and pulling herself upward. She nipped at his neck, his jaw, and then his lips, sliding her tongue slowly across them and into his mouth.

Hadn't he learned she wouldn't play his games?

Amethyst slid her hands downward and Siilas' eyes displayed a mixture of desire for her to toy with him and the urge to push her down and consume her. He kissed her fiercely, pushing against her again, now toward his bed.

Amethyst pulled back, slowly tracing her finger across his lip. "And I thought I was coming for dinner," she whispered before leaving his cabin, just as she had the night before.

She could only imagine his frustration. She smirked to herself at the thought. Would he attempt again? She moved from his cabin onto the deck, pale moonlight shining brilliantly downward.

Amethyst gasped as a hand gripped her and she turned. She hadn't heard Siilas following due to the waves against the hull.

"What is it?" he asked. His voice was almost pleading.

She smirked. "I won't play your games."

"Neither I yours. What game *do* ye play?"

"I'm no common lass to swoon at the thought of being desired by ye. Me choices are me own, an' I'll do only as much as I desire."

"Do ye not desire me?" he asked.

She laughed. "If I do it's only for me own gain an' purposes."

He released her arm, smoothing back his hair and once more donning that simple smile. "Very well, lass. Perhaps ye aren't a treasure to be conquered," he mused.

"Nor is any woman," she retorted.

He laughed then. "I'm a pirate, lass. To conquer all is my venture."

"As is mine," she said.

She brushed past him and toward his cabin once more. Perhaps she'd at least grant him his satisfaction.

He followed her with that simple smile.

As soon as the door closed, she turned the tide for his actions. She pushed him into the door, gripping him and devouring his mouth with her own.

He smirked and she knew he hadn't ever encountered a woman such as herself.

The next morning, she returned to her cabin to find Darien up and waiting for her. "I assume you've overcome your challenge?" he asked.

She shrugged with a smirk. "Like putty in my hands," she mused.

Darien released his breath. She knew he didn't approve, but he bit his tongue.

"I won't be returning to Siilas' cabin, Darien. I only wanted to prove a point and teach him a lesson." She paused, "And, of course, I'd have a little fun while I was at it." She giggled softly.

Captain Siilas didn't ask for her again. In fact, she became like any member of the crew with duties and plunders and drinking her rum. When she desired the pleasure she craved, she pulled the captain aside, and he seemed rather content to let her.

A Name is a Reputation

After several months of sailing the northern waters and discovering nothing, they turned westward. Amethyst decided it was time to join the next crew.

Once they made port, she told Captain Siilas she'd be making her way toward her own goals and left the *Bloody Moon.*

Amethyst continued in such a pattern for a couple of years. She joined a new crew, seduced the captain or one of the crewmembers she deemed either desirable or a challenge, and began to proclaim herself a temptress.

Aboard several ships, there were men that attempted to push her down and force her will when she toyed with them, and she just as quickly showed them to their fate. Some she held at sword's tip to walk the plank, while others she challenged to a duel before the rest of the crew and slaughtered them on the deck. Still others shared Sedra's fate, their blood spilled from their necks as she drank away their life. She continuously observed the ways different captains ran their ships and also spread her name and reputation amongst pirates.

As she moved to different ships, Amethyst listened for rumors of notable pirate and merchant captains and any news from the fae territories. She learned of a variety of captains with reputations of mistreating their crew, killing innocent villagers, or participating in various trafficking rings. She kept a personal list of each of them.

There were three particular captains Amethyst made special note of: Zeake, Nathal, and Ektolyl. Captain Zeake of the *Goblin's Bluff* was particularly nasty. He was known for trickery and deceit in trades, and he frequently had to acquire new crewmembers. He either killed them or they left from his withholding their share of loot. Captain Nathal of the *Roaring Lion* was known for his ability to take on warships and plunder them and thus often had high-priced goods to trade.

Captain Ektolyl of the *Laughing Skull* was notorious as one of the few pirate captains who planned each battle as though he were a war general and hunted down merchant ships of various trades. He avoided battles he knew he would lose and had a reputation as both a great ally and a formidable foe.

She also learned that the Fae Navy was looking for the runaway fae maiden, but no one knew it was her specifically, in part because the Navy had little information other than that she had fled to the sea. However, there was an enormous bounty for anyone who turned her in.

The most recent crew Amethyst had joined was a rough bunch that she quickly grew tired of. It hadn't been long since she'd become one of their members, and she and Darien decided it was time, once more, to move on to the next ship. She wondered if she'd have a difficult time. She had grown a reputation for being an able deckhand and helpful in a plunder, but also seductive and terrible to those who tried to subdue her.

They made port at Port Mirka and while most of the deckhands aided in removing the merchandise for trades,

Amethyst and Darien went ashore toward the *Goblin's Goblet*. It was where she'd had her first luck. Perhaps she'd find more. She had seen enough of the other pirate ships to know what it took to be a captain and how realistic her desires actually were.

Amethyst ignored the typical shouts as she entered the pub, going straight to the bar and demanding rum. She sipped her glass, gazing at the wall on the opposite end of the room as if it would somehow provide her answers.

"What's a pretty lass like ye doin' at tha Goblin's Goblet, eh?"

Amethyst turned. What met her gaze were laughing brown eyes set in a strong, tanned face and flanked by brilliant red and sandy golden locks. His body was powerfully built and he was dressed in a loose pale shirt and dark pants. He looked older than most others she had met: probably in his late forties or early fifties.

She let a coy smile tug at her lips. "What business is it of yours?" she asked.

The man only laughed, placing both elbows on the bar and looking at her from the corner of his eyes. "A lass like yerself doesn't belong in a place like this," he said.

Amethyst pursed her lips, feeling the fire of her temper starting to simmer in her chest, "What sort of girl does, then?" she asked, a spark in her gaze.

The man turned his face so that both of his eyes met her squarely. "Well, lass, there be pirates about here and there's no tellin' what might happen to a fine lass such as yerself. I bet ye'd fetch a fine penny."

Amethyst's fangs and nails elongated and a snarl formed. "Perhaps you would like to see, sir, what might happen to you if you even try." Darien's firm grip on her shoulder calmed her, and she turned toward the bar, grasping the mug once more and gulping at the rum.

The red and golden-haired man eyed her a moment. "Easy there, lass. I've no intent of harmin' ye. Yer friend would see to my death, no doubt, eh?" he asked, gesturing toward Darien who only nodded silently. "It's not often we see wenches 'round here. An' I get the feelin' ye're not here just for the rum and a little runaway mischief."

Amethyst was silent a moment, looking the man over. There was something warm in his brown eyes and she believed him when he said he meant her no harm. Perhaps he had only been teasing her. She wouldn't be surprised. "I'm looking to become a first mate, and my companion a quartermaster," she said matter-of-factly.

The man almost fumbled his mug of ale at her words and laughed again. "Are ye, now?" He paused, his eyes staring into hers a moment. "Well ye be in luck, lass. It isn't often pirates allow a female aboard. But as ye'd have it, I don't believe in superstition, and I recently lost a few members of me crew. I could use new deckhands. But tell me, lass, why should I give ye the job?"

Amethyst felt her brows rising. Her gaze met Darien's briefly before she turned back to the man. "We've sailed aboard various pirate ships for the last several years, actually. We can do anything you ask, and more. Repairs, cleaning, cooking, and you won't find another as skilled as we are in battle," Amethyst let her tongue slide slowly over her lips and smiled. "I'd wager we could take on a whole ship by ourselves."

The man seemed to consider her reasons and at last smiled. "So yer the lass the other scalawags talk about," he mused softly.

Amethyst quirked a brow at his statement, though said nothing.

"Name's Captain Adair, but ye can call me Ady, if ye prefer. Ye can come with me after we leave," he said.

"Amethyst," she said, stretching out her hand. "And my companion, Darien," she added with a gesture in his direction. There was something about this man. He was different than many others she had met. Perhaps it was his age, but he seemed more carefree and full of life.

Adair shook her hand after a brief hesitation, and smiled. "Welcome aboard, lass."

Not long after, they made their way back to the docks and to Adair's ship, the *Fiery Stallion*. It was a large balinger with two square-rigged masts and two decks. A balinger was commonly seen in the hands of pirates, but not one of this size. The ship was a deep but brilliant brown with lighter accents. Spaces for oars were set in the hull and she knew it was built for both speed and to give its crew a winning chance in a fight. In her years with the merchant sailors, she had witnessed the advantage such a ship gave during a raid.

As soon as they were aboard, no announcement was needed. Clearly, the deck hands weren't used to having a woman around. Cheers and hollers resounded and while most of them continued with their work, a few approached – perhaps out of curiosity. "Blimey! Tha Cap'n's lost his marbles!" one said with laughter.

"Nay, lads, he's tha same as ever, eh, Cap'n?"

Adair nodded with a grin. "Always willin' to 'elp a fellow pirate," he said.

"Well c'mon, lass! Yer just in time fer supper," said one of the men who had initially approached.

She nodded and Darien and herself followed them below deck to the mess tables. As they ate, she discovered the men were incredibly inquisitive, or just nosy. When they learned her name, she received a mixture of hollers and jokes concerning her reputation.

"Better steer clear o' this one, lads!" one said.

Amethyst rolled her eyes, sipping her rum. "No one receives a fate they don't deserve," she said, a bit harsher than she had intended.

The men only laughed and clashed their mugs together before drinking their ale. At least they were a lively bunch, she noted. She also told them of her life on the seas since she'd become a pirate, in particular her personal victories in battle. They seemed to respond well to those tales.

The next day, Amethyst and Darien once more settled into ship duties. Amethyst sat with one particular group that carefully repaired one of the sails. They had gone through an especially nasty storm recently.

She looked up. It was strange how comfortable she felt here. She realized that if she didn't have goals to become a captain herself, she could imagine herself staying. This crew reminded her somewhat of the crew she wished to have, though hers would be more mannerly, she thought with a smile.

Across the deck, Amethyst noticed one of the men eyeing her. She pretended to ignore it and returned to her work. She shouldn't be surprised, she thought.

A few hours later it was a bit after mid-day and she stood, dusting off her clothes.

Amethyst was more than ready to take a break and put something in her stomach. She made her way below deck, hoping to find fresh fruit. As they had recently left port, it would still be good. As soon as she'd picked what she wanted from the lower deck, she moved toward the mess tables on the second deck and sat.

"Care if I join ye, lass?" asked a voice with deep tones.

She looked up. It was the same man who had been eyeing her earlier in the day. He reminded her of Captain Adair. He was young, probably in his twenties, with tanned skin, broad shoulders, laughing brown eyes and curly sandy-blonde hair. She shrugged.

He sat down. "I'm Leonard... but everyone jus' calls me Leo."

"Amethyst," she said in turn.

He nodded with a grin, eating some of his food. "So are tha stories true?" he asked.

She quirked a brow, "What stories?" she asked.

He chuckled. "Well I 'eard ye can take down a ship all by yerself! And tha' yer a feisty one t' handle."

As he paused, she smirked. "Perhaps ye'll learn fer yerself," she said.

"With a reputation like that, I'm surprised yer not a captain," he mused, taking another bite.

"Not yet," she said.

At that he looked up. He was silent a moment, and she felt as though he were trying to read her. "How do ye plan to become a captain?" he asked.

Did he genuinely want to know?

"When I decide I'm ready, I'll capture a ship for meself, win the crew, and me reputation will be one unlike any on the seas."

"Somehow that I believe," he said, drinking a bit of his ale.

"And what of ye?" she asked, "Are ye, by chance, related to the Captain?"

At that, Leo grinned. "That obvious, eh? The Cap'n's me dad. Me mum was lost to tha sea when I was young."

"I'm sorry," she said.

He shrugged, "It was a long time ago."

"Well are ye planning to take over yer dad's ship, then?" she asked.

"Nay, Amethyst. I also plan to take a ship for meself. Perhaps during a plunder."

"Well maybe we'll be allies," Amethyst mused, finishing the last of her rum. At that, she went on her way.

The next day, Leo joined her for lunch, once again of his own accord. At first he merely asked if she were becoming accustomed to the ship.

She only replied, "Aye."

After a bit of silence he asked, "Amethyst, what do ye ultimately hope to achieve as a captain?"

She couldn't help noticing the way he called her by her name instead of merely 'lass' or 'wench' or anything else. "Freedom," she said with a smile.

"Don't we all," he mused softly.

"And ye?" she asked in return.

"Perhaps the same. To go where I please and see more of the world than what I already have."

She nodded, eating her food, sipping her rum, and watching as he gained a distant look.

"Well, someday," he said suddenly, meeting her gaze with his own warm smile. Their meal was done so with that, they parted to resume duties.

The next day, similar conversation occurred between them, and did so the days after that.

The days blended into weeks and Amethyst learned Adair plundered only targeted merchants who he carefully followed on trade maps or those he deemed deserving of whatever fate might fall in a raid. After all, it wasn't just pirate captains and ships that had reputations, various merchantmen did as well.

The loot they didn't desire from their plunders was traded or sold at port for things they needed or wanted and life was merry.

Amethyst quickly had taken a liking to Leo, and the feeling was mutual. She suspected he believed it was more, and she allowed it, if that were the case. Eventually their relationship grew physical and she was content to find pleasure in her nights as opposed to her relentless night terrors. She enjoyed watching the way he laughed heartily at the smallest of things, and was fearlessly impulsive.

The moon had long since risen over the ship which currently sailed away from Aeidahs, a large and well-known island chain between Vorda Isle and Orlesce.

Amethyst lay awake, thoughts circling her mind. The memory of her most recent conversation with Leo came to mind.

"I'm curious, what's been holdin' ye back?" he'd asked.

She had paused, hardly wanting to spill *all* of her issues and secrets, but of all the ones she had been able to trust so far, other than Darien, Leo was the most genuine. She almost envied the way he was so carefree and honest. It was refreshing, and was part of the reason she had taken a liking to him.

"Perhaps fear," she had said finally. There were so many ways to fill in the question of what for her, but she hadn't elaborated. "Though, perhaps it's time I put that aside. I've seen enough and learned as much as I can without actually being a captain."

"Ye know Adair will aid ye," Leo had said.

She wondered if the captain knew of her true goals.

Then again, it wasn't unheard of for a pirate captain to give a captured ship to a trusted member of his crew. She wanted to be her own, and she'd hate to eternally be in his debt. No, she'd capture her own ship – as she'd first said she would. Still, she knew Leo's intentions were the best. Perhaps she should at least ask the captain. He may even suggest something with his knowledge of the trade routes.

She'd decided to tell Captain Adair tomorrow.

Amethyst glanced toward Darien's sleeping form on the bed across from hers in the cabin they sometimes shared when she didn't spend her night with Leo. She smiled to herself. *'We're going to achieve everything at last.'*

The next day, Amethyst joined Darien for duties, as she often did. There was rigging to check and repaired sails to hang.

"You know what Leo said the other day?" she asked.

Darien met her gaze a moment and shook his head.

"It's time we take the next step, take a hold of a ship and make her ours," she said, a sparkle in her eyes.

Darien paused in his work, putting down the ropes and the tools. "Well you didn't need Leo to tell you that," he said.

She grinned. "Aye. Though I wanted to truly gain an advantage over all the other ships and their captains. I've taken my time for good reasons, my reasons. But I am ready. Otherwise we might remain on Ady's ship forever."

"What of Leo?" Darien asked.

"What of him? He wishes to become a captain of his own ship. We'll go our separate ways as all the others have." She shrugged.

"And if he offers an alliance?" Darien pressed.

She scoffed. "Why, Darien! I haven't fallen for him. He's merely another to bring pleasure and good taste. Like my rum."

Darien only shook his head. "Very well. What are your plans?"

She didn't fail to note the way he abruptly changed the subject. "I'll learn from Ady and when the Fiery Stallion attacks another ship, we'll take it for ourselves.

"Aye, aye," Darien said.

Afternoon passed and the sky darkened. With it came a small storm, only enough to rock the waves though it still created a soaking downpour.

Amethyst approach Adair's cabin, immediately becoming soaked through, to discuss her plans as Leo had suggested. She slammed his door open, too excited to knock and wait for his reply.

Adair looked up with a start.

"Ady, it's time you were aware of my ambitions and my true reasons for seeking out your pirate's crew," she announced, stepping toward him.

Adair smiled and sat back. He'd been standing over his desk, poring over maps and merchant trade routes. It was high time for their next raid. "Well, blimey, Amethyst, shut the door first," he said.

Amethyst paused, glancing back at the door. Feeling impatient, Amethyst merely kicked the door closed and continued forward before sitting dramatically in one of the chairs near Adair's desk. "I know you're planning another raid so we won't be running out of goods. I'm going to take my own ship."

Ady stroked his beard as if debating how to respond. She knew better, so she continued. His laughing brown eyes gave away his thoughts. "I've long sought a life of freedom where I set my own rules and live my own way. But more than that, I want a group to call my own who would never betray me and would follow me to the ends of the world. I'll give my crew true freedom like they've never before experienced."

Ady was silent another moment. "Do ye not have the freedom ye desire here?"

Amethyst laughed. "Ady, it's more than being a mere pirate aboard another's ship. I'll captain my own ship, and become a queen of the seas. And more than that." She stopped there, unwilling to tell him the full extent. Unwilling to share she had spent so much time learning the pirate world in order to know exactly which ships to hunt down and which to leave alone.

She watched Adair's lip curl upward into a smirk of interest. "Of course. Alright, I'll help ye," he paused, leaning forward as his eyes gained a spark of danger, "But don't try taking any of me crew with ye."

Amethyst smirked, "Wouldn't dream of it, Captain. That wouldn't be any way to repay the man I will owe."

Adair shrugged and leaned back, gesturing toward the maps he had been scouring before her entrance. "Ye should already be familiar with tha merchant trade routes. Several shipments o' various goods set sail only two weeks back an' we'll cross their paths soon. We sail here," he pointed to an intersection of two trade routes, "to up our chances."

There was a knowing glint in his brown eyes.

Amethyst frowned, "We're taking on two ships at once?"

Adair shook his head, a grin on his lips. "I'll be taking on one. Ye and Darien can take the other."

Amethyst smirked when she realized that Adair had known her ambitions before she'd come and had been planning to help her all along. "What do these ships carry?" she asked.

"One silk and other clothin' materials. The other," he paused, "has slaves."

Amethyst frowned. The mere thought disgusted her, but there was also another risk. The fae often captured those they saw as lesser and those they defeated in conquest as slaves. There was a chance this ship he spoke of belonged to one of the Fae Navy, and if that was the case, she wasn't certain she and Darien could take it alone.

Further, if it were the opposite – fae slaves captured by retaliating traffickers - she may still be discovered. As a fae herself, they would most certainly attempt to take her and sell her as well. Amethyst breathed out slowly. She wasn't alone.

"What better chance to gain a loyal crew than to free captured slaves," she mused. "Though perhaps they'd only wish to be returned to their homes and families."

"Perhaps. Or perhaps they'll find they can send their families more money than they ever dreamed. I'll even share the merchandise from the other ship."

"At least I've got one ally," Amethyst said.

"Aye, ye've got that," Adair said.

"When should we expect to cross paths?" she asked.

"Without interference, by sundown in two days."

"I'll be sure to be ready," Amethyst said. She stood, glancing out of the window nearby, then turned and headed toward the door.

She slipped below deck and toward hers and Darien's cabin. As soon as she entered, Darien looked up from a book. Amethyst plopped down on her bed. "That went better than expected," she said. "We're taking a ship in two days."

Darien smiled, "Aye, aye, Captain."

Amethyst laughed.

"It's the last merchant ship we'll rob," Amethyst said, "at least one undeserving of wrath."

"So what are the plans, exactly?" Darien asked.

Amethyst filled Darien in on the details from her conversation with Adair. Darien frowned at the mention of the slave ship, probably coming to the same conclusions she had. "I'm not going to hide myself any longer," Amethyst said. "We have an advantage, and we're taking it."

Darien put the book down, and she knew he was about to protest.

"Don't. I've made up my mind."

He sighed, closing his silvery eyes. "Very well. I will remain your protector and companion to whatever end."

Amethyst had learned sometime before that most pirates rarely plotted raids like soldiers did for war. They typically roamed freely where they wanted and if a ship did cross their path, they would see it as an opportunity and take advantage. The only plotting otherwise was in intentional intersection with another ship.

Pirates were hardy, rough, and merciless. Their lack of inhibitions granted them their hearts' desires of luxuries, especially against common merchant ships, the crews of which struggled to keep the pirates at bay.

Despite all of that, Amethyst had taken the time to plan. She could be rash, but in this case, she knew the chances of running into fae as her enemy were high and she wasn't going to risk failure.

She simply took precautions. She wasn't about to be taken back to the fae territories and subjected to whatever cruelties she knew would await her. Or worse: sold into trafficking or sent to the bottom of the sea.

Darien helped her. He had seen more of war firsthand in his life than she had and was able to provide a strategy of sorts.

Two days went by swiftly, and everyone aboard felt the anticipation, especially once the ships became visible in the distance.

Even if the ships they had targeted tried, they would never be able to out-run the *Fiery Stallion*. Perhaps the two ships would sail closer together to try and crush the *Stallion,* or at the least have double the man-power against the approaching pirate ship. Neither case would surprise Amethyst, but before they even got close, she was already going to implement her plan.

She had been getting ready all day. She and Darien had some belongings, but she wasn't worried about those now. Once the ship was hers, she could take her things from the

Stallion, and she knew Adair would be more than willing. She doubted he would suddenly turn on her.

Instead, she took only what was essential. She was dressed in a simple pale pirate's shirt, dark britches, and plain dark leather boots. Several daggers were hidden about her person, despite the simplicity of her clothing, including one tucked neatly into her cleavage. She couldn't help a light smirk at the thought. Her ringlets were tied back with a leather strip.

Today would be the day she would finally take her freedom from the world.

Distinguishing which was the slave ship was difficult. One of the ships was a fluyt, a square-rigged ship with two masts and two full decks built solely for cargo. It would be an easy take-down. There would be no guns aboard save what the crewmembers might carry on their person and at that, the crew would be small. The fluyt didn't need a lot of man-power.

The other ship was a schooner, and would prove trickier. It also only had two masts and two decks but it was fore-and-aft rigged, meaning it would have better maneuverability. Plus, she knew it would have gun-power though the crew was probably a similar size to the fluyt.

Neither of the ships waved the flags of the Fae Royal Navy. That still didn't mean she was in the clear. Regardless of which ship carried the slaves, Amethyst made up her mind to claim the schooner then and there. She knew she wouldn't need to convey this to Adair. As an experienced captain, he would pick up on the details for himself.

Without further hesitation, she dove into the sea. There was no way she would cover the distance faster than the ships would meet, but her purpose was stealth. The sea was both deep and unclear, which would perfectly mask her movements.

The sea vibrated as the cannon fire began and she swam as carefully as she did swiftly. Even if the water slowed projectile movements, it didn't mean she couldn't be hit with something and injured.

Amethyst surfaced only moments later as she reached the stern of the schooner. She had already let her nails elongate into claws and she began climbing her way up the hull of the ship. As the battle had already commenced, she knew the sailors' focus would be on the *Fiery Stallion* and there wasn't much chance they'd notice her climbing up the back.

She felt bad about marring the surface, especially if it would soon be hers, but she had no choice. The sound of her digging into the wood was masked by the shouts and explosions of cannons. If she had used a dagger, she would have risked anyone on the gun deck spying the tip of the blade poking in through the boards and she couldn't have that.

Amethyst reached the small quarterdeck and climbed over the railing. There were two sailors, guns pointed at the *Fiery Stallion*, shouting, "Take 'er down, mateys! Protect tha cargo!" The rest of the crew was on the lower main deck, firing at the *Stallion*.

Amethyst had never had much interest in guns, but neither was she human. She could fight well without them. Silently, Amethyst slipped across the deck. There was a brief crack as she twisted the neck of one of the sailors. He fell limp and tumbled overboard. The other sailor jumped, his gun clicking as he aimed it toward her. With a flick of her wrist, a dagger was plunged into his chest and she dove to the side as he fired on his way down.

She rolled, catching herself in a crouched position and stood, peering over the edge. Where was the captain?

Amethyst spied him quickly. A dark, feathered hat sat on his head and he was shouting orders to the crewmembers while engaging the oncoming pirates. He wasn't bad in a fight. Already some of the pirates had tried to board and he had sent a couple of them into the ocean.

She grabbed the sword from the sailor she had slain still aboard and leaped from upper deck. She landed just behind the captain who was focused on the oncoming pirates. Without hesitation, she drove her sword through his middle and leapt back.

"Amethyst!"

Her eyes swiveled sharply, and she saw Darien. He dove over her, pushing her down to the deck and then stood quickly.

Just as he had pushed her down, a few guns had fired and missed her form. "Thanks," she said, rising enough to give herself momentum and kicking her leg in a semi-circle. Several of the sailors crumbled, losing their balance entirely.

That was all she needed.

Amethyst lunged forward, retrieving another sword and roughly picking up the body of the captain to use as a human shield. Instead of simply moving forward with it, she shoved it into the group of sailors, many of them diving out of the way.

"Darien!" she said, summoning him to her side.

He backed toward her, sword raised and eyes sharp.

Placing one hand on her hip, she raised the other to her lips and released a shrill, loud whistle. The sailors focused on her, some of them guns raised. "Listen up! My name is Amethyst of the fae. But don't think I'll be easily used to fetch a fine penny. I seek a life of true freedom on the seas and this ship is officially under me as its captain. All who unite with me will find a life like never before imagined. But anyone who resists or betrays me," she paused, her fangs protruding slightly as her lips curled into a smirk, "Will meet either my blade, or be forced to walk the plank with a cannonball tied to his feet!"

The sailors glanced at each other, then one particularly large man stepped forward. "We're not pirates, lass. We may be sailors, but we're respectable men, and we won't cast our pride into the sea for a petty wench's dreams. Prove ye can e'en sail a ship! The likes of ye is no captain o' mine!"

Jeers and hollers followed.

Amethyst stepped forward, eyes gleaming. "First, I'll prove my skills with a ship. Then, if ye still wish to challenge me, lower yer gun and use yer sword!" With that, she stabbed her sword into the deck and moved toward the main mast. She swiftly climbed to the crow's nest and loosened the rigging from the mast until the sail drooped. Then, she secured the rigging once more and descended the mast before, again, grasping her sword.

"Any able-bodied man c'n do that," the sailor scoffed and while he did lower his gun, he lunged for her with his blade.

She stepped to the side and parried. Amethyst remained in constant motion. She dove in, and he cried as she plunged a dagger through his middle. Moments after, she gasped at the feel of his blade in her skin and tumbled. She caught herself and lunged again, the sailor also lunging toward her. "Say yer prayers, wench!"

She smirked and at the last moment lunged back, watching as he stumbled and caught himself on the deck. Amethyst swiftly brought her sword downward through his heart.

She whirled, preparing for another attack from the crew. They had different reactions. Some were staring at her, jaws agape. "Can ye truly offer us such freedom and luxuries?" some were asking, while others were either stepping backward away from her or stepping toward her with red faces and hands on their swords. One even said, "I could never trust a captain who would so easily kill one of her crew."

"Do all of ye wish to walk the plank?" she demanded, her lips curled in a snarl.

Several sailors stepped forward in unison. Their eyes were alight. Perhaps they thought they could take her on as a group. Or perhaps they wanted to stain the deck with her blood like she had their fellow sailor. Perhaps both.

The soft thuds of Darien's footfalls as he stepped forward to aid her alerted her to his approach, but with another twitch of her ear, he stopped.

Amethyst removed some of the hidden daggers from her clothing and with a flick of the wrist, several sailors stopped in their tracks, groaning. The daggers were buried in the legs of two of them and in the shoulders or arms of the others. She had intended to stop but not necessarily kill them. Amethyst rushed forward, catching the remaining three off-guard. She shoved her elbow into one sailor's gut and her fist met his chin, sending him backward. She dropped, swiveling her leg and knocking the one next to her to the ground and the last one, she pointed her sword to his chest. A few curls had broken loose of the leather tie and dangled about her face, her breath coming short.

The sailor dropped his weapon.

Without a word, Amethyst grasped him, shoving him toward the plank. With her sword at his back, he inched forward until he plunged into the sea.

She turned, the remaining sailors looking at each other and then back at her.

"Listen up, scalawags! Whether ye like it or not, your captain is gone. An' I would wager every one o' ye has wished for somethin' more. Wages. Food. Luxuries. Ye're no longer merchants or starvin' sailors for an organization. And as such, ye'll only be able to eat if ye choose to aid in the plunder and hunts. Ye 'ave one o' two choices. Ye can fight and share in whatever we gain. Or ye can die o' starvation. Hell, if ye choose the latter, ye can walk the plank right now!" She paused, her gaze meeting each of the other sailors.

Amethyst wondered how they would respond. She was somewhat uncertain about her methods, but she had also felt she needed to show them she would not be easily overcome. In her mind, how could she captain a ship of men if they felt they could push her around and not take her seriously? In her time at sea, she had learned one thing. As a woman, she was viewed as weaker, and in order to prove otherwise, she had to make herself intimidating.

They looked at each other hesitantly. Finally one spoke, "We'll join ye," there was a pause, "Captain."

Amethyst smiled, putting her sword in its sheath.

"Then back to work, lads. We sail toward the *Stallion* to take our wages. Know now that mutiny or any talk of it will result in a worse fate than these bilge rats, but as promised, those who stand with me will have only better days ahead."

Amethyst moved toward the body of the captain, taking the hat from him and squaring it over her curls. "Your first mate is mage Darien. Any issues or requests you have will be brought directly to him. Anyone who whispers of me to another soul will meet death quickly." She paused, looking over them with a smirk and a glint in her eyes, "Oh, and no woman is *ever* allowed on my ship."

Amethyst wondered if those aboard would understand. While she had fought for men to accept her as a good sailor, a good pirate, and still a woman, she still had to contend with her nature. As a fae woman, she couldn't ignore her territorial instincts. She had felt them toward her ex-husband, as much as she had hated it, and she felt it toward her ship now. She was terrified that another woman would attempt to take away what she had gained, including her newly found captain status, as well as any potential she might have to earn her crew's trust. No woman aboard could ever be tolerated.

She paused, making her way toward the stairway to the lower deck. "What cargo do you carry?" she asked.

"Slaves, Cap'n," responded one of the sailors.

So, she had picked the correct ship regardless.

"Release them," she ordered. She gestured and several sailors followed her below deck. They quickly set to work removing the chains and moving the slaves on board above deck.

The slaves were a mixture of races, though were mostly fae, something she had expected when seeing the crew of the ship were not so. She couldn't deny the profitability, but she could never condone slavery, especially of her own kind.

The slaves had had awful conditions below deck. They were unsightly, unhealthy, and some of them had died. Amethyst commanded their bodies be set adrift in honorable fashion.

As soon as the living slaves were above deck, Amethyst moved to quarterdeck and looked down. "From this moment, these slaves are free men. You all heard what I spoke before and it still stands. Whoever unites with me will find themselves a life of freedom never before imagined. I have no interest in slave trade, so those of you who do not join me will join your deceased companions. I have neither the time nor can I risk taking any of you to port."

The slaves all looked at each other but said nothing. They simply stayed put and placed one hand over their breasts, signaling their pledge. She assumed that meant their loyalty, though time would tell.

With that, she moved toward the rails of the main deck to where the remains of the fluyt still were afloat, though no trace of the cargo remained, and the *Fiery Stallion* sailed beyond. She was certain Adair had taken the cargo with him.

After Amethyst released a shrill whistle, she saw the unmistakable forms of Adair and Leo waving in response. She waved back for a moment. She knew they would understand she was grateful without her having to say it. Still, she was not going to part ways just yet. Perhaps they were making their distance in case she had failed, though she hoped Adair would have known better.

Amethyst turned back to her crew. "You will each tell me your names and then those of you that have sailed the longest will teach the new men of the ship."

She stepped forward, and took the time to remember each of them. It was the first step in preventing mutiny. Among them were some extremely tenured members: Serafin, Artemas, who she learned everyone called Artie, and Cyran; there was also one slave who had survived below deck longer than the others: Hiram.

"Alright ye scalawags," she said, "We catch up to the Stallion, and then we'll repair the ship!"

"Aye, aye," voiced enough men for her to assume they were resigned to do as she said for now.

To Become a Captain

It did not take long for them to once more be broadside the *Fiery Stallion*. "Permission to board, Cap'n?" she asked. Even if she knew she was welcome, she was officially a captain now, and she was determined to maintain proper behavior. As proper as pirates could be, anyway.

"Permission granted, Amethyst," Adair responded back, a spark in his eyes.

A smirk tugged at the edges of Amethyst's lips and once the plank was set, she moved across. Darien remained aboard the *Nightingale*, the ship they had just captured, though he watched her closely. She trusted him not to let the men try to overthrow her so soon after her conquest.

"Well, Captain, do we still have a deal?" Amethyst asked, stabbing her sabre into the wood of the deck and resting her hand on its hilt.

Adair only smiled, nodded, turned, and made his way across the deck toward the stairway to lower deck. She sheathed her blade and followed suit. Some of the *Stallion*'s crewmembers followed.

As soon as they reached the loot, Adair gestured toward a separated group of barrels. "Take it t' git yerself started, lass. An' when ye've gained more, ye'll repay it."

Amethyst stepped forward, peering into the barrels. There were a handful of maps, some clothing and fine silks, some salted meats, and also a barrel of rum.

It would at least give them a start. Satisfied with their contents, she nodded.

With that, Adair motioned and the men with them carried the barrels to the main deck.

"I'm in your debt, Adair," Amethyst said, smiling at him as well. "You have my word that I will repay it."

Adair grinned and slapped her on the back. "Ye best be careful from now on, Amethyst. Ye'll have to make it on yer own, and I'm already at risk of the other captains believin' I've gone soft!" A bellow of laughter escaped him.

Amethyst shook her head, coughing as his hand made contact with her back. "Perhaps ye should fire a few rounds as I sail me vessel away, hmm?" she shot back with a grin.

They once more reached upper deck, and the men from her newly acquired crew quickly took the barrels aboard.

Amethyst extended her arm and Adair grasped it firmly. Finally, she returned to the *Nightingale*, ordering the men to draw in the plank, and she made her way to her own upper deck.

She ordered the freed slaves be given the clothing. The meat and rum was to be divided equally to last until their first plunder. The maps she took to her quarters. She needed to know them intimately. In her travels she had learned much, but to see it laid out before her so plainly would give her a great advantage. From her years at sea, she knew well the waters in which those she hunted sailed as well as the trade routes other sailors took.

Within her gut, Amethyst suspected not all of the men would remain under her leadership. She felt they might resist on their first raid and perhaps even rally behind those they attacked to try and sink the *Nightingale* to ocean's bottom.

But she had already formulated a plan against it.

If she wanted them to rally behind her, she had to show and prove to them the value in her goals. She would get there in time, but first, she needed to decide in which direction to go.

Within her quarters, Amethyst studied the maps, and finally summoned Darien.

"What do you think, First Mate?" Amethyst asked, her eyes meeting his on entry.

Darien looked down at the map she had on top, dashed lines of varying colors in different directions all across it and a small key in the corner.

"Perhaps our first aim should be in strengthening the crew," he replied in his ever soft-spoken manner.

"Aye," Amethyst said with a nod. "Food and drink, and the taste of battle." She pointed toward one dashed line in particular that within a few days' time sailing east they would intersect. "Let's show these lads what it will mean to sail beneath us."

Soon they were sailing full speed ahead due east. A part of her feared a potential encounter with the Fae Royal Navy, yet she knew their raid would take place before coming anywhere close to the Fae Territories and as of yet, her name would not have reached their ships. If they were looking for her, she doubted they'd suspect a stolen slave ship.

Over the course of the next few days, Amethyst spent time amongst her crew getting to know them more closely. She could not be their leader, she felt, if she only demanded fear without building somewhat of a friendship with them. She talked of her time spent as a sailor, and also as a pirate, and finally aboard Adair's ship and the difference she had already seen and felt.

One night, she stood on the main deck, gently swaying a goblet of rum back and forth. Artie approached. She heard the thuds of his boots behind her before she knew who it was.

"Evening, Cap'n..." he began.

She smiled at him, "Evening," she responded.

He was sipping on a mug of ale. He leaned on the edge beside her, watching the waves a moment. "Might I ask ye somethin'?" he asked.

She met his gaze, trying to assess his features. "Aye," she said.

"What is ye purpose? Ye capture our ship, force us to obey ye, an' at tha same time promise freedom?"

Amethyst smiled again, taking a swig of her rum. "I was a sailor as you lads were for many years. And I'll admit it was honest pay and we worked for our food and clothes. I only mean honest in that we earned it. It was hardly good pay." She paused. "But it wasn't living. I became a pirate, but ultimately it wasn't quite what I was looking for."

"And ye'd ask us to become pirates? Ye'd rather us steal from those workin' honestly then do so ourselves?"

"Perhaps ye'd look at it that way. Except those that might join me wouldn't be among the robbed, would they? To merely plunder and live like a barbarian is not my end goal. I desire only to take what I must and prove I can be anything I wish to. Eventually, I will live freely and everyone both on sea and land will fear and respect me. Not just for my capabilities, but for my accomplishments. No one will contest me."

Amethyst paused. "Ye should know I don't plan to merely raid and plunder merchant ships as a pirate. I intend to hunt down those captains, merchant and pirate alike, worthy of my blade. Those who take mercilessly and those who have care only for themselves." Those that had wronged her. Images of a few captains in particular crossed her mind.

"What of the territory soliders? The navy ships that hand out free trials and hangings to every pirate caught."

"If they can catch me," Amethyst retorted.

A smile filled Artie's lips. "I'm a sea dog either way. I suppose there's nothing to lose, eh? If we follow ye, there's gain to be had, and if we don't, we'll be worse off?"

Amethyst grinned. "Well I'd only throw ye off the plank if I suspected mutiny. But if ye wish to go yer own way, ye won't find such a life anywhere else."

"Perhaps. But we'll stick it through with ye."

Amethyst nodded. "Aye, aye," was all she said in response. She suspected her words would carry to the rest of the crew, but if not, she would repeat them as many times as necessary.

They sailed through clear waters for several days, ever on the watch.

"Sail ho!" cried the lookout, the men rushing to the sides of the ship. At last, the ship they sought was coming into view. The *Silver Lady,* sailed by Captain Rada. Its amber hull glistened in the sunlight with large pale sails and its figurehead of a siren. Amethyst still remembered the way Rada treated his crew like rats while he stuffed his belly and often took whatever pleasures he wanted. He saw women as nothing more than another form of earnings. Yet the reason she had hunted him down was for revenge. As payment for accepting her and Darien to his crew, Rada had used her body and threatened to end her life had she rejected him. Amethyst had vowed to give him a just reward, in her eyes, and that time was near.

Rada was also elusive and knew well how to avoid pirates. But as she had sailed aboard his ship, and she now sailed aboard a ship not yet recognized as a pirate vessel, she doubted he would escape her. It would not be well-manned, and was somewhat of an easy target.

At least, Amethyst hoped it would be. She tied her hair back with a pale ribbon.

"Ready yerselfs, lads!" Amethyst shouted, "soon ye'll taste the pleasure of freedom!"

Amethyst was confident that if nothing else, the prospect of a full stomach would be enough for the crew to do as they must.

As they drew nearer, Amethyst met Darien's gaze and he gave a brief nod. He was to remain aboard their ship while she went ahead.

Her gaze remained fixed on the merchant vessel until they were drawing broadside. The lookout threw down a rope which was attached to the foremast of the ship. She caught it and pushed away from her ship, swinging aboard the *Silver Lady*. Her sword was drawn as soon as her feet touched the main deck and she clashed with one of the sailors, pushing him back.

Soon, the men from her ship swarmed aboard, swords drawn, and followed after her. Her goal was to make as little damage as possible lest they drown their loot.

Amethyst made her way toward the captain's cabin while the crew fought the sailors. She flung a dagger into one sailor's shoulder and he let out a cry as he sank to his knees.

The fight was over quickly. The sailors not only recognized they were outnumbered, but lacked the strength to truly fight back.

A loud bang resounded as she flung the door to the captain's cabin open, and Rada startled, eyes wide and mouth hanging open as he looked up.

"Th-Th-Thea?" he whimpered.

"My name is Captain Amethyst, and you don't deserve to captain this ship."

"P-Please. I'll give you whatever you want," he stammered, the items on his desk clattering as he struggled to stand.

Amethyst moved forward swiftly, stopping just in front of the desk he stood behind. She reached up and drove her sword through his heart, before turning and leaving the door open behind her.

Amethyst shoved away the memories that had resurfaced from her time aboard this ship. It had felt good to spill Rada's blood after everything he'd done. She only hoped she wouldn't begin a blood rampage after getting a taste of revenge.

She made her way toward upper deck, observing the bodies about the main deck and the few crewmembers that remained. Many of the merchant sailors had been pushed overboard and those who hadn't knelt with their hands up, weapons dropped.

"I am Captain Amethyst! Your captain was unworthy to hold his title. You can join me and fight those like him who robbed your bellies and your pockets, or you can walk the plank with your fellow sailors."

The crewmembers slowly stood, regaining their weapons and gave shouts of agreement. Among them were several Amethyst recognized, including Darrell. His eyes met hers a moment and she wasn't sure if it were shock or admiration she saw. Perhaps both.

"Load the ship!" Darien hollered as soon as it was clear they'd have no more fight back. Immediately, the crewmen set to work taking the merchandise aboard the vessel. They collected salted meat, rum, clothing and even some ship supplies.

"Set it ablaze, gents!" Amethyst ordered as soon as they had taken what they required. "Let this be the first to warn the world."

Finally, she accompanied the crew and returned to her ship, moving toward Darien who was standing on upper deck.

"Well done, Captain," Darien said with a small smile.

Amethyst placed a small kiss on his cheek. "Every last one of the bastards like him will suffer his fate. Everyone on the seas will know not to trifle with me."

They set sail south after that. Amethyst determined to ruin the ship of the first pirate captain she had tried to join. The one who had attempted to dominate her and instead had ended with his blood spilt on the beach - Sedra.

She had learned after leaving him there that his first mate, Tavur, had taken over the ship, the *Dragon's Curse*, and that its reputation was one of trafficking and raids of seaside villages. The crewmen would rob the villages and rape the women and sell those from the villages for whatever price they could fetch, leaving the villages in ruins. Amethyst couldn't wait for her blade to taste their blood.

Her crew spent their time as they sailed mending the ship and gaining their strength.

Amethyst discussed plans with Darien. Already, she had a list of ships to hunt down and destroy, though she wondered if she'd truly be able to with such a new and inexperienced crew of pirates. Although there were numerous fae aboard and they had magic as a distinct advantage, she didn't want to fall back on it. She wanted to prove herself outside of magic.

They were at least four months away from the ship they sought and she was determined not to waste the journey. Each day, Amethyst and Darien spent time training the crew. She hadn't spent time in her youth among the fae learning how to fight for nothing. She was determined to build a crew of more than mere sailors – a crew of skilled warriors.

At first, the crewmembers struggled and were easily defeated. The men looked at her with fear every time she pushed them down, her sword always pointing at their throats or their hearts. Yet soon, they began to not only defend themselves well, but even pushed her back on some occasions. She was a skilled fighter and was not easily overcome.

In turn, she learned more of the cannons and guns commonly fought with. She knew of them, but her knowledge was less in comparison to her swordsmanship.

In the time of their journey, they encountered a small handful of other ships, two merchant vessels and three pirates' ships. The others were small and Amethyst's crew outnumbered them easily. She overcame each of them in a similar fashion to her first conquer, her crew overwhelming those on board and her leadership leaping ahead into their midst urging her men onward.

They did not utterly destroy the ships, but merely forced the crews to surrender and took the goods they needed, before returning to the *Nightingale* and continuing their voyage. Amethyst had chosen to plunder the vessels out of need for supplies and for the crew to further grow their skills in battle, but not to kill the unworthy. She knew the battle upcoming would be a true challenge.

As they were nearing the ship they hunted, night had fallen. It was a clear night, the moon only half of itself and the stars glimmering brightly.

Amethyst stood on upper deck, her hands grasping the wheel, her gaze searching the horizon. She wanted to spot them before the lookout did. She had already instructed him not to shout when he did, but rather to return to the main deck. The men were waiting, breathing in the breeze that swept across the seas before them.

Darien stood beside her, the wind whipping his hair about his pale, angled face.

"Do as you wish with the crew," Amethyst murmured, "Tavur is mine."

Darien nodded, glancing at her briefly, before his gaze also returned to the horizon.

It was not often that a pirate ship would attack another. Amethyst wondered if by now word would have reached others on the seas and they would know it was a pirate's vessel approaching. And further, know it was hers.

She spotted the other ship, raising her arm and gesturing to her crew. In the moonlight the *Dragon's Curse* was a dark form on the horizon.

"Draw your scabbards, mateys," Darien called, "and sink this bloody ship to Davy Jones' Locker!"

They had prepared for this.

As they drew closer, the details of the other ship became visible. Its hull was a deep brown. It was a chebec, a ship with three fore-and-aft-rigged masts. It was designed for speed while still carrying a great amount of cargo. In the hands of merchants, it was hardly a threat, but in the hands of pirates, many of the oars were replaced with cannons and the crew would also be well-armed. Further, it was a ship designed to keep up with warships. It would not be as easy a fight as the ones before it.

Amethyst was determined to defeat it. She knew her own three-masted fore and aft rigged schooner could also hold its own, as could her crew.

Already, she had gained some respect with the crewmembers in teaching them and demonstrating her knowledge and skill. And they had seen first-hand the luxuries they enjoyed as pirates as opposed to under-paid sailors. She silently hoped they would fearlessly rally behind her and this victory would seal their ties.

She could already hear the shouts and battle preparations aboard the *Dragon's Curse*. As she hadn't had a white flag raised, they must have been alerted. She wasn't sure. "Light the torches, ye dogs," Amethyst called. The men followed suit, each holding a small flame licking at the sky in one hand and prepared to leap aboard the *Dragon's Curse*. Then they were drawing broadside with the other ship.

"Fire!" Darien shouted as cannons blasted and debris began its rain on the seas.

"Behind me, lads!" Amethyst called. Before the plank was even lowered, they were swinging aboard the enemy ship and each man threw down his torch to the deck and drew his sword before landing, meeting many of the crewmen in a clash and sinking their bodies into a heap with their blades.

Gunfire resounded from the *Dragon's Curse* and those remaining aboard Amethyst's ship responded in kind. Amethyst surged forward with the first group, even as some of their members fell. She was not going to stop until she had spilt the captain's blood. The sound of cannon and gun fire echoed round after round and the clashing of swords was shrill.

Sweat began to glean on the pirates' brows and the fire which had begun from the torches already greedily ate away at the chebec.

But the battle was not yet won.

A flash of silver out of the corner of Amethyst's eye made her turn toward upper deck. She swung her sword, causing a dagger aimed for her to clatter away and overboard into the sea.

Where was the one who had thrown it?

There! Standing on upper deck was a lean sailor, not particularly tall, with several daggers hanging around his person. Already he was poised to throw another.

Amethyst didn't hesitate as she pushed her way toward the stairway and climbed to upper deck. Her days of training had paid off. She raised her sword and blocked another on-coming dagger, finally reaching the raised tower which was upper deck. Once she got close, the man with the daggers drew his sword, attempting to block her attacks. She learned quickly his skills lay in long-distance fighting rather than close-quarters combat.

She pushed his sword back with hers and lunged in close, ramming her knee into his gut and her fist into his face. He stumbled back, dazed, long enough for one of her crewmen to deal the final blow.

Just beyond him, she spied the captain gripping the wheel of his ship, his face clearly displaying his torrent of thoughts. His muscles bulged as he kept the ship steady. It appeared it was all he could do to keep his ship afloat and bellow orders to his crew.

A smirk curled its way onto her lips. "Captain Tavur! Yer filth will no longer stain the seas!" she called as she ran toward him, her sword drawn.

He released his ship to defend himself, his blade clashing with hers equally. "As if I'd be cut down by a puny wench," he spat. "Maybe I'll let ye live so ye can watch me take yer ship and spill the blood of yer crew!"

"Proud words uttered by greedy scum," she murmured, blocking one of his blows and driving her sword against his side making a nasty gash. He yelled at the blow and she stumbled as his hilt dealt a blow to her shoulder. He had missed her neck, barely.

Amethyst turned, widening her stance to steady herself and lunged for him again. Just as he moved downward with his sword, she dove to the left, thrusting her sword upwards toward his ribcage and piercing through its gap into his lung. As swiftly as she had issued the move, she pulled her sword back and as he stumbled, she jammed her elbow into his cheek, pushing him toward the surface of the deck.

At least she'd assumed correctly that her swordsmanship exceeded his.

With the help of two of her crewmembers who had followed her to upper deck, she pushed Tavur overboard. The splash of his body was barely heard above the cannons, guns and roars of the fire.

Amethyst didn't linger on it. Instead, she rushed to the edge of the upper deck, surveying the battle. Her crew was struggling against the enemy pirates. She made her way toward the main deck once more, aiding her crew in their battle, the others who had held back now joining them as well.

With the focus on the quickly disintegrating deck of the *Dragon's Curse*, the battle didn't last much longer. Many had fallen, but victory was theirs.

"Back to the ship!" Amethyst shouted with a wave of her hand. "Leave these cursed bilge rats to the fire," she said, not turning her gaze away as they set sail.

Amethyst turned only as Darien shouted, "Victory is ours!"

Shouts and cheers echoed.

"Lower the sails, lads. We sail for Port Mirka!" she finished.

Darien's eyes met Amethyst's and he moved toward her. She nodded to him, moving toward her cabin.

"Amethyst, we've lost many and the ship needs repairs," Darien said as soon as they were alone.

"We'll light torches for those lost. But forget the ship, Darien," Amethyst said.

"Captain?" Darien asked.

"We're taking another ship," Amethyst said. She felt resolute. The schooner had done well, but she wanted something more suited toward her end goal. Something other pirates, even if they didn't know who she was, would look at from a distance and never dare to approach.

"Amethyst, perhaps we should make repairs before—"

"Do you question me, first mate?" she asked, a coy smile tugging at her lips. "Or do you trust me?"

Darien sighed, studying for a moment. "What are you planning?" he asked finally.

"Port Mirka is a pirate's port, as you know. And when we get there, the *Laughing Skull*, the *Goblin's Bluff,* and the *Roaring Lion,* will be docked in order for their captains to negotiate trades and sailing in consort. While Captain Ektolyl, Captain Zeake, and Captain Nathal are busy drinking ale, we're taking what we see fit. And that includes one of their ships," she explained.

"Ah, yes," Darien said slowly. She watched his face closely, his eyes softening and his mouth finally curving upward. "My captain is a pirate among pirates. We aim for the *Roaring Lion*, then?"

Amethyst only nodded. The *Roaring Lion* was a frigate, a formidable warship and a true treasure for any pirate that sailed it. Most other types of ships were nothing in comparison. Captains Ektolyl, Zeake, and Nathal, and their ships were among the most well-known on the seas, both to other pirates and to merchants. She could only imagine should she succeed in this next venture, that she would be just as well known.

"To Port Mirka," Amethyst offered, gesturing toward Darien with a bottle of rum she'd retrieved from her dresser.

"To Port Mirka," he echoed with a smile.

Commandeering

everal days passed with no disturbances. Amethyst's crew seemed content to busy themselves with ship duties and simple repairs. Even with plans to take another ship, they needed to remain afloat long enough to get to port.

At last, they were nearing the isle. Amethyst was in her cabin, arms folded over her desk as she discussed capturing their next ship with Darien.

"Land ho!" cried the lookout.

Amethyst looked up, a glimmer rising in her eyes. Her ears twitched at the sound of the cheers coming from her crew. Without hesitation, Amethyst stood and made her way toward the main deck, looking over the edge of the ship toward their destination.

The great mountain at the center of Vorda Isle was a clear dark form silhouetted against the setting sun in the distance and she knew they would make port within hours.

Darien climbed the steps from the main deck and approached.

"Darien... First Mate. Alert the crew to our plans. Anyone who even hints at betrayal is to be thrust to ocean's bottom.

We'll need every man we have to be completely on the same page."

"Aye, Captain," Darien said.

At last, the ship was pulling into the bay. "Drop anchor!" was heard before the clinking of chains as the men threw it into the sea.

The moon was no more than a rising sliver and the stars were few above. The water which rippled around them was dark. It was perfect to hide the men as they carried out her and Darien's carefully formed plans. Nothing was going to stop her now.

The crew began to unload some of the captured merchandise onto the docks. While they worked, they talked with other pirates there. Many of the crewmen from the other ships at port had already headed inland to drink and converse for the night. Through conversation, the men quickly learned the worth of what was aboard the other anchored ships.

One of those ships was the *Roaring Lion*, which featured two full decks, several smaller decks, and three square rigged masts. The hull was deep brown in color and the sails pale.

Some of the men returned to Darien and reported. Immediately, one group of deckhands lowered rowboats into the sea and made their way toward the frigate. Stealth and surprise were on their side as they boarded, swept across the ship and threw overboard the few crewmembers aboard.

The rest of Amethyst's crew began dropping the barrels that would not be offered in trade from the schooner into the sea and tying rope around them. They swam, pulling the barrels behind them, to the frigate where they loaded them onto the ship.

Meanwhile, Amethyst slipped into town.

An eruption of shouts hit Amethyst in the face as she stepped into a pub known as *Wenches, Ale, and Gemstones*. It was not far inland near the docks. Jeers and pounding of mugs on the bar and the tables resounded. She made her way toward the midst of the crowd. Part of her still wanted to lay somewhat low. As a mere member of other pirate crews, she had been able to keep her name from spreading as someone notable to the Fae Royal Navy. However, she knew the moment word got out of her being a reputable force on the seas, the Fae Navy would be after her, among others.

At the same time, she intended to make herself known as someone more than capable and it was time for her to stop hiding anyway; she would never achieve her goals if she did. She wanted to be both known and feared.

As she was not particularly tall, Amethyst grasped one of the wooden chairs and stood on it, despite the protests of the bartend. "Listen up, ye mates!" A shrill whistle echoed around the room after she put two fingers to her lips. "I'm lookin' for Captain Ektolyl, Captain Zeake, and Captain Nathal."

All heads turned in her direction, some hoots and hollers sounding as well. Though no one acknowledged being who she sought.

Her ears flicked against her head, but she stifled her annoyance. Brutes, the lot of them. "I am Captain Amethyst and I'm looking to trade."

Laughter followed and some returned to their conversations. One shouted,"Captain of what?"

More laughter followed, "Wouldn't trust a wench far as I could throw 'er!"

"Run along now, lass."

Her lips curled, her fangs glimmering in the pale light of the torches. Even the men who she knew would at least have heard her name seemed to take her lightly. Did they not believe she could rise to captain her own ship?

Amethyst drew a dagger and all conversation stopped again as a loud thud resounded, the dagger firmly planted in the opposite wall of the pub. "I'm no mere wench," she said.

Instantly the men stood, hands going to swords and the room growing tense. "There's no need to threaten bloodshed, lass," said one man.

"I'll do what I must. Now which of ye are tha Cap'ns I seek?" she asked.

A few men slowly released the hilts of their swords and shrugged. "Alright, lass, ye've got our attention," one voiced. "I be Captain Ektolyl. I'll see what ye've got." He paused, gesturing toward two others. "C'mon, then, lads. Let's entatain tha lass, eh?" he said with laughter.

Amethyst smirked and leaped down from the chair, making her way toward the door. She remained alert, her ears flicking back to listen for their movements. She wouldn't be surprised if after her stunt one of them tried to stab her in the back.

They made their way back to the docks, and she confidently approached her captured schooner, raising her fingers to whistle once more.

Darien waved from upper deck and the men from Amethyst's crew still aboard the schooner gathered on the main deck.

Amethyst led the men from the pub onto her ship where the provisions they had held back were already waiting.

Several men had followed the three captains from the pub. She wasn't sure if they were the members of their crew or if they had tagged along for curiosity's sake. She heard the men talking amongst themselves, and a smirk once more graced her lips as they realized this to be the very merchant ship that had been making its way for a slave trade to the north of the isle at Port Blaise.

Although, she also noticed the snickers as some of them mentioned its tattered state. They joked she was the captain of a sinking ship as the only reason she could claim such. She dismissed it.

Amethyst stopped and turned, the captains and those that had followed from the pub stopping abruptly at her motion. She made a sweeping gesture with her arm, her other hand grasping a dagger snuggly tucked into her belt. "Ye'll stay aboard me ship only as long as ye're examining the loot," she announced. "And ye'll offer me fair trades," she added.

The captains moved forward, rummaging through barrels and eyeing the goods like a starving man eyeing meat.

Finally, Captain Zeake stepped toward her. "Ye've got some amount of worth, lass." He presented a small pouch of animal hide, the contents clacking softly. "I'll give ye these sapphires for the whole lot."

Amethyst grasped the pouch, peeking inside. There were twenty round gems within. She drew one out and examined it. They were small, probably less than the standard measurement of a carat. As a fae herself, she was well versed in the various types of gems and their value. She knew these were zircon. Even if they had been true sapphires, there were not nearly as much to the gems in this pouch as she knew her loot to be worth.

She dropped the gem she had taken back into the pouch and turned her gaze sharply to Zeake. "You insult me," she spat. A soft zing of metal echoed followed by a soft thud. Captain Zeake cried out and gripped his arm as he stumbled back. Her dagger had landed in the flesh of his palm. He would not be able to use that hand in the future for some time. Zeake stormed away from the ship, a slew of curses escaping his lips.

Immediately, those that had followed from the pub drew their swords, prepared to attack.

Amethyst raised a hand and snapped her fingers. Instantly, the men onboard her ship moved to surround those from the pub, a mixture of guns and weapons drawn.

"Perhaps, gents, ye'd like to reconsider. After all, these barrels are still up for a *fair* trade," Amethyst said after placing her other hand on the hilt of her sabre. She tucked the first pouch of gems she'd received into her belt.

Slowly, the men returned their swords to their scabbards.

The man that had told her there was no need to threaten bloodshed at the pub placed his fists on his hips, his lips curled into a frown. "I be Captain Nathal."

"Isn't it hypocrisy for a pirate to protest violence?" Amethyst said with a laugh.

Captain Nathal ignored her and held up a similar pouch to that Zeake had offered. "Tell me, lass. Is it truly gems ye seek? Or do ye wish to trade loot for loot?"

"I can attain any loot I desire," she said, "the point is to gain something I don't already have."

Nathal only shrugged and tossed the pouch to her. "Perhaps ye'll be more pleased with me offer than Zeake's, then," he said with a slight smirk on the corner of his lips.

Amethyst only opened his pouch as she had before and removed one of the gems from within. They were a pale brilliant blue, and each one a different size, she noted. "What do ye claim these to be?" she asked.

"Tourmaline Paraiba. A fine rarity which can buy much, lass."

Amethyst laughed, her finely pointed fangs glimmering. "Ye seek to educate a *fae* on the rarity and value of a gem? These are mere topaz!" At that, she drew her sword, pointing it toward his chest.

"Yer insult is greater than Captain Zeake's. Ye'll walk the plank for yer arrogance!"

Nathal raised a hand for his crew to stay back as he drew his own sword, lowering his stance. "I be a captain, lass. Ye insult me at the notion I'd walk yer plank. No one interfere! I'll show ye yer place, *wench*," he snarled.

Amethyst smirked. "Well then perhaps we should test who be the better captain, eh?" She lunged toward him, their swords clashing in a brilliant cry of metal.

He blocked her, but stumbled back.

She didn't remain in one place but rather constantly shifted her position. He swung his sword and she caught his blade, throwing it sideward as she dove and thrust upward. She licked her lips as her sword sliced into his shoulder and a satisfying yell escaped his lips.

He faltered, but swung his sword downward once more.

She drew her sword back and leaped backward with it, narrowly avoiding his blade. Her eyes were brilliant in the darkness and she danced around him. A few ringlets had escaped her bundle and clung to her forehead; she paid them no mind.

Nathal whirled. His swings were wide and left him open. Slowly, she was pushing him toward the edge of her ship.

In a lunge forward, she slid past his thrust and buried her elbow into his stomach. She turned, grasping his wrist and he dropped his sword as he coughed.

She kicked the blade away from him, dancing outward again and pointing her sword to him.

"Now turn an' walk tha plank, ye bloody dog!" she said.

Nathal stepped backward, tripping as he found nothing behind him but the short board leading away from the ship.

"Perhaps ye'll offer will be better should ye ever wish to trade from me again," Amethyst said, stepping forward once more.

He stepped back again, a yell escaping him as his foot found nothing but air and he tumbled into the water below.

Amethyst turned, sheathing her sabre and moved toward the middle of the deck. "Now, then. Captain Ektolyl. Perhaps ye have an offer worthy of me loot?"

Ektolyl stared at her a moment. She wondered if he were shocked at what he had just witnessed. Finally, he cleared his throat. "Nay, lass, there be nothin' I'd offer ye for yer loot. Instead, I'd like to extend an alliance."

Amethyst raised one brow, scrutinizing Ektolyl for a moment. He must realize her actions toward the other captains had been because they insulted her. Their offers had not been fair to the value of her merchandise, and they had lied about what they were offering her, trying to fool her into believing common gems were actually rarer ones. She wondered if he held a fair value for her trade, but saw that she was formidable and had chosen to ally himself with her for his benefit.

Regardless of what he was thinking, Amethyst felt he showed her respect, recognition, and his own intelligence by his gesture. Finally, she extended a hand toward him. He grasped it, his grip firm. "Let's draw up the paperwork," she said, glancing toward Darien briefly. He nodded and soon, a parchment with ink was brought forward. She wanted to make the alliance official.

"Listen up, gents!" Amethyst said, her gaze traveling around the group of men gathered on her ship. "Clearly yer previous captains couldn't be trusted! If they weren't willin' to give a fair trade, who's to say they weren't keeping more than their share of yer loot, eh? They used ye fer their plunders and didn't give ye any of yer worth! Join me, and ye'll discover freedom ye've not yet known," she challenged.

The others stared at her for a moment, and slowly some of them began whispering amongst each other.

"Why would we trust ye, lass, if ye so readily cut down fellow cap'ns?" one challenged, some shouts of agreement following.

"Aye! What's t' say ye wouldn't dispose of us also?"

They had a point. "I only slay those who would suggest mutiny or betrayal. Or those who don't treat others with respect. Yer captains were worthy of my blade. Ye gents, however, have done nothing to warrant it."

The men around her finally seemed to consent, some nodding their heads while others shrugged their shoulders. They agreed to join her crew; the increase in number would be necessary to man the frigate.

Amethyst noticed some that left and made their way back up the beach, but she let them go. Perhaps they would serve to spread what had happened and that she was not to be easily contended with. At least, she hoped so.

"Well, gents, it seems there be a couple o' ships in this harbor that no longer possess a captain. Tha frigate be mine, lads. Ektolyl, do ye desire to keep yer ship, or take another?" she asked.

Ektolyl glanced toward the remaining unclaimed ship. The frigate had been Nathal's. Amethyst knew that Ektolyl's brigantine, the *Laughing Skull,* - with a combination of square and fore-and-aft rigged sails and excellent wind-maneuverability - would pale with the prospect of sailing the nearby barquentine, the *Goblin's Bluff,* - similar in rigging but with even greater sailing abilities regardless of the wind and the cargo aboard, as well as requiring an even smaller crew to perform the duties and sail the ship.

She wasn't surprised when Ektolyl met her gaze once more. "I'll pass me brigantine to me first mate."

"Aye," she responded. "As allies, we'll all share whatever loot we gain when our paths cross in days ahead, savvy?"

Ektolyl nodded and with a shrill whistle, he turned. He made his way off Amethyst's ship and toward the brigantine. Amethyst assumed he would converse with his first mate and perhaps gather his belongings before commandeering the barquentine.

As soon as he was gone, she gathered her crew.

"To the frigate, gents! Ye've earned a night of merriment and the ship is ours!" Cheers and shouts echoed in the night air. Some of the men made their way toward the pub to have drinks while others were content to drink aboard the newly acquired frigate.

Soon, the schooner was abandoned in the bay. It was hardly anything worth sailing at this point.

As she approached her new ship, Amethyst slowly took in its features. Its hull was a dark brown. It appeared almost black in the darkness. Its sails were pale, though they were raised while the ship wasn't at sea.

Most notable was the figurehead at the prow of the ship. Its form was a pouncing lion, claws unsheathed and mouth wide open. Its lips were curled in a fierce snarl and its eyes peered downward at the world below.

It didn't quite strike the fear she desired. But she could change it later.

Amethyst boarded the ship, her gaze sweeping about the main deck. She was impressed by its size. She made her way toward her new cabin. It was spacious with a medium-sized closet to her right and glassless windows in all of the walls other than the one with the door. To her left was a simple dresser – it was nothing extraordinary - and against the far side of the cabin was a large bed.

Men. They had no appreciation or taste for elegance, in her experience. But she would make her cabin how she pleased in time. First, she was content simply to take it in and relish in the fact this ship was hers.

Amethyst turned and left the cabin. She wanted to thoroughly explore the ship. Across from her cabin was a stairway leading below deck. She descended the steps, taking in the second full deck. It was lined with spaces the length of the ship. Every other space had a cannon chained to the deck in front of it and in between the cannons were short benches. Under each bench was a fastened oar.

Amethyst continued down the stairway. The third deck wasn't a full one, but it was spacious enough. What was before her was a long hall on either side of which were the sailors' cabins. She finished the final steps and turned. On the end behind her was the galley. The iron stove in the center was the biggest she had seen on a ship, though the cabinets held nothing more than plain dishes. She had somewhat been expecting to see something more elegant.

Amethyst moved out of the galley and down the hall, peeking into the cabins. They were as simple as any she had seen though somewhat more spacious.

Finally, she reached the end of the hall where there was a plain door. She stepped in to a small room. Directly in front of her was a desk with a window on the opposite wall. To her left was another door. She approached it with curiosity and beyond it found another stairway.

Amethyst climbed it quickly and as soon as she reached the top, she realized it led straight to the main deck outside of the captain's cabin.

Well, that was convenient. Perhaps she could make the room below her personal study aside from her cabin. She wasn't sure what other purpose it possibly could have served.

She made her way to the front of her cabin once more where yet another stairway led to the quarterdeck. She climbed the stairway and breathed in deeply as the sea breeze swept over her. At the end of the deck, Amethyst noted that there were two upper cabins above the captain's cabin. Both were as simple as the cabin's on the lower deck and she wondered if Darien would use them.

In front of the cabins toward the edge of the upper deck was the ship's wheel. One last stairway led to the roof of the upper cabins, which was also the poop deck. She felt no need to see it.

Instead, Amethyst gripped the wheel, staring into the distant darkness. She tried to imagine herself sailing into the wind.

The Ship Is Mine

Amethyst's crew spent the next week becoming more comfortable aboard the *Roaring Lion*. They needed to adjust to its size and assign duties amongst themselves.

"The Roaring Lion isn't me, Darien," Amethyst announced as she aided the crew in some of the work.

"What will you call it, then?" he asked her. Darien had ropes slung over his shoulder and was hauling them toward the main mast at the center of the deck.

"The Gargoyle," she exclaimed without hesitation. "It's fierce and others will think twice before approaching. And like the statues that guard beautiful buildings..." she trailed off.

Darien glanced toward the prow of the ship.

Amethyst followed his gaze. "Aye, we'll have to make some adjustments." It wouldn't be terribly difficult to alter the figurehead, she thought. They were already docked at port and they could use materials from the schooner they had abandoned if need be.

They removed the outstretched arms of the lion and added two long pointed horns to its brow. The men carved down its mane and added ridges to its face. They cut upward through its open mouth until its teeth gleamed from a wicked grin. When the work was done its face peered at passersby fearsomely.

Meanwhile, some of the others had taken down the sails and sewn green and grey gargoyle faces into the canvas.

Some of the loot they had gained from taking the *Gargoyle* had included pieces of furniture. There was a desk which some of the crewmembers helped Darien move to the upper cabins. He made one his own while the other became a study of sorts.

Not everything Amethyst desired was already theirs, however.

Amethyst shopped at port, hoping to further spread her name as a new captain. She traded some of the gems she had acquired from Nathal and Zeake and bought herself a wardrobe and a bathtub, a shower head and towels as well as a simple dressing table complete with a round mirror and hair accessories. As a captain of no small ship, she had already determined she would have whatever luxuries she desired, simply because she could.

She gave the gems she didn't use to her crewmembers for them to do with as they pleased. She assumed some of them would waste them on ale or perhaps a high-priced courtesan. Perhaps they might even stuff them in their pockets. She also demanded they buy several lengths of pipe and a bath of some sort. She ignored their confused expressions.

As soon as she was done shopping, a few of her crewmen helped her take her new belongings aboard.

"Blimey! Are ye tryin' ta furnish a mansion?" asked one man as he eyed her mirror and dressing table suspiciously.

Amethyst laughed, tipping her head back as she did so. The many silver hoops in her ears jingled. "No! Ye'll see, lads. Our ship will truly be like no other. So long as yer sworn to secrecy," she said, a glimmer in her eyes.

They made their way down the beach and up the plank. "Do ye really need all this, Cap'n?" another man asked.

"Aye!" Amethyst insisted, "I'm still a woman, after all. And a fae at that. I'll do as I please and have what I want."

The man who had spoken eyed her incredulously, his jaw falling for a moment, and then clamping.

Amethyst helped the men with the dressing table, as she could only carry one of the things she had bought. She moved backward, setting the table down only a small distance away from the far right corner of her cabin, against the wall opposite from the bed.

"Place the wardrobe there," she instructed, pointing toward the corner to the left of anyone walking through the door. "Any of you can take the old dresser and do with it as you please. I have no use for it," she added with a wave of her hand.

Some of the men glanced at each other. "This dresser's far better than tha one in me cabin! Help me out, lads. I be takin' it for meself," one said with a toothy grin.

As two of the men removed the old dresser, some others brought in the bathtub Amethyst had bought. Apparently her previous responses kept their questions in their throats, though she could read the question all over their faces. She smiled.

"Place it in the closet on the far wall," she told them. "I'll take it from there." The closet in question was large enough to become a bathroom; she could use her wardrobe for her clothes. A little magic and it could be just as she wanted it.

As soon as she was once more alone, Amethyst fixed the showerhead she had bought into the wall of the closet and beside the tub she hammered in a simple rack she had bought also for her towels.

At last, Amethyst felt the ship was truly her own.

As they sailed from Port Mirka, the sun was rapidly falling. Amethyst stood on the main deck, hands grasping the railing. Her gaze was fixed on the horizon, and her curls freely danced about her figure.

Since she had let those who hadn't allied with her go, an unsettling feeling had risen in her stomach. So far, they had been met with one success after another. Was she just experiencing good luck? No. She had worked for every bit she had taken and had proven her worth as a captain time and again now. Few remained, she hoped, that would question her or rally against her. Though she suspected if she faced a fleet, it would be her greatest challenge yet.

The unsettling feeling was something else, but she couldn't name it or think of what could possibly be causing it. Instead, she turned toward other thoughts. After so much time, she now captained a ship she was proud of with a crew that rallied behind her. A confident sort of smile found its way onto her lips.

Amethyst pushed away from the side of her ship and made her way toward Darien's study. She knew it was only fair she discuss any decisions with him before making them final. She knocked softly and her ears flicked slightly at the sound of his voice.

"Come in," he said.

The click of the door handle turning was barely heard and the door creaked open. "Darien, there's something we must discuss," she started, closing the door behind her. The soft thuds of her boots on the boards beneath her echoed as she made her way across the room. He looked up at her briefly, and then back down. An array of maps and documents lay on the desk he had set up for himself

"The Gargoyle is mine. Ours, and I wish to make it entirely comfortable for myself other than the physical luxuries."

Darien chuckled for a moment. "Ah, yes. The lads told me of your spending spree."

Amethyst frowned. "Don't laugh. I am still royalty, you know."

"After everything you've been through, you deserve whatever you want. I only laugh at the crew's reaction. Don't forget they don't know who you are, even if they know you're fae."

"Nor will they ever. That's strictly between you and me. No one can ever know who I really am. Even the fae among the crew." Even if the fae knew *of* her, few had known her specifically. Only those within the city of Clozaa had seen her, and even fewer knew her name. Many fae named their children after gemstones, and the fae people had referred to her as *mah sieei ueltho,* her royal maiden, in the fae tongue.

Darien's eyes met hers, his features softening. She knew he already knew the importance of what she had spoken. There had been no need for her to iterate it, but it was already done, so instead she moved on.

"I wish to weave magic into the ship," she said, getting to the point of why she'd come.

"Don't you think that will put everything you've acquired at risk?"

"No. It is common for fae to use magic. I only haven't thus far to prove I could gain where I am without using it, and to prevent the Fae Navy from trying to locate me through my magic print."

The Fae Royal Navy was the greatest and most feared of the fae armies. The Fae Navy alone had conquered numerous lands and races throughout history and the mere sight of it struck fear and caused other ships to flee. They were a great fleet of ships captained by the most ruthless warriors of the fae people, fearless in pursuit of others and in using magic to their advantage. The generals answered directly to the *iist,* the lord of the fae, and as such if he would have sent anyone to find her, it would have been the Navy.

"What's changed?" Darien asked.

"Now that I've announced myself to the world as a fae pirate captain, it's only a matter of time. The Fae Navy will be hunting me down anyway. I just have to elude them."

Darien frowned. "How will *using* your magic help you elude them?"

"Well, Darien, that's part of me being who I am. I am privy to magic in a way very few are. Even among the fae." She paused.

Darien nodded.

"I'm going to make it possible for hot showers or baths, for the food to last longer than ordinary, and for anything we can make on land to be possible on the ship. That includes cooking. We'll probably even be able to have milk aboard. Feel free to use what magic you desire as well, Darien. Don't forget there are others among the crew who can use magic, such as the ones that we freed on the schooner. They can help as well. Aboard the *Gargoyle*, we'll welcome fae crewmen. They'll be free to do as they please, so long as they respect me, and keep the magic a secret from anyone who isn't a member of the crew."

There were two reasons to keep the magic secret: she didn't want anyone to say she gained her reputation using magic as an advantage, and she didn't want to risk someone who reported to the Fae Navy learning any more than they might already know.

Darien nodded. "Aye, aye, Captain," he said.

As soon as she left Darien's study, she moved toward the inward edge of the upper deck. The men lounged about, some in conversation and others content to sip their drink or stargaze.

She raised two fingers to her lips, issuing a shrill whistle.

"Who among ye can use tha magic?" she asked.

At first, the men glanced at each other hesitantly. Outside of the fae territories and conquests, most didn't announce their magical abilities, even if others could infer based on race. Many of the non-magical races feared magic and attempted to subdue those who could use it. Those who flaunted their magic sometimes found themselves captured and forced into slavery, perhaps simply for the non-magical races to prove they didn't need magic and were just as capable as those races who could use it.

"Why do ye ask, Cap'n?" one man voiced after a moment.

Amethyst smirked, holding out her hand. Her eyes took on a soft glow as she formed a small ball of light that grew to the size of a cannonball and then vanished. Immediately, her eyes returned to normal. "Ye needn't fear t' use what ye have," Amethyst responded to the question. "I wish to enhance the ship."

The men slowly gathered, and those among them who could use magic voiced it. There were a handful of fae males, mages, and others that either carried the blood of a magical race or were creatures that had taken on human form such as centaurs, griffins, and even one who claimed to bear dragon blood. Their magic abilities would be specific to their race, but she wanted them at least to know they were free.

Admittedly, Amethyst was glad they had chosen to remain in human form for the time being. She had witnessed most of the other creatures in beast form and they were certainly a force to contend with. At least they were on her side.

To weave magic into the entirety of the ship as well as its merchandise would take much time and energy, even with as many aboard that could use magic as there were. Those that couldn't use magic performed the daily tasks and maintenance required while the others set about enhancing the ship.

They started with the food. Salt and brine already preserved the meat, but with a brief spell, the mages enclosed the barrels in ice and with another spell, the fae prevented the ice from melting.

Afterward, they moved to the cabins. Slowly, one by one, they set pipes into the walls and floors of the ship, using magic to aid in the process. It was much simpler to magically move boards and replace them as opposed to using ordinary hammers and nails.

Amethyst made sure the pipes led to a handful of openings in the hull beneath the surface of the sea. Magic would prevent the ship from flooding and also allow for the men to draw water from the ocean and filter and heat it, if they chose, for bathing purposes.

She had considered making the process simpler by merely allotting a part of the ship to public bathing, but quickly changed her mind. For one, there wasn't a particular deck that would be adequate to use, and for another, she wished to give her men the same option of private bathing that she would have.

The piping alone took several days.

Finally, they moved on to the body of the ship itself. They laced the hull with both protective and masking magic. It would help to prolong the life of the ship as well as make spotting them more difficult.

Amethyst felt an incredible drain on her body. She wasn't used to performing magic as much as she once had, but she knew that she would regain her stamina now that she had openly used the magic, and that she had a bit of time to rest.

She resigned herself to her cabin. "Enjoy yerselves, lads, and take some time for merriment," she told the crew.

Amethyst remained content for a few days to sip on rum and lounge in the sun when she wasn't pampering herself in her cabin. She hadn't enjoyed regular bathing since her days with her ex-husband and the feeling of water pouring over her skin was exhilarating.

On one of those days, she emerged from her cabin without any clothing at all, only a folded blanket over her arm.

She ignored the men as they gawked in shock. "Cap'n, have ye gone mad?" someone asked.

"Nay, lads. I merely desire some sun," she responded with a wide grin.

She climbed the steps to upper deck and thrust the folded blanket outwards before laying on her stomach and gently pushing her long curls to the side. After so much time at sea, her naturally light skin was brilliantly tanned, but she desired a flawless color without any lines or marks. As captain, she felt entirely comfortable. She had already demonstrated countless times what would happen to anyone that dared disrespect her in any way.

By the time she had laid on the deck a few times in the midst of the day, the crewmen barely paid her mind, or at least, they didn't respond.

Amethyst was lying on the deck during mid-afternoon and opened her eyes sharply at the feel of cloth against her hardened stomach.

Darien's slender yet toned figure was outlined by rays of sunlight and his face was scrunched in a frown.

"What is it?" she asked, her tone a little sharper than she intended.

"Ye'll want to see for yerself," he said, the words almost a murmur.

Amethyst sat up, the cloth she had felt earlier rolling onto her thighs. It was a simple white tunic. She picked it up and slipped it over her torso before grasping Darien's extended hand and rising to her feet.

Darien pointed toward the horizon where several brilliant white flags were waving. They weren't the sort raised in surrender.

Amethyst felt the blood draining from her face. "It can't be," she whispered.

For only a moment, Amethyst remained still. The Fae Royal Navy. After all this time. She could only imagine they had found her so quickly because her name was on the lips of many since she had made such a show of becoming the newest captain. She was certain Darien would say, *"I told you so,"* with how much magic they had been using, but he was gracious enough to say nothing now.

Well they might think they were gaining on her, but she was determined to escape. She rushed to the edge of the upper deck, grasping its rails as she looked to the crew down below. "Lower tha sails, lads! Rowers, get below deck!" Her tone was both commanding and sharp. She looked to Darien, who gave a brief nod.

Instantly, the men rushed into action. Some climbed the mast and with a whoosh and the sound of billowing linen, the sails tumbled down and out as they caught the wind from the sea. At the same time wooden oars were pushed outward by those that had gone below deck and began to propel the ship forward.

Darien had also slipped below deck. Shortly after the rowers had begun, the oars flashed a brilliant green and soon began moving at an incredible speed.

Amethyst hadn't been caught yet, and she wasn't going to be now. While the men worked below, their captain grasped the wheel and steered their direction.

Amethyst looked back for a moment to see if the Navy ships were gaining any distance. The fae soldiers appeared to have enchanted their oars as well; their ships were moving as swiftly as hers. Was there nothing more she could do to escape them?

"Taz, Elias!" Amethyst hollered at two of the crewmembers near the main mast. "Fetch the others who can use magic. I've got an idea."

They nodded and scrambled below deck, soon returning with every member of the crew besides Darien who could use magic. The first mate had to keep the oars moving. "Gather around the edges of the deck, lads, and move the waters with control spells. We'll open our own path through the sea!"

"Aye, aye!" they shouted, and immediately those gathered did as she instructed, their voices blending together as they spoke spells in their own tongues and the ship lurched forward faster than ever before.

While the fae were among the most powerful in their control of magic, Amethyst felt she had an advantage having such a variety of users. The fae could only control magic in certain ways, whereas Amethyst's crew could each use their own way to bring about even greater results.

Even after the brilliant flags were no longer in view, Amethyst still felt shaken. Her entire body was tense. She stepped away from the wheel, signaling the men to pull in the oars and resume their leisure.

She had known at some point she would face the Navy, but she hadn't thought it would be so soon. Still, she was determined to evade them whatever it took and continue the life she desired at sea. Even with that decision, if it was the case that her name was on enough lips to get back to the Fae Royal Navy, she decided she shouldn't make port for a time. She didn't want to sail into an ambush.

"We'll rely on a few raids for supplies for now," she told her crew.

Amethyst spent a decent portion of her days going over the trading maps and tracing the merchant ships' paths with

Darien. She didn't want to remain in one area or along one particular route for too long. It was too risky that word would reach unwanted ears and she'd be hunted.

Perhaps after she'd gained plenty of booty, she'd make port off of the Orlesce country and trade some of her plunder. Orlesce was the farthest country she knew of away from her homeland. Or at least as far as she'd ventured.

It would take several months' time if not more. Plenty of time for her to gather her thoughts.

They planned each plunder carefully, each route specific to what they needed as well as optimum for changing directions.

When they weren't going over the maps, Darien gave the crew their bearings and aided with ship duties while Amethyst attempted to dismiss her anxiety.

The first ship they encountered was a simple merchantman which carried wood, tools, and other supplies. The captain, Mather, was one she had encountered during her days as a mere crewmember who was known for fae trafficking. He disgusted her, and his defeat was swift.

The *Gargoyle* turned northward afterward, their next target another small merchantman carrying clothes and fabrics. Among the goods, she found a long dark cloak and scarlet hat that she took a special liking toward.

As time passed, Amethyst felt her fear of sailing into the Fae Royal Navy growing and her plunders became more coldblooded. She desired only to gain what they needed without concern for where it came from, and her terror at being recognized and turned in spurred her to leave no survivors. Her attacks had less reason behind them. She could feel herself changing from her original ideals about piracy, but she also couldn't subdue her fears.

Amethyst felt her worries slowly disappear with each battle. She felt powerful and it didn't hurt that the fights eased her tension.

They only encountered one ship which they were unable to conquer. It was another frigate, as armed as the *Gargoyle* with guns and weapons. At first, they had attempted to approach, but as soon as parts of Amethyst's ship began to splinter and it was clear the other ship was prepared for attack, she ordered her men to steer clear and be on their way.

They turned their voyage southwest. There was a certain point between Vorda Isle, Tysck to the north, and Orlesce to the south that many merchant vessels had to pass. Amethyst doubted she could take on multiple ships at once, but she knew she'd encounter one particular merchantman that would have a bountiful supply of food and drink as well as some other supplies.

It would have just left Port Blaise and its journey would be toward Bohai island, a small isle in between the two land-masses above and below it that served as a perfect recuperation spot for ships with long voyages. It was similar to Vorda Isle in its position between the rest of the continents.

Within a week the merchant vessel was in sight. It was mid-day and the sun shone down on the ship, a fluyt, its white sails glistening. The men aboard the *Gargoyle* were ready as the lookout shouted they were approaching and those below deck loaded the cannons.

Amethyst looked through her spyglass. Those aboard the fluyt were scrambling, turning the ship so that it sailed with the wind, and attempting to prepare defense. There were passengers aboard being ushered below deck. Fools. She lowered her scope and drew her sabre.

"Prepare to board, lads!" Darien shouted.

Soon, the *Gargoyle* was drawing broadside the fluyt and the pirates' shouts were drowned out by the explosions of cannon fire.

The pirates threw the plank across the distance and rushed aboard the fluyt, others using ropes instead.

Amethyst barreled into one of the merchant sailors, pushing him back into one of his fellow seamen. "Force them together!" she commanded. Her crew surrounded the lightly-manned ship, its sailors slowly pushed into a circle backs against each other.

"Drop yer weapons," Darien ordered them. The *Gargoyle*'s crew stood around them, swords pointed at their necks.

They obeyed, their swords and guns clattering as they hit the deck.

The ship was captured and its sailors subdued. Those that hadn't been forced into the circle had been pushed overboard and lay at ocean's bottom.

"Listen up!" Amethyst began. "Those of ye who wish to join me crew, speak up now! Ye'll find both yer bellies and yer pockets full!"

Silence rang a moment other than the sound of the waves crashing against the ships.

A few of the merchant sailors stepped forward, nodding their heads.

Amethyst nodded toward Darien.

"Tha rest o' ye walk tha plank!" Darien finished for Amethyst. Even if Darien were opposed, she knew he would wait till later to voice it to her. The sailors' faces grew pale and one by one, they were pushed into the sea.

"Gather tha loot, lads!" Amethyst ordered.

"Aye!" they shouted and soon, the merchandise from the fluyt was stored aboard the *Gargoyle*.

Amethyst returned to her ship, intent on seeing to it the new crewmembers received their fair share. She slipped below deck to see what all they had gained, yet as she was passing the second deck, her ears twitched upward at the sound of a woman's voice. A snarl formed on her lips and a glimmer in her eyes.

Amethyst slipped down the hallway toward the noise.

One of her crewmembers looked up sharply as the cabin door slammed open, Amethyst's form casting a shadow through the doorway.

She took in the scene before her, a skinny human wench half-naked and draped over the bed. She had blonde locks tumbling down her shoulders and cheeks as rosy as spring flowers. She must have been one of the passengers from the fluyt.

Her territorial nature as a fae gripped her. Without saying a word, Amethyst moved swiftly across the room. "Did I not make myself clear? No wench is ever allowed aboard my ship!" she bellowed. She grasped the wench's hair and proceeded to drag her out of the room, the girl wailing as she did so. "Ye presume to lay your hands on what is mine?" Amethyst asked the lass.

"You mad fae scum. Get your hands off me! I can do as I please," the girl shouted.

Amethyst's slap across the girl's cheek resounded and she pulled her upward toward the main deck. Finally, in the open night air, Amethyst forced the other to her feet, drawing her sword. "You'll be a spectacle for all to know what becomes of any lass that dares come close to everything I have achieved. Walk."

The girl sputtered, but backed up, nearly tripping over her dress. At last, Amethyst stopped, the girl's back to the edge of the ship.

"Turn around and keep moving," Amethyst demanded, her eyes fierce.

Tears began dripping down the wench's cheeks, and Amethyst only smirked. She watched as the lass moved forward, hesitating at the edge of the plank. "Would ye rather jump, or have my boot in your back, wench?"

The girl only shook her head, sputtering. "Please, please, I'll stay away. Just let me go."

"You should never have trifled with my ship," Amethyst murmured, sticking her sword outward until its tip was near the girl's body. "Now jump!" she demanded.

The girl screamed on her way down, the sound ending as her body splashed into the sea. The only thing that would save her life was if she knew how to swim, assuming some sea animal didn't get her first.

Amethyst didn't watch to find out. She simply turned back, her crewmembers watching with shocked expressions.

"No wench is ever allowed on my ship!" she barked with a snarl.

"Ye'd rob us of that pleasure, Cap'n?" one protested.

She snapped her gaze to the one that had spoken. "Ye do as ye please elsewhere. We'll make port plenty soon enough. But never aboard my ship," she snapped.

"Aye, aye, Cap'n," the men answered.

With that, Amethyst pushed past them and moved toward her quarters. "Divide the spoils as you please. First Mate Darien will answer your questions." She paused, turning back for only a moment. "The next lad found with a wench on my ship will walk the plank behind her," she warned, before continuing her way.

Once inside her room, she grabbed a pillow from her bed and screamed into it. *'How dare they question me. A petty wench will threaten everything! Fools!*

Didn't they understand? Another woman aboard could be her undoing. She could steal the trust and hearts of the crew and cause mutiny. She could take away from everything Amethyst had gained with her crew, and most of all, could blab secrets she learned to untrustworthy ears. Amethyst could not see past her natural fae instincts. Her territorial nature and her impulses made her blind to anything but seeing other women as a potential threat.

No wenches would ever be allowed near her beloved ship.

She grasped a bottle of rum from her dresser, tipping it to her lips. Would the men whisper of mutiny after this? Or would they respect her instructions? Amethyst replaced the bottle and moved out to the main deck once more. The crewmembers had resumed work. She had told them they could do as they pleased elsewhere, and they docked at port often enough. Surely they would recognize she hardly meant to rob them.

Finally, Amethyst pushed her worries aside. She had already made her statement, and she was not going back. They were sailing away from the ship they had just raided, and she was eager to make port. She had goods to trade, and something in her gut told her it was time.

"Lower the sails, lads! We sail for Orlesce!"

Shouts echoed in response.

They sailed with little disturbance for some time, the days passing by peacefully and full of merriment.

They were still several more weeks' time from the coast when the lookout cried, "Sail ho!" from the crow's nest. All aboard the *Gargoyle* rushed to the edge of the ship, peering outward.

Amethyst lengthened her spy glass and put it to her eye. In the near distance, two ships came into view. One was a clipper, a three-masted square-rigged ship that was built for speed. Its hull was narrow for its incredible length. It was a merchant's ship; Amethyst knew aboard would be a wealth of supplies for trade, and that it would be poorly armed in order to make more room for its goods. The clipper was known for avoiding raids by mere evasion rather than winning battles.

But it was the other ship that more closely caught her attention. It was another frigate. Its hull and sails were black, edged in silver, and a brilliant red reaper was sewn into the canvas'. The *Reaper's Scythe* was etched in red into the stern of the ship. It was a pirate's ship, and it was also pursuing the clipper.

Amethyst lowered her spy glass. Between the two of them, the clipper had little chance of escape. But she wasn't about to hand over her goods to some other scumbag.

"Speed the ship up!" she called. Amethyst ran across the deck toward the bow. "Ready the ropes and the torches, lads! The clipper is ours!"

The wind whipped through the sails as they gained on the merchant ship. But the other frigate was closing in too. Amethyst felt her lip curl into a snarl. Even if it was another pirate, she'd sink his ship too if she had to.

"With me!" Amethyst said to several of her crewmembers a short distance before they would reach the clipper. She climbed to stand on the railing of the *Gargoyle* and dove into the sea, swimming toward the merchant ship. Those she had commanded dove in after her.

Soon, they reached the hull of the clipper and Amethyst drew two daggers from her person, beginning to scale the ship. The crewmen with her followed suit. Within no time, they reached the deck. The sailors aboard had been scrambling to prepare defense at first sight of the pirate ships and hadn't seen as Amethyst and some of her crew dove into the water. Now, they were distracted as the ships approached. The pirates boarding their ship from the water's surface had an advantage.

Amethyst leaped over the railing, flinging one of her daggers into the chest of a sailor and diving to the deck to avoid a gunshot from another. She sprang to her feet once more as cannon fire exploded around them and battle cries ensued. She knew Darien would be directing those aboard the *Gargoyle*, and assumed the *Reaper's Scythe* was firing as well.

As soon as the *Gargoyle* was broadside the clipper, the crewmembers threw a plank to the clipper and ran across. Some of them dropped torches to the ship's deck while others captured several of the merchant sailors.

"Oy! Are ye mad, lass?"

Amethyst's ears twitched at the smooth rumbling voice and she whirled after having slain another of the sailors, her fangs bared.

What met her gaze was a tall man, his shoulders broad and his jaw well-defined. His shoulder-length brown hair had broken free of its bundle and wisps clung to his face. He was dressed in a pale loose pirate's shirt, dark britches, and a black belt from which a collection of daggers and vials hung. She could only guess at what they contained. On his forearm was a tattoo of a grim reaper. He must be from the other ship. From his ears dangled a couple of golden hoops, but she noted he was clean-shaven and there was something about his deep black eyes as they met hers. Something mischievous, laughing, gentle even, perhaps. Something calming.

"This ship be *mine*," she responded, ignoring his question.

"Nay, lass. This ship be almost tha seas'. It's already sinkin' from yer fires." At that, the man placed the tip of his sword into the deck and rested his hands on its hilt. It was a sabre, similar to her own.

Amethyst scowled. "Not before tha merchandise be aboard me Gargoyle." She glanced around the ship. Even before she'd said so, her men had already begun moving the merchandise from the clipper to the *Gargoyle*, and it seemed the other crew had been doing the same.

"Well, lass, ye didn't have t' kill all tha merchants t' take tha loot. Ye could've jus' captured an' forced a surrender. It's clear ye can handle a sword, an' they were hardly armed."

"What's this? A pirate with morals?" she asked, tipping her head back with a sharp laugh. It was impossible, wasn't it? After all, even with her notions of being different than other captains – it was mostly in actual ways of life aboard the ship. Even she knew her ideas of doing away with those who had wronged her or the innocent was only her justification for her own raids and murders. She was a pirate, after all, whose love had become for the sea and for her ship and for living life the way she pleased, whatever that took.

Was he not the same?

The mysterious man only watched her with those dancing black eyes. What was it about this man? She felt not fury, but rather intrigue.

Finally, she snapped her fingers. "Back to tha ship, lads!" She whirled once more, making her way to the *Gargoyle*.

Amethyst turned back, lifting her ears and her brows slightly at the sound of another voice. "Wait!" Its sound was a smooth tenor, different from the man who had questioned her actions.

A young man was running toward her furiously from the other pirate's ship. Brilliant red-orange locks swayed about his pale angular, though boyish, face from which brilliant golden eyes shone. His ears were as pointed as hers, though the scent of the fae wasn't on him. It was a different scent. And she noted he lacked the pointed fangs associated with her kind. What was he?

"Take me wit' you," the lad demanded as soon as he was standing just in front of her. He was tall, though clearly young. Twenty at the oldest, she judged, though maybe it didn't matter. Appearances could be deceiving. She and Darien barely looked in their twenties by human standards also, she remembered.

"And ye are?" Amethyst asked, crossing her arms.

He may be young, but he was handsome, Amethyst noted.

"Mikhail," the boy said with a grin, stretching out a pale but strong hand.

"Ye'd reject yer crew so easily?" she asked, not quite taking his hand.

"My crew?" The lad laughed. "I 'as only along fer tha ride. Aye. This bloke," Mikhail jabbed a thumb toward the first man who had spoken, "don' have an ounce o' bloodthirst in 'im! I can tell yer worthy o' capturing tha seas."

Was he a suck up? Or was he truly honest? Was he referencing the way she'd mercilessly cut down the clipper, perhaps?

She slowly looked him over once more before stretching out her hand. "Captain Amethyst," she said simply, and then turned once more.

Mikhail didn't hesitate in following her aboard her ship.

She couldn't help wondering what this lad's story was as she watched him introduce himself to the crew.

"We continue sail west," she announced. *'Away from the fae territories, and hopefully the bloody Navy,'* she thought.

"Aye, aye!" the crew answered.

For the first few days after the raid, Amethyst noted the boy Mikhail saw fit to prove himself to the crew as a worthy sailor and make himself comfortable. She wondered if he was a bloody cutthroat.

The second day, he removed his shirt while he helped some of the men adjust the rigging after their battle. Just his muscled chest and middle would have drawn her attention, but the brilliant red, orange, and yellow tattoo emblazoned across his front truly drew her eyes. It was a large phoenix in flight.

He couldn't be... could he?

Well, anything was possible.

The phoenix-kind were incredibly rare to encounter. They typically kept to themselves, but they were also enormously powerful. Amethyst found herself becoming more curious about this boy.

The Phoenix Lad

$\mathcal{I}$t had already been a week since their encounter with the clipper, and they hadn't crossed another ship.

Amethyst lay in her cabin, having no interest in lounging in the sun for the moment. She was content to stare at the seas out of her window and sip on her rum.

Her mind wandered over her journey thus far. In truth, she was just a woman with simple desires, but she felt in order to have them, she must uphold a certain reputation. She must present herself as unbreakable in order to hold respect and fear among other captains.

There were times when the desire to merely be a woman and not a ruthless captain overcame her, and she didn't quite feel comfortable even letting her crew see her that way. She had only just gained their trust and respect, though she suspected they knew her conflict to some degree already. Still, until she was entirely ready to show her moments of vulnerability, she remained in her cabin during those times.

Her gaze snapped to the door as she heard a soft knocking.

"Enter," she commanded.

The door creaked as it opened and Mikhail stepped through the doorway.

Amethyst sat up, quirking a brow. "What is it?" she asked.

"Are ye comin' to dinner, Cap'n?" he asked.

Why did he care?

Amethyst shrugged and smiled. "Aye."

She rose. Might as well.

"Are ye alright, Cap'n?" Mikhail asked her.

She paused in her step, startled, then continued.

"Ye seem..." he paused, as if deciding the right word, "troubled."

'Troubled?'

"Er, lonely, perhaps," he said.

Amethyst laughed, her curls bouncing with her movements. And there it was. As she'd suspected. No man truly cared for her, except Darien. Love was merely a game to be played. She raised a hand and patted his shoulder gently. "Aye, Mikhail. I'm just fine," she said, moving past him and out of her cabin.

He followed after her silently.

She made her way below deck where the crew was already gathered at the mess tables.

As she ate and sipped at her rum, she eyed Mikhail as he talked with the crew. He was a handsome lad and she found she was rather curious about his details. Perhaps he would provide entertainment for the time being.

Amethyst slipped away as soon as she was done eating. The stars were particularly brilliant, she noted, already shining in the last fading lights of sunset, and the sky was cloudless. She lay back on the deck and made herself comfortable, a bottle of rum in hand.

Her mind drifted once more toward the Fae Navy. She had evaded them for now, but she couldn't remain at sea forever, no matter how powerful her ship. Even if she gained supplies from raids, she knew at some point or another she'd have to make port. She wondered if she could reach out to allies in order to avoid any ports where she may encounter them.

Mikhail's face once more came into view and Amethyst's hand snapped for one of her hidden daggers. She frowned. She hadn't even heard him coming. He was above her head, peering over her.

"Do ye have a death wish, lad?" she asked him. She relaxed and returned her gaze skyward.

"Pardon?" he asked.

"Never sneak up on a fae."

"I didn' mean t' startle," he said.

He reminded her somewhat of a puppy. He seemed to always have to know what she was doing or where she was. She wasn't quite sure how to deal with it.

"What is it, lad?" she asked.

Mikhail shifted to sit next to her, his fiery gaze moving between her face and the sky. "Like I said, Cap'n, ye seem lonely."

Was he only wishing to keep her company? She couldn't tell. He didn't seem to make any advances. Perhaps she shouldn't toy with him so easily as she had so many others.

For a while they sat in silence.

"Mikhail," she addressed him, "What made you leave home?"

He raised a brow at her and then grinned. "The need for adventure, Cap'n!"

Silence resumed and Amethyst shifted.

"Well, if you must know, I don't really have a home," he said. "Nor have I ever. Or if I did I don't remember. I woke up as a child surrounded by woodland and ventured off until I found a small village by the sea to the north. I stayed there for a while until I discovered my phoenix form and the village burned. From there I travelled across Tysck trying to avoid humans for the most part until I could learn to control the phoenix. I was near the sea most of my travels. I never went too far inland. Eventually I stopped at a port to get something to eat when I met Cadell - the captain of the Reaper's Scythe. He offered a place with his crew and the idea of adventures on the sea was appealing. I hoped being at sea would prevent another fire catastrophe. I hadn't been with Cadell long when I saw you." He stopped.

Amethyst took it all in. Part of her felt sympathy for him, but she still couldn't help wondering why he had so readily jumped after her and her crew. "So why me?" she asked. "Why the Gargoyle?"

"Cadell can't use magic. He wouldn't be of any real help to me, nor would he be able to do anything should I choose to toy with fire and it went awry. Besides, there's something similar between you and I. I can tell." He grinned at her and offered a confident wink.

Amethyst continued to stare skyward. What similarities, she wondered? But she didn't prod the question.

"So what about you?" he asked her.

She hadn't been expecting that. "I simply desire to live life as I please without anyone else to tell me what to do."

"So, defiant runaway, huh?"

She scoffed and looked at him for a moment. "I am not a child."

"Okay, *princess*," Mikhail said with a laugh.

Amethyst felt frustration rising in her chest that he felt so comfortable addressing her in such a manner and teasing her. Yet she couldn't quite bring herself to be angry with him or to retaliate. Instead, she glanced away.

He continued to chuckle, looking away from her.

What was so funny? She wanted to know what he was thinking. Instead, silence resumed.

Amethyst glanced toward him once more as he stood, his warmth shifting away from her.

"Well have a good night, Cap'n," he said merrily as he left.

The next evening, Amethyst watched Mikhail approach Darien. Her first mate's gaze met hers briefly and then shifted toward the phoenix-lad. She chose not to eavesdrop on their conversation. She knew if it was pertinent, Darien would tell her later.

In the morning, even as the first touches of sun graced the horizon, Amethyst stood against the edge of the deck staring seaward.

"Good morning, Cap'n." Mikhail's voice tickled her pointed ear.

Amethyst jumped slightly, once more reaching instinctively for her dagger before she settled, her lip curling slightly above her fangs.

Mikhail chuckled, moving to stand next to her. "Are you always so on edge?"

She glared at him, forcing herself to relax. "Are you always so devious?" she retorted.

Mikhail only laughed again. "Forgive me, Cap'n."

Amethyst breathed out slowly. She couldn't decide whether she was annoyed by Mikhail or if she enjoyed his constant presence. He barely left her alone. It was nice on some level, but he didn't seem to understand she enjoyed her space.

"So Cap'n, I've been wonderin', why is the Gargoyle laced with magic but ye never practice it?"

"That's none of your business," she said bluntly.

"Must you be so guarded?"

"Aye," she said.

"Why?"

Amethyst paused. Should she open herself? Should she take a chance and let him in? Even a little? He had shared some of his past, but he had done so willingly, she felt.

"My ex-husband tormented me in many ways." First, he must know where she'd come from for him to understand her pursuit of her accomplishments. "I've worked for what I've gained on the seas; they are my only solace. My ship is both a formidable warning to others, and a sanctuary for me." It was all she was willing to say. Even speaking of details of her past would be unbearable. She had managed to shut out that part of her life. But she would never forget. She must remember so as never to make the same mistake or forget the one who had wronged her so should she ever get her revenge on him.

She felt the phoenix-lad's fiery gaze on her face and she glanced at him only briefly before looking away once more. His eyes had softened as if he understood beyond what she had spoken. She looked down as his hand covered hers, a touch that he gave and then removed as quickly as it had come.

"Have you never tasted something gentle?" he asked.

Amethyst thought back over her time on the seas. The many pirates she had toyed with for her own pleasure but never letting it go farther than physicality. One step wrong and she had either sent them to Davy Jones' Locker or left their ship in disarray. She hadn't ever allowed the tenderness some had spoken of or offered. Too much risk of vulnerability.

"Do you want to?" He hadn't even let her reply to his first question.

Something in her stirred. "I need time, Mikhail," she said.

He only shrugged as if he couldn't care either way. But she saw the look of disappointment in his eyes. Still, she appreciated he didn't simply go after her with his desires.

"Join me for dinner," she offered him.

He grinned. "Aye, aye, Cap'n!" With that, he left her to her thoughts.

Amethyst still couldn't figure out what to think of Mikhail or how to react to him. He was still so boyish in some ways. So carefree and ambitious.

She went about her day debating what to say to him in the evening. Whether she should be open to his suggestion or not. Should she allow him a chance?

Finally time for dinner came and she had it set up in her cabin. She even dressed up a little with a full red dress and a red flower pinned in her tumbling curls.

Amethyst glanced toward the door as she heard a knock. "Come in," she said.

Mikhail had also dressed up to some degree. He had donned a gentleman's coat and tidied his brilliant orange hair. He certainly was an attractive one, she noted.

His boots made dull thuds as he crossed the room. "All this for me?" he asked, a mischievous sort of grin on his face.

"Don't read too far into it," Amethyst responded, though she realized what it must look like to him.

"Aye," he said with a chuckle.

Amethyst took her seat and he did the same. "Ye look stunning, Cap'n," he said.

She nodded and smiled at him. "Thank you," she replied. She could feel his eyes drinking in her figure, or so she thought.

"So, Mikhail, you haven't answered one question," she said.

He raised a brow, his fiery eyes almost looking puzzled. "And what question be that?" he asked.

"What makes you think I can help you with magic?"

Mikhail grinned at her. "Well, that wasn't specifically a question you asked," he said. She only held his gaze unwavering, waiting for his answer. "Just a feelin', Cap'n. I could sense the magic on yer ship the moment we crossed paths. An' even if ye can't, I feel far more comfortable than on the Reaper's Scythe."

Amethyst shrugged. "I hope ye don't think magic is an integral part of my conquests. I used it for my ship and that is all. Otherwise, I don't rely on it."

Mikhail watched her a moment.

Despite his efforts thus far, she still couldn't dismiss her experiences with males in the past. She admitted he was different in a way. But ultimately his goals were still the same, she felt. But then, she couldn't really say much, she supposed. She had toyed with others without care for their feelings for her own gain to discover her realm of control, her limits, her own urges. And he seemed to pry into her feelings before her body.

Amethyst ate delicately. Their conversation moved to idle chatter, though her thoughts continuously swirled between her past experiences and her current arising feelings. She found herself thinking that if Mikhail did advance, she would accept him.

"So, Cap'n, what of my question?" Mikhail asked her.

Amethyst felt she knew what he meant. But she shot back the same response he had given her. "What question?"

"Have you tasted gentle pleasure?"

Had he read her torment of thoughts? She swallowed the bite she had taken and sipped at a bit of her rum. "No, I haven't," she said plainly.

His movements were fluid as he stood and closed the gap between them. He was so near her, and his scent was of a burning ember and the sea. It was an odd combination, though pleasant. "Allow me to only offer a taste, Cap'n, and ye can decide whether ye desire more or not."

It was only a suggestion. An offer for her, if she wanted, she knew.

Her gaze was glued to his, and her lips parted ever so slightly. "Very well," she whispered.

There was a stir within her at the brush of his hand on hers and he placed the lightest of kisses on her lips. It was so foreign, this kind of kiss. Her mouth tingled, and she forced herself to remain calm.

She knew right then and there that, as sweet of a taste as Mikhail might leave on her tongue, he wasn't what she truly needed. She felt as though she must hold back all of her raging desires lest he become overwhelmed or dominated. She could sense his male need to be in charge. Perhaps he even viewed her as a lady to be treated with tenderness and respect. But that would only drive her insane. That was exactly the life she had left behind. She wasn't a prim and proper lady. She was an impulsive pirate captain prone to her emotions and her drives and one who reveled in being able to do as she pleased when she wanted to.

Perhaps somewhere in the world was her perfect match, but it wasn't this lad before her.

Still, she felt she couldn't simply dismiss him now, so she let him reach up and gently place her chin between his thumb and forefinger before he kissed her again, more firmly. She let him trace his fingers down her jaw-line and neck to her arm, naturally sending shivers down her spine. He deftly lowered her already draped sleeves. Then he effortlessly pulled apart the strings in the back that held her dress around her and it fell to the floor with a gentle whoosh. And then she let him show her his own desires.

Amethyst woke with a start, peering around her cabin. Moonlight was shining brilliantly through her window, casting a pale glow over the furniture. She groaned softly and wiped at her brow before glancing at Mikhail's sleeping form next to her. She was glad her own disturbances hadn't woken him.

Slowly, Amethyst got up and moved to her wardrobe. She donned a simple silken robe and moved out of her cabin toward the quarterdeck. Would she never be rid of her nightmares?

Despite how many different nights she spent with another, it was always the same. No comfort ever seemed to come to her.

She gasped softly at the sound of boots against the deck and turned. Her muscles relaxed as she took in Darien's form.

"Is it so wise for you to welcome him into your bed?" His voice was as soft as ever.

Amethyst frowned. Had he come to scold her? "That's my decision to make. He's incredibly persistent."

"Aye," Darien said. "He asked me about you."

Amethyst nodded.

"I only told him to be careful and not to expect too much."

Amethyst nodded again. "Do you think I'll ever have peaceful sleep as a norm, Darien?" she asked, changing the subject.

She saw out of the corner of her eye as he faced her, leaning back against the side of the ship. "I feel when you no longer worry about the Fae Navy you'll sleep better, at least."

"Mmm, that's true," she said. After a moment of silence, Amethyst met his gaze. "I'll return to bed."

Darien nodded with a smile.

"I don't wish for Mikhail to suspect or know beyond what he's already learned."

With that, she returned to her cabin and her bed, though she didn't return to sleep.

Mikhail woke with the first touches of sunlight. She knew, because he stirred and then his arm wrapped around her middle and his lips gently kissed her shoulder.

"Good mornin'," he murmured.

"Morning," she said back.

"So, Cap'n... I'll be awaiting your response," he said.

The memory of only hours before flashed across her mind. When they had fallen back into the sheets, he had laid beside her, tracing patterns into her skin and asked what she thought, and if she desired more. She'd said she'd let him know in the morning.

"Aye, Mikhail, there's something sweet about your gentle ways," she said with a smile, meeting his gaze. She had decided she was content to see where it went for the time being.

He grinned victoriously and kissed her lips before moving out of the bed.

After that night, Mikhail spent most nights with her. He talked of his dreams for the future and how he wanted to settle with her someday and provide all the safety she could desire.

She laughed each time he brought it up and avoided specifically dismissing the notion. "My heart is to my ship," she told him now and then.

He didn't seem to understand her goals, but she grew more comfortable with him and was somewhat envious of his naivety. Still, she never could quite open up to him. She answered his questions in such a way that she didn't reveal much but still satisfied his curiosity.

Time began to pass more quickly for her as they continued their journey to Orlesce. The weeks turned into months and at last they were reaching the coast.

She was eager for the trades and to buy more rum.

The crew burst into activity as soon as they docked at Port Drelle, another port commonly visited by pirates. Amethyst joined them, aiding in moving barrels onto the docks.

"Darien," she called to her first mate.

He looked up from his own activities and moved toward her.

"Will you finish the trades?" she asked.

He produced a small coin purse from his pocket and dropped it into her hand. "Don't spend it all at once," he said knowingly.

Amethyst only laughed as she turned to leave. He knew her so well, she thought.

She paused as Mikhail grasped her hand. "Can't I come?" he asked.

She glanced toward the rest of the crew and offered a brief shrug. "Very well," she said.

Amethyst first made her way into the market where she mostly spent time window-shopping. Nothing looked incredibly appealing, until she passed one particular building with enormous glass windows. She paused, taking in the dresses displayed behind the glass. They were exquisite. This was what she was looking for.

She stepped into the shop, breathing in the scent of new clothing and a bit of dust which collected between the floor boards. Without hesitation, she began sorting through the hanging dresses. Some had lacy frills while others had slits or corsets. Within little time, she found a flowing silver garment decorated only with blue curls that flowed gracefully in a variety of directions on its edges. Two white gloves hung to its side as accompanying accessories. An excited smile graced her lips.

"Why not this one, Cap'n?" Amethyst glanced toward Mikhail. He was holding out a dark crimson dress with a sinful slit to the thigh and a dark leather band about its middle. She frowned and shook her head.

He pouted, looking disappointed, but after all she wasn't really buying something for *him*, she thought.

"I'll have this, please," she said giddily as she handed the shop keep the silver dress she had chosen.

He only nodded and accepted her coin quickly. Perhaps he wished for her to leave. She wasn't sure. She dismissed it readily and made her way toward the street once more.

"Join me for a drink, Mikhail," she exclaimed as she made her way toward one of the local pubs. The sign above the doorway had a simple skull carved into the wood and read *Skull's Mark*. The inside was spacious with several lanterns hanging about the room and long oval tables filling up the dining area. A long stairway at the back of the pub suggested there were rooms on the floor above available for a cost and three large doors behind the bar counter indicated rooms beyond.

Amethyst moved toward the bar, demanding rum from the barkeep. Once she grasped her goblet, she made her way toward a table at the back of the pub. She was a little surprised to see Mikhail hadn't followed her.

Instead, he had remained at the bar counter and was talking with another there. Amethyst wasn't entirely sure who this other man was - an old friend who had grabbed his attention, perhaps?

She watched them, focusing her attention until she could hear their voices.

Mikhail's head was tipped back in continuous laughter.

"So I hear ye've joined tha Gargoyle," the other man said.

"Aye! Cap'n Amethyst is..."

Her heart began to race as one of his fingers pointed in her direction and briefly, both of their gazes met hers before returning to their ale.

"Oh, are tha rumors true 'bout that one?" the man asked.

"Which rumors, hmm?" Mikhail asked.

"Well I hear she's a merciless bloodthirst, that one. There are rumors she's a vampire. An' they say t' stay away from her if ye value yer life."

Amethyst couldn't help the small smirk as she heard the rumors. While she absolutely was not a vampire, it seemed she had at least succeeded in building her reputation.

Mikhail got excited, and then the blood drained from her face as he gained control of himself and calmed from his laughter. He said, "A *vampire*? Nay! Amethyst is fae. And between us, mate, I think she's nobility. Or at least someone of importance. But the rest of it ye should definitely believe."

Amethyst assumed Mikhail said the last bit either to affirm her reputation or from his own selfish desires to keep her to himself. Perhaps both.

She stood, her fingers suddenly feeling antsy for her dagger. She felt perhaps Mikhail trusted this friend too much. That she was fae, she wasn't too concerned with. But he had shared too much. As far as she wanted anyone to know, she was no one. If anyone suspected she was of import, she feared being turned in to the Fae Navy for a price.

And if her name were mentioned to them, there was no doubt in her mind they would know who she was, even if the rat didn't.

No, she couldn't risk it.

She slipped out of the pub. '*Mikhail... you're too naïve.*'

Amethyst returned to the *Gargoyle*, looking for Darien. It was time to go.

"Where be Mikhail?" one of the crewmen asked her.

"He's chosen to go his own way," she said simply. At that moment, she spotted her first mate, helping another secure new sails to the main mast.

"Darien!" she called, waving a hand.

He glanced at her and smiled, waving back.

She approached him, looking upward to where the sails waved wildly in the wind coming off the sea.

"What is it, Captain?" he asked.

"Mikhail is no longer trusted. He's a liability. We need to set sail before word reaches the Fae Navy, alright?"

Darien only nodded. She knew she needn't tell him more details at that precise moment.

"Have you finished all the trades we need?" Amethyst asked.

"Aye, Captain," he said.

Amethyst nodded and turned away. Perhaps she was overreacting. But if she didn't trust her instincts, she knew sooner or later it would cost her.

"Raise anchor!" Darien called. "We sail east!"

As they sailed away from port, Amethyst glanced to the shore where she saw an orange tussle and pale figure standing on the beach.

She set sailed southeast, hoping to avoid any territories at all for a while.

Sanctuary

For several weeks they sailed without sight of land or another ship. Amethyst began to wonder if they should change course. They were entering uncharted waters. She hadn't ever been this far south and so far as she knew, there was nothing beyond.

Her thoughts drifted to Mikhail. She felt awful leaving him behind as she had, but there was no turning back now. She'd already left him behind, a swift decision from her fears. Perhaps they'd cross paths again, but for now, she needed to survive. She doubted he would be one to turn her in, but she didn't trust the others who would learn about her from his lips.

Amethyst busied herself with helping the crew and, when there wasn't work to be done she took brief swims or lay in the sun. They continued sailing and she couldn't help thinking she would be perfectly happy sailing forever, however impractical it might be.

"Captain! Captain!"

Amethyst awoke quickly at the sound of pounding on her door. It was the midst of the night but the ship quaked and rocked like a shaken doll. She hurriedly threw on her britches and boots and ran out.

"Captain! Tha storm has blown tha riggin' together. We'll have to cut it free from tha mast!" Even with her enhanced hearing, she could barely hear him over the wind and the crashing waves against the hull.

"Have ye lowered the top-sails and fastened the storm sails?"

"Aye!"

She looked up to where Cyran pointed. The sound of the ropes straining blended with the storm and it was clear the mast was falling also. If they didn't act soon, the ship would perhaps even turn over into the raging sea.

"Hand me a dagger!" Amethyst told Cyran.

He produced it swiftly and she placed it between her teeth, grasping hold of the mast. It quaked between the pressure of the storm and the lines pulling it downward.

Amethyst struggled, the wind whipping her hair into her face.

It took some time, but at last she reached the crow's nest and she grasped the dagger she'd been biting. Amethyst reached high, striking at the rigging until it snapped and broke free of the mast. The ship would need repairs, but at least it wouldn't go down.

She slipped down once more, handing the dagger back to her crewmate. "Get below deck! We'll ride this storm out!" With that, she made her way below also toward the cabins. She wanted to be sure everyone was okay, at least. Amethyst didn't return to sleep but rather remained with the crew for the remainder of the storm.

She climbed upward to look out as soon as the seas calmed. Where were they?

It seemed the clouds had dispersed with the coming of morning as the sun shone down casting a fading red glow on the seas. The white foam of the waves drifted casually until it broke against the hull of the ship.

In the distance, a rocky mountain was dark against the horizon and the unmistakable glimmer of sands reflected the rising sun.

It was possible the storm had blown them west once more toward the Aeidahs island chain. But somehow, with how far south they had already sailed, she doubted it.

"Fetch me the maps," she commanded to one of the crewmembers near her.

"Aye, aye, Captain," he said with a nod before disappearing.

There was one benefit to the fae's relentless conquests in ages past. They had mapped out Aseath and all of its territories.

Was it possible?

The crewmember returned and handed her several rolled pieces of parchment.

She bent down, splaying them out on the deck and tracing her finger over the territories and the oceans. Then, she looked up, her brow slowly furrowing further and further.

This island wasn't on the map.

A smirk formed on her lips. "Full speed ahead!" she ordered. "This isle be ours, lads!" She was glad they weren't terribly far. Even with the magic imbued in the ship, the storm had wreaked its havoc. Perhaps at worst, they would find trees and wood enough to make repairs to the ship after the storm.

"Weigh anchor!" Darien shouted as the ship entered shallow waters.

The rowboats were lowered and the crew began making their way toward the shore.

Amethyst's eyes swept along the shoreline. Past the beach lay towering palm trees and dangling coconuts, beyond which were rising bluffs and rock. Seagulls cawed loudly as if protesting the intrusion of new inhabitants.

She couldn't help wondering if, and daring to hope that, they might be the first to ever set eyes or foot on these shores. Could it be possible she'd found her own personal sanctuary?

Before she would make that official conclusion, she determined they should explore the island and gather as much about it as they could.

"Alright, gents! We split into groups of three and search the island. We'll meet back when the sun is highest at midday and discuss what we've found, savvy?" Amethyst said once those who weren't remaining aboard the ship were together.

Shouts of, "Aye!" were heard in response and the men set off.

Amethyst and her group moved forward straight into the group of palm trees and further inland. At first, she hadn't been certain if the isle were nothing more than a solid block of rock surrounded by beaches and trees.

But she had noticed the seagulls flew downward and disappeared beyond the rock. It had raised her suspicions.

The trees stopped abruptly before the wall of rock and bluffs. Ridges were naturally carved into the surface and dark caverns were visible scattered throughout.

Amethyst motioned with a hand and moved westward, staying close to the rock wall. She stopped as she came across one of the caverns which was relatively near the base of the wall. A shallow rock path led to its entrance and she climbed the small way until she was standing inside the cavern.

She whispered an illumination spell and a brilliant ball of light burst forth against the darkness. The cave was nothing special; there didn't even seem to be a glimmer of precious stones within its walls, nor was there water it seemed.

Amethyst moved forward again, her fingers twisting ever so slightly as she controlled the movements of the light.

It traveled around the cave's walls and ceilings until it reached the farthest corner. Her brows furrowed as she moved closer. A small draft tickled her skin, hardly noticeable at first.

The footfalls of herself and her companions echoed in her ears, but more than that was the soft sound of moving air. The cave led to an underground tunnel. She wondered where it might lead. She'd heard of underground tunnels where people got lost, and there were ancient legends of fearsome beasts living in such places waiting for prey to devour. If these were the same, even with her slow age rate and magical abilities, she wouldn't last long without sustenance. At the least, she needed more than only the small group that had accompanied her to fully explore the tunnel.

"Let's return after we've met with the rest," she said, turning briskly and making her way out of the cave. As she stepped outside once more, she let her gaze travel up the face of the wall. It didn't go forever.

Perhaps going over would be wiser than going under.

They made their way back toward the ship, content to eat the meat of the coconuts they gathered and wait for the other crewmembers' return.

As soon as the sun was highest, the others had gathered.

"Further south and to the east, the rock collides with the sea and plunges into its depths. The beach itself seems to slowly vanish giving way to the rock."

"We found tha same on the west side of the isle, Cap'n. There was one visible entrance, but the waves would destroy anyone against the rock afore they could get close."

So, the rock wall went around the entire island. Amethyst nodded, envisioning what they were describing. It was possible the isle really was nothing more than a massive mountain. But something in her gut told her there was something more.

"We discovered a tunnel beneath the mountain in one of the caverns at the wall base. We'll need a decent group to go deeper though."

"But, Cap'n, couldn't the tunnel only lead to nowhere? Who knows what's down there?"

Amethyst smirked. "Nothin' the crew of the Gargoyle can't handle, lads. An' with plenty of hands, should it lead nowhere, we'll be able to make our way back, eh?"

"Aye, aye!" said several of the men in agreement.

"We'll gather a few supplies and leave immediately while the day is still full. Those of ye not accompanying us through the tunnels will give those aboard the information." With that, Amethyst once more went aboard her ship. The crewmembers moved after her.

She helped gather supplies, and briefly told Darien what they had found and where they were going. He stayed behind to help the remaining crewmembers tend to the ship.

Once the explorer group returned to the beach, they had several bunches of rope, flasks of water, and a slew of weapons. Some of those that could use magic also came along to summon light as needed.

Finally, they set off toward the cave Amethyst had discovered.

Once they found it, Hiram, one of the fae crewmembers, summoned a similar ball of light to that Amethyst had only hours before and the crewmen set off into the tunnel.

Her first instinct that it was an underground maze proved correct. As they set forward, Amethyst was grateful for the light that illuminated the path ahead. Water dripped somewhere in the distance and echoed off the walls. Every now and then a rodent's screeching echoed also with the sounds of low growls and something sharp scraping against stone.

At each twist and turn, Amethyst instructed one crewmember to make an unmistakable mark in the stone should they need to retrace their steps and go another direction.

They stopped as they encountered an enormous cavern deep within the rock. Stalagmites and stalacites jutted up and down from the floors and ceilings and glimmered softly in the magical light from the crewmembers.

A small pool lay at the opposite end of the cavern and its waters caused rippling reflections on the rock above. Amethyst led the men downward and toward the other end of the cave, where three other tunnels split away into the darkness. She moved to the first, closing her eyes and letting her other senses take hold. The air from it was damp and musty and she wrinkled her nose.

She opened her eyes and moved toward the next tunnel, stepping in only slightly and once more closing her eyes. That same slight draft she had felt when first discovering the tunnels gently tickled her skin and there was a fresh sort of scent. Having found what she was looking for, Amethyst ignored the third tunnel. She doubted it led anywhere important, and for that matter, she was ready to get out of these tunnels.

"This way," she murmured, continuing forward down the tunnel.

The darkness seemed to stretch onward and onward. She wasn't entirely sure which direction she was going anymore.

Finally, that same small draft she had discovered in the beginning began to grow stronger. Either she was making her way to the outer face of the wall once more, or she was getting further inland.

"Dissolve the light," she said. Immediately, they were consumed in darkness, surrounded by the sounds of each other's breathing and their footfalls against the floor. The sounds of the rodents' screeches and whatever had made the low growls grew dimmer and dimmer.

It took a moment for Amethyst's eyes to adjust, but a smirk formed on her lips as soon as they did. The dimmest of lights reflected off the stone in the distance and she moved toward it, her heart beginning to race with excitement and curiosity.

The light grew brighter and brighter and the feeling of wind stronger until she could see earth in the distance.

She ran faster, and at last she emerged from the tunnels.

Amethyst stopped, trying to take it all in.

Before her lay an exquisite oasis. Tall green grasses waved gently back and forth and wild flowers colored them. The grasses stretched far to her right and left until they curved along the interior of the rock wall and disappeared to the far side of the island. Rising trees dotted the area and slowly condensed until all that could be seen were dark trunks and shadows which then fanned out southward until the forest also stopped at the rock wall.

Amethyst was shocked at the calm within the walls, other than the wind coming in from somewhere on the isle's other side and the gentle sound of gurgling water somewhere ahead.

She moved forward slowly, glancing to the faces of her crewmembers. Their eyes were large and some of their mouths agape.

Amethyst turned, facing them. "Split up again, lads. We'll meet back here once we've thoroughly explored this place."

"Aye," the men responded, collecting themselves.

Amethyst set off straight once more, determined to find the source of the gurgling water. She moved without hesitation into the condensed trees at the center of the island. As the forest thickened, so did the foliage and underbrush. She discovered berries thrived and there was even wildlife that scampered away from the sound of her footfalls.

She stopped as she discovered a small clearing ringed by the trees. Near where she stopped was a brook flowing toward the other end of the clearing and disappearing into the trees beyond. Rocks and pebbles formed both the riverbed and its bank. Its source appeared to be a simple spring, bursting forth from the earth.

She continued, following the water's path as she made her way once more into the cover of trees. The brook twisted and curved as it led her to the opposite end of the oasis and through the trees. Her ears twitching at the sound of the sea crashing into the rock in the distance.

The trees began to thin and opened to a canal of sorts. The brook grew wider and tumbled downward as the earth turned from dirt and grass to sand and stone. It met with the sea, flowing into a small bay. The seawater there was calm, gently lapping at the interior beach.

From where she stood, Amethyst could see that the rock wall indeed formed a complete circular shape except for this one break in its surface. An enormous doorway in the stone opened to the ocean, light pouring in and sea mixing with the fresh water from the brook. She imagined this was what her men had described from the outside when they had explored the isle on first arrival, in which case this entrance was both obscure and dangerous for anyone trying to come in through it.

A little help from magic would not only make it impossible to enter but also completely invisible.

Amethyst turned back toward the cave system that had led them to this hidden sanctuary in the first place. She followed the brook and then made her way back up the way she'd come. At last she was climbing the brief slope to the cave entrance.

Some of the others from her crew were already waiting and those that weren't were not far behind.

"We'll make our way back, lads, and meet with the rest of the crew," Amethyst said. Thoughts were swarming her mind. Was it by mere chance or by fate that she had found such a place? It was clearly undiscovered, but more importantly, it was a perfect sanctuary. If she could make it so that no one else ever discovered it in the future, she could find safety and rest here when she wished to remain hidden from the world. And better yet, it was the perfect place to elude the Fae Navy.

She couldn't help the excitement welling in her.

As they made their way back through the tunnels, Amethyst was glad they had marked the path. Before long, light was once more before them and they exited the cave they had first entered. Amethyst had a feeling there were multiple entrances, but there would be time to fully explore later.

She breathed in the fresh air from the sea and led her crewmembers forward through the palm trees, toward the beach and her beloved ship. It was a dark form against the horizon. Their venture had taken away the day and the sun was setting, casting the sea and the sky into a blend of reds, oranges and yellows.

"Captain! We were beginning to wonder if ye'd return!" shouted one of the crewmen.

Amethyst grinned. "I appreciate the concern," she said. "We shall have a feast tonight, lads! In celebration of discovering our own island!"

Cheers and shouts followed.

"Eat, drink, and be merry! And tomorrow we will conceal this isle from the world so that only we may enjoy it. Our private treasure."

There were more cheers and the men set about filling their mugs. Those that had accompanied her told the others of what they had discovered while Amethyst slipped toward her first mate.

He was in the galley, helping the main cook, Vince, prepare that day's meal.

"Darien," Amethyst called as she stepped in.

He looked up, his eyes softening as he met her gaze and a smile curved his lips upward.

"Welcome back, Captain," he said.

"You won't believe what we've discovered," she exclaimed. "Within the mountain is a hidden oasis. It's... magnificent." She paused, glancing toward Vince. "We're going to celebrate tonight, so be sure the crew has a feast," she said with a smile. He nodded at her enthusiastically.

Amethyst returned her gaze to Darien, "Wait until you see it."

Darien moved toward her. "I'm thinking we'll make this place our priority for the time being. Gather supplies and goods and make it a place where we can find rest when we tire of the sea or need to get away for a time."

Darien nodded. "Yes, it's truly fortunate."

"I'm going to call it Aeoumrese," she said, glancing toward the towering rocks visible from the single window at the back of the galley. The name meant 'sanctuary' in her native tongue.

Darien nodded again. "It's fitting. Now, go and celebrate with the crew," he urged.

"You're coming?" she asked.

He only grinned and gave a small shrug. He did enjoy cooking, and perhaps he wished to help Vince in preparing the feast.

With that, she spun and left, eager for a night of rum and laughter.

Amethyst was up and about early the next morning. It would be no small task to entirely hide and then make the island home, and she couldn't wait to start.

"Join me at first light," she had told the members of the crew who could also use magic, particularly the other fae aboard. The sun had not quite risen, but even so she stood on quarterdeck and stared outward over the sea.

"Mornin', Cap'n." Her ear twitched slightly at the sound of boots against the deck and the voice of Serafin, one of the crewmembers who had been with her since her capture of *Nightingale*.

"Morning," she called lightly, turning to offer him a smile. He joined her at the edge of the deck and glanced toward the wall of rock. Its dark form was illuminated by pale moonlight for the moment. "It is beautiful, Cap'n," he offered.

"Aye," she said, "and ours."

"We're lucky we didn't get dashed against those rocks and sent to Davy Jones' Locker," he said with a laugh.

Amethyst smirked. "Or perhaps incredibly skilled. If fate meant us to find it, it wouldn't have so cruelly sent us to our deaths before discovery."

Serafin laughed heartily. "Indeed, Cap'n."

At last the first light was rising over the sea and the others slowly joined them. Some were woozy from the night before, but Amethyst trusted they would sober quickly, given the task.

"Ready yourselves, lads! This be far greater than merely protecting the Gargoyle."

Amethyst raised her arms, "Focus yer energy on the isle!"

The others followed her lead.

Her eyes took on a brilliant glow and she uttered a spell in her native tongue.

The crewmembers with her again followed suit, a pulse of light beginning as the last words were spoken and spreading until it covered the entirety of the island before them. The task took much time, the sun climbing to its highest point and beginning to fall before the spell was complete.

Amethyst knew the final step must be to tie the spell down with an eternal link. Otherwise, in time it would fade away or constantly be a drain on her and those that had cast it. With a few more uttered words in her native tongue, the light cascaded to the sea surrounding the isle and collided causing the waves to spill backward for only a brief moment. For any passing by, unless they were seeking its sanctuary, they would only see the ever flowing waves colliding against each other.

At last, the glow faded from her eyes and she gasped softly, grasping the edge of the ship for support. Such an amount of magic, even supported by many from her crew, was exhausting, yet she couldn't simply retire to her cabin for the remainder of the day.

"Take the goods ashore, men!" she instructed the crewmembers, in particular the ones who hadn't used magic. "The isle is ours!"

"Aye, aye, Cap'n!" echoed from the crew and they set to work.

By nightfall, they had managed to take what goods they would keep on the isle to its center. It was enough for them to build the beginnings of a base, but more supplies were needed.

Amethyst returned to her ship and her crewmembers followed. "Rest up, lads! Tomorrow we get back to work. We'll plunder what we need to truly make the isle our sanctuary."

"Aye!" shouted the men once more.

While the crew ate dinner at the mess tables and drank their fill, Amethyst moved toward quarterdeck. Darien followed.

"What do ye plan after we establish the isle, Captain?" he asked.

Amethyst looked at him and smiled. "A life of true freedom, of course! I can take what I please, do what my heart desires, and if the Navy finds me, I have somewhere they'll never reach me."

Darien nodded, turning his gaze seaward. "And what of your reputation?"

"I'm already half-way there. I'll also be known as one who cannot be caught and cannot be defeated. And any who try will find themselves at ocean's bottom."

Darien only nodded once more. "To freedom, then," he offered.

"To freedom," she agreed.

The One Who Calms
the Nightmares

Once the men had their fill and night had fallen, they sailed from Aeoumrese. "Cap'n, once we leave, won't it also be hidden from us?" one of the men asked.

"Nay!" she cried with a grin. "It's the beauty of us casting the spell."

They set their path north toward the Braza island chains. Amethyst hoped to find a bounty of ships.

A few weeks passed before white sails could be seen against the horizon.

The dark form of the *Gargoyle* was masked under a dark sky. "Dim the torchlights," Amethyst commanded, "Ready yourselves, lads."

Most of those aboard the merchant vessel were asleep. Only the lookout and a few deckhands kept watch.

Only once the pirates were near enough to fire cannons, if they had chosen, did the lookout shout and began to madly ring the alarm bell.

The *Gargoyle* drew broadside the other vessel within moments and the pirates stormed the deck with ease.

Merchant sailors rushed to the deck, though quickly learned they didn't stand a chance.

"Cap'n, there's nothing here," called Artemas as he returned from below deck.

Amethyst shoved one sailor aside and moved toward Artie. "What do ye mean?" she demanded.

The merchant ship's captain approached, hands held upward. "We were on our way to port for supplies and to rest. We ran out of what goods we had the other day. Please, we didn't ask for any of this."

"No one asks for the hand they're dealt," Amethyst retorted. She frowned. He could be telling the truth. Should she take that chance?"

"Let's go!" she yelled, pointing the tip of her dagger into the other captain's stomach. "Darien! Take the trading maps," she ordered.

Amethyst turned abruptly and made her way back to the *Gargoyle.*

Once she had returned to her ship, she lay the maps out for the others to see also. "We'll use these to find the next ship. We need building supplies for Aeoumrese and a store of other goods." She paused, tracing a finger along the various trading routes. They were indicated by dotted lines across the pages. Each map was labeled with a different trade: silks and fabrics, clothing, jewels and adornments, coal, slaves, wood. Finally she found one which she knew included the goods she needed: tools. Certainly there would be saws, hammers, nails, and other supplies. There were plenty of trees on the isle to use as long as they had the supplies to shape them.

For the time being, she dared not make port. Any port. She worried still about crossing paths with the Fae Navy too soon. Or ever. So, she needed to rely on trades for everything.

"We continue sail north," Amethyst said, rolling the maps together once more. "I trust you'll set our course?" she asked, her eyes meeting Darien's.

He nodded and moved away with several of the other crewmembers.

Amethyst hoped they had taken enough goods with them after leaving Aeoumrese. Even with magic prolonging what they had, time at sea took its toll. She knew they needed a good plunder before they would run out.

Days began to blend together as they sailed for the trading routes and their prey.

The first merchantman they encountered was another fluyt and was easily conquered. They took all the weapons from those that had sailed aboard the ship as well as what building supplies and tools they could carry.

Before they left the ship, Amethyst pressed a dagger against the captain's neck and demanded to know the details of some of the other trade routes. She learned a carrack had set sail from Adriac some weeks before and was making its way toward Tysck to the far northwest. If she could gain the goods from the ship, she knew it would be a true treasure chest.

A carrack was an enormous vessel that despite its numerous decks and sails was slow and not well armed, at least in the hands of merchants. Its capacity to carry merchandise was incredible, and even if those aboard were prepared against an attack, Amethyst was confident they could overcome it.

The carrack's route was a fairly straight one, with a stop at Port Blaise on the north side of Vorda Isle. Amethyst intended to overtake the merchants before they reached the port. With their current course, they'd intersect the carrack in a few days just past the Braza island chain.

She instructed the crew that they would take down the ship in the way they had their first raid against the merchant scum she had once sailed under. She didn't want to set the ship ablaze on their first attack in case they could use some of its materials.

The men worked to sharpen their weapons and some even sparred with each other. Amethyst hoped the plunder would go smoothly.

At last the carrack was in sight and a whoop resounded from the crew. The winds were also in their favor as they sailed for the other vessel.

Though Amethyst didn't look through her spyglass, another ship on the opposite side of the carrack became visible as they neared it. It was the *Reaper's Scythe*. They had beaten her to the merchant ship, but she was still determined to take her share of the loot.

Amethyst led a handful of crewmembers and used ropes to swing aboard the carrack instead of waiting for the plank, though the others soon followed as the booms of cannon fire exploded into the air.

The carrack fired back. Its crew was a decent size, and those that weren't already engaged in battle with the *Reaper*'s crew met those from the *Gargoyle* head on.

Amethyst collided blades with one of the merchant sailors and found she was somewhat impressed by his swordsmanship. She hadn't quite been expecting that. Still, she didn't falter, and instead continuously lunged in and out. He may be skilled, but he couldn't match her speed. Soon, her sword was plunged through his stomach and she moved on.

If only she could subdue the captain, their capture would be complete and they could take what they wanted. Her eyes searched the ship.

Then she stopped, sucking in her breath slightly.

Locked in combat with the merchant captain was the man she had met in a similar fashion during another raid. Was he the captain Mikhail had mentioned? What had he said the name was? Cadell.

Amethyst moved forward once more toward the two, observing their battle closely. Would Cadell prove himself a hypocrite, she wondered? He had been lecturing her on her savagery last time they'd met, though perhaps he fancied himself one who only took lives when necessary.

She scoffed at the notion. They were pirates.

Before she even reached them, the clanking of metal hitting wood echoed as the merchant captain's sword was knocked from his grasp and clattered to the deck. Cadell stepped forward, his sabre's tip tucked under the captain's chin and pointed toward his throat.

"Surrender," Cadell said, "and we'll be on our way."

"That's it?!" Amethyst asked, making her presence known.

The merchant captain's hands slowly went up, his stance wavering. "Arms down, men!" he barked to his crew. The sounds of battle slowly dimmed as the various crewmembers turned their attention on the captains.

"Well, if it isn't the fae captain," Cadell said, though his focus remained on the merchant captain.

She quirked a brow. "Aye, fancy coming across ye again." Amethyst frowned.

"Take tha loot, gents!" Cadell bellowed, his sword unflinching from the captain's neck. "She is ours!"

"Is she now?" Amethyst said, her fists firmly planted on her hips.

"Aye," Cadell responded. "Perhaps ye didn't listen last time we met."

She drew her sword.

"Ye wish to challenge me for tha loot?" Cadell asked her.

"Aye. What need have ye of it other than food and drink?" she demanded.

"None," he said with a grin. "But we only take what we need."

Amethyst paused, assessing him a moment. She moved forward, grasping the merchant captain's arm firmly. He screamed as she shoved him overboard. He would survive.

Afterward, she turned and faced Cadell. "Perhaps ye are mad, lass," he said.

"I'll do as I please. And you couldn't focus on me with your sword at his neck. Now he's out of the way," Amethyst said, forsaking the sailor's way of speech for a moment.

"What need of ye for the rest of tha cargo?" Cadell inquired, ignoring her quip.

"My business is my own. Stay out of it. And that includes *my* plunders," she said, meeting his gaze. That mischievous black gaze that drew her attention. What was it about this man?

He grinned. "Well, I'll accept yer challenge, lass. If nothing than for a bit o' fun."

She frowned at him and without giving him a chance to prepare or attack, she lunged for him.

His blade met hers in a resilient zing of clashing metal. She pushed back, lunging in again. With each swing of her sword, he met it and deflected her blade.

Their feet were in constant motion, a swordsman's dance.

He swung low and she blocked, diving in for a blow with her arm.

Yet, he caught her elbow in his palm and pushed her back.

It seemed his skills in a fight were both precise and agile. He was strong, swift, adept. They were equally matched.

Sweat dripped from her brow down her face, and she could see the same was true for him.

Amethyst stepped back and to her left, watching for his movements. He seemed to be doing the same.

How was he so quick to respond, she wondered?

She lunged toward him again, purposefully swinging wide. Her aim was to pull his stance open so she could dive in close and strike.

Cadell lunged also, catching her wrist with the back of his arm and her fist in his other palm. His blow to her sword hand tried to loosen her grasp. Instead, she gripped it tighter.

At the same moment, he pushed her back with his forward movement, his momentum colliding with hers and causing them both to tumble to the deck.

She grunted as they rolled. Amethyst landed a solid punch to his face, but as their tumble came to a stop she found herself lying face up, his body over hers.

He was supporting himself with one hand beside her on the wooden surface of the deck, one knee down, and the other pulled to his stomach in his crouch. His free hand was grasping his sword which was pointed toward her throat.

He grinned. "It seems I've won the duel."

She laughed with a glimmer in her eyes. "Are ye certain?"

She watched the realization slip across his features and his smile fall as he noticed then her hand-dagger pointed at his heart.

Truly, they were equally matched.

He chuckled and pushed himself upward to his feet in a fluid motion, sheathing his sword as he did so.

Amethyst tucked her dagger away against her person. She started to push herself up; she stopped when she saw Cadell's hand extended toward her, a smile on his face. She hesitated, somewhat baffled. Was he truly such a gentleman? It was odd. She normally scoffed at the notion of chivalry. Men only wanted to demonstrate kindness for ulterior reasons: either because they saw women as lesser and weak, or because they wished to lure them and woo them.

Somehow she sensed neither intention behind his gesture. Rather, there was just something in those dancing black eyes that told her he genuinely meant well and only wished to show courtesy.

Could that really be right?

They had only just been attempting to injure, perhaps even kill each other. Who was this man that lived the life of a pirate and also believed in such behavior so wholeheartedly?

Her heart was pounding, but she attributed it to their recent skirmish. Her hesitation lasted only a moment. She dismissed his hand and pushed herself upward and on her feet. As much as she wanted to grasp his hand, in part for curiosity about the feel of it and what might happen at its touch, she was stubborn and felt the need to demonstrate the strong, capable woman she was.

Amethyst put her sword away. She had no idea what to make of him. "Take the rest," Amethyst called to her crew. She brushed past him, not failing to note the way he shook his head to himself at her refusing his hand.

The merchant sailors had gathered into a group, waiting nervously for the pirates to finish their business and leave. She was certain they were also eager to rescue their captain from the waves.

Her crew finished gathering the goods they had been after, including several crates of livestock which they had been both pleased and surprised to find, and finally they returned to the *Gargoyle*.

"Turn course," Darien ordered the crew. "We sail for Braza!"

"Aye, aye!" shouted the crew as the ship changed its direction.

The island chain wasn't far behind them. The *Gargoyle*'s crew had taken gems from the carrack as part of their loot and Amethyst wanted to purchase food and drink before they returned to Aeoumrese. What they would have gained in sustenance had been taken by the *Reaper's Scythe*, with the exception of the live animals, she thought with annoyance.

Still, her frustration was overpowered by her intrigue over Cadell. The way he didn't spill the merchants' innocent blood and allowed the ship to continue its sail. The way he took what would please and fill his crewmembers but no more. The way he seemed to genuinely live by the honor he exuded, if there was even honor among pirates.

Perhaps she had become caught up in her path for vengeance, and she had become numb to the bloodshed. Or perhaps she was too paranoid that survivors would report her to the Fae Royal Navy and she'd be caught. She briefly remembered her notions of what her ship would be like. Well, her crew was still one with dignity. They behaved themselves, dressed well, kept themselves clean and refrained from flashing their belongings for all to see.

She pushed the thought from her mind.

They stopped briefly at a port on one of the smaller islands. Anyone she would've wanted to avoid would most likely be at the larger ports or easy to spot from the smaller port and she was in and out.

Once more, the *Gargoyle* set sail and continued south past the island chain. "We return to Aeoumrese!" Darien instructed the crew.

The rest of their voyage remained uneventful. Within a few weeks their island sanctuary was once more in sight.

They set to work, moving their gathered supplies and tools into the heart of the island and making it home. They used some of the resources the island already provided, such as the trees for extra wood. They built huts, food stores, and stores for the drinks to remain in reserve. They also formed and sharpened some of the rock into weapons and training materials.

As they finished each structure, those with magic cast spells so they wouldn't wear away from the weather or from lack of care while they were out at sea. Amethyst intended for the isle to be one where she and her crew could get away and recoup, or train, or simply live, if they wished to escape for a time.

They led the captured livestock through the cave tunnels and released them into the heart of the island. There were few, but a decent variety including sheep, cattle, and even a couple of dogs. The canines would keep the other animals in check. Given the grasses, trees, and spring, the livestock would expand on their own. They would be another source of meat should the crew ever run out of food.

A little more than a year passed and their project was finally complete. Certainly, it had been enough time for Amethyst to return comfortably to the seas. Being so near the sea on the island wasn't quite the same.

As they pushed out to sea for the first time in those months, Amethyst couldn't help the feelings of excitement that flooded her system. She was glad her crew hadn't become bored with so much time on land.

They set sail northwestward toward Tysck. Perhaps they'd encounter one of the pirate captains from her days as a mere crewmember and have a bit of fun. Perhaps they'd sail together for a time, enjoying drinks and feasts. If it was one she didn't like, then she'd have a decent battle.

As they sailed, other thoughts periodically crossed Amethyst's mind, such as those about the captain of the *Reaper's Scythe*. The thoughts persisted no matter how many times she attempted to brush them off.

The sun was reaching its highest point and shone brilliantly on the azure seas. Rather than climbing to upper deck, Amethyst merely flung her blanket on the edge of the main deck and flopped onto her stomach for her daily dose of sun.

She stared into the distance, her mind wandering. She had learned his name only from Mikhail. But who was he really? If she were honest, he'd demanded her thoughts since their parting.

'Bloody hell...'

She needed to remove these thoughts. They were of no use to her. She hadn't sensed any amount of desire from him as she had from others, and he had seemed as though he would remain indifferent if she ever tried to seduce him. She supposed she couldn't know that for certain. Was he merely keeping himself contained? There was no way she could ignore the way he had ignited a fire in her skin. She sipped at a bottle of rum, yet it seemed the rum only brought on the thoughts more – like some sort of tidal wave.

Amethyst growled in frustration and rose to her feet. Forget today. She'd soak in sun some other time. She whipped her blanket into the air and flung it over her shoulder before making her way back to her cabin.

When she emerged, she was dressed in simple pirate's clothes with her hair tied back.

The lookout was shouting the sighting of wreckage in the distance. As they sailed closer, Amethyst saw a scene similar to the one when she had first encountered pirates. Scattered pieces of wood and merchandise floated on the waves and smoke was rising from the burning remains of the ship. Amethyst grasped a spyglass, peering through it. A tattered flag broke free of the splintered mast and drifted down to the water's surface. It had a skull and crossbones; this was the remains of a pirate ship.

Amethyst frowned. "Steer clear of the debris, lads," she ordered, "continue toward Tysck." She wondered what had happened. Had the ship attempted to plunder a merchant vessel and had, instead, been torn apart? Or had it been a fight between pirates to begin with? She considered the fact she had gone after pirates she had felt did not deserve to continue sailing. Could there be another captain doing the same?

Before long, the wreck was behind them and they continued toward clearer skies. Still, Amethyst couldn't push aside her curiosity about what she had witnessed.

Several more weeks passed in which they encountered two more tattered remains of pirate ships. Finally, the lookout was shouting the sight of an intact ship and Amethyst grinned. Perhaps she could find some answers to her mind's questions. She grasped a spyglass, peering through it.

Amethyst felt her brows rise. It was Leo's ship, the *Golden Lion.* Through the spyglass she could see red flags waving about the masts with a crouched lion sewn into the fabric. It was not uncommon for pirates to cross paths now and again without intending to do so. She lowered the glass. So it was true; he had gone and become a captain. She gestured for them to sail toward the other ship.

As they got closer, she thought about how ever since she'd become captain, she'd attempted to keep her distance from the other pirates for the most part unless she was hunting a ship down to send it to Davy Jones' Locker. She wondered just what her reputation was now.

Soon, the two ships were broadside, and a plank was thrown across the gap between them. Leo stood on the edge of the *Golden Lion's* deck, watching her with his laughing brown eyes as the sea wind danced through his curled sandy-colored locks.

"Permission to board?" Amethyst called.

"Blimey! I can't believe it," Leo said with a laugh. "Come on aboard!"

Amethyst moved across the plank and gasped slightly as Leo yanked her into a hug. "Nice to see you again too," she said.

"I heard ye were a cap'n, but ye disappeared," Leo told her with a chuckle.

"Well, I heard ye've been takin' names for yerself," Amethyst retorted.

"Aye," he said.

"Care to show me around?" she asked with a grin.

"Aye," he said again with another chuckle, turning and leading her across his ship.

It was a brig, a square-rigged two-masted ship with two full decks and several other partial decks.

"Care t' join me fer dinner?" Leo asked when they had returned to the main deck.

Amethyst hesitated a moment, debating his intentions, and then nodded. "Aye."

He grinned at her. "Return to me ship in a few hours, then."

She made her way back to the *Gargoyle,* deciding she may as well dress for the occasion. As such, she moved toward her cabin.

Her crewmembers were content to befriend or catch up with those aboard the *Golden Lion* and they shared tales and talked of the latest gossip. At least they could comfortably enjoy themselves and their drink for a bit.

Amethyst spent the next couple of hours preparing herself. She fingered through her collection of dresses and accessories as well. She glanced toward the door when she heard a knock. "Come in," she said, turning her gaze once more toward the mirror on her vanity and applying red lipstick to her lips with a brush. She could see from the reflection that it was Darien. He stepped in and closed the door behind him.

"It's wonderful to see a friend and ally, Darien, isn't it?" Amethyst said, glancing toward him and smiling.

"Aye," he responded, smiling back at her.

"Is everything alright?" she asked.

"Shall I join you this evening?" he asked her.

"Do you wish to?" she asked him.

He shrugged, taking a seat on her bed. "I wish to protect you."

"I'm sure Leo is the same as ever. He wouldn't hurt me or try anything questionable."

"Aye, that rings true for him. I only meant that an alliance hasn't officially been made and you both are two distinct captains."

Amethyst laughed, rising and smoothing out the dress she had chosen. It was a maroon red, the seams designed to hug her figure and the skirt flowing with her movements. "Well I'm sure Leo is the last person I'd need to suspect of betrayal or an attack. I suppose we'll see how the evening goes..." she trailed off, pinning a clip into her dark purple ringlets. "Now, how do I look?" she asked.

Darien sighed, standing once more. "Like you're dressed to kill," he said, smiling at her again.

"Thank you, lovely," Amethyst told him, planting a kiss on his cheek. She smirked at the red print that was left behind. "Ye might want to wipe yer cheek though," she said with another laugh.

With that, she left, making her way back toward Leo's ship.

"Well ye didn't have to get so dressed up for me," Leo said with a chuckle on her arrival, "Though ye do look amazing," he added.

Amethyst smirked. "Well it's not every day you encounter an old friend."

He nodded, and led her to his cabin where a full table was prepared. There were steaming turkey legs at the center surrounded by glistening golden-brown rolls of bread and a variety of colors from the dishes containing fruits and vegetables. Truly a pirate's life was a pleasing one, Amethyst thought.

She took her seat, not failing to note the goblet with rum already poured for her. Perhaps he felt she hadn't changed much either.

"So you became a captain," she said with a grin.

"Aye," he replied, "though hardly a tale as exciting as yours, I'm afraid. I was given this brig at Port Drelle some time back," he added with a laugh. "I suppose being Adair's son gave me an advantage. Tha cap'n was lookin' to sell 'er and when he learned who I was he gave 'er to me at a bargain."

Amethyst smiled. "Well the tale of my capture isn't so much more exciting," she said.

His eyes met hers. "Every lad on tha seas knows it, lass," Leo said. "Tha savvy female pirate captain who can't be fooled or tampered with and takes what she pleases."

"Is that what they're saying about me?" she inquired.

"Aye," he replied.

"Even after I disappeared, as ye pointed out?"

He grinned. "Just because there aren't any new tales as of late don't mean yer reputation would fade. I assure ye they'd still know it had they crossed paths with ye as I did."

She nodded, sipping at her rum. "I should hope so."

"Where have ye been anyway?" he asked her.

"Exploring uncharted seas," she said with a smirk. She didn't elaborate further.

"Well that explains why no one's seen ye. Ye just suddenly decided to return to the world of the living?" he joked.

She shrugged. "Perhaps I missed the taste of battle and other pleasures." She paused. "And what of the world since

I've seen you? We've passed the remains of other pirate ships on our voyage."

He was silent a moment. "There's been more skirmishes between pirates as of late. Rumor says there is some sort of power that can grant humans access to the magic, and some are hunting it along with any pirates that claim to have knowledge of it."

Amethyst nodded, "That explains much," she said. Humans could be greedy and irrational when it came to power. For that matter, so could anyone. The history of the fae, full of conquest, was a prime example.

Amethyst changed the subject, "I'm glad to see you're well, Leo."

"Aye, I've no interest in riskin' me life fer tha mere rumor of power," he said with a shrug.

Amethyst smiled. "I'd hoped to encounter an ally on our journey to Tysck. I was worried I'd see nothing but wreckage, or perhaps even cause wreckage myself."

"Well perhaps fate crossed our paths then, eh?" He moved toward her.

Amethyst was pleased with the idea. He would be a pleasant distraction at least for the night. Yet despite their friendship in times past, he remained just that. A friend to share pleasures but with whom she couldn't imagine herself remaining. She wondered about his feelings toward the matter, but didn't ask. Instead, she simply allowed herself to enjoy their fun.

The next morning, Amethyst returned to her ship after saying her goodbyes to Leo and his crew. She was feeling restless, even after the previous night. They continued sail toward Tysck where she would look for some new crewmembers.

As they sailed, Amethyst continued to grow more restless, though was uncertain of the cause. Darien had several theories. They were possibilities, but regardless it didn't ease her. He thought perhaps she had found peace at the island and that now she was at sea once more it was bringing back her torment at night, or that it was an underlying fear of the Fae Royal Navy showing itself.

She dismissed it. No matter the cause, her nightmares had returned and violently.

Night after night she woke in a cold sweat during the earliest hours of the morning, gasping for air or sometimes crying.

She kept a bottle of rum nearby, always in reach, though its effects only seemed to dull her senses. They failed to banish her torturous dreams.

Amethyst found herself sitting on the upper deck during the night, hoping the wind over her face would calm her and during the day she dosed off during her sunbaths to try to keep up with her lack of sleep. She felt that, during the day, it was easier for Darien to keep an eye and wake her.

Several weeks passed and the coast of Tysck was in sight.

Amethyst debated whether she should make port or not, but finally settled on it. Some of the crewmembers desired to visit a pub and others wanted to trade.

The crew was already in action before they dropped anchor, preparing to make room for new goods and move others ashore for trades.

Amethyst took a small pouch of coins and headed toward the marketplace. Perhaps she should do some shopping and focus on something other than her ship.

She dressed in a simple blouse and flowing skirt, making her way up the dock and toward the shops. There were various shops she expected to see such as those selling clothing, books, various food stalls, and other sorts of supplies. There were also some she didn't expect to see, including one displaying paintings and sculptures.

She stopped in front of a shop showcasing the latest weapons, looking in the window for a moment at the various swords and guns.

Her ear twitched at the sound of a low, smooth voice behind her.

"...we'll take it back to tha ship an' Aurek can decide what to do with it."

She turned, brows furrowing. Where was he?

Moving steadily down the road that divided the market was Cadell. Another man walked beside him, holding something in his hands.

Amethyst's eyes followed them a moment. Confusion filled her mind. Why should she bother? It wasn't as though they had some sort of relationship, as she and Leo did for example. And yet, this man so strongly drew her intrigue. Why had her heart stopped when she'd heard his voice? What had demanded she look to make certain it was him? It was more than mere curiosity.

She breathed out slowly and continued moving past the weapon shop and toward the clothing shop beside it. It was a place where she was less likely to encounter him, she thought. She hadn't even noticed his ship at the docks, although she realized he could have arrived after she did, or that she simply hadn't paid too close attention.

Amethyst didn't stay in the shop long. She selected a pale blue dress with white accents on the sleeves and hem of the skirt and made her way back to her ship.

"We leave as soon as night falls," Amethyst announced to Darien once on board.

"Aye, aye. I'll prepare the ship. You should alert the men at the pubs, though," he told her.

Amethyst huffed. She should've known.

She only nodded, and after dinner, she made her way toward one of the pubs near the beach known as *Siren's Song*.

The pub was bursting with life and banter, shouts heard even before she opened the door. The sun setting over the sea cast brilliant orange and gold light about the main area of the tavern and the barkeep was attempting to push drunken sailors from the bar. The round tables about the room were full of mugs or goblets and several of the men had paid wenches draped over their shoulders or pulling them toward the stairway at the back.

Amethyst felt tempted to get a drink herself, but focused on finding her crewmen. They were seated near the back of the pub in a group and watched the rest of the banter as though it were a theater. She couldn't help smiling to herself slightly.

Such behavior would never be permitted aboard the *Gargoyle*. They may be fearsome to battle and bloodthirsty cutthroats, but they behaved themselves and had to demonstrate manners at the least. Particularly when eating and drinking.

Amethyst approached the group.

"Oy, lads, tha cap'n's arrived," Cyran said with a grin.

"Only to gather ye," she replied. "We'll set sail by nightfall."

"C'mon, then, Cap'n! Share a drink afore we leave, eh?" Artie said, raising a goblet.

She sighed, giving in. "I'll order me a drink, and that's it," she told them. With that, she moved toward the bar, gesturing toward the barkeep. He hurried toward her, smoothing himself and trying to catch his breath.

"A goblet of rum," she told him, and he nodded.

While she waited on her drink, she glanced toward one of the tables near the opposite end of the room. Cadell sat, sipping on a mug and laughing. Several men sat around him now as opposed to how she'd seen him earlier in the day. Was fate toying with her, she wondered?

Amethyst turned her gaze back toward the barkeep as he placed her goblet in front of her. She dropped the pay into his hand and moved toward her crewmembers. They cheered, all raising their drinks as she spoke. "We'll spread tales of tha Gargoyle across all tha seas and be known by all!"

She sat with them as they laughed and discussed some gossip they had heard on the docks, such as which captains were gaining reputation and which had been captured by warships. As they talked, Amethyst glanced toward Cadell's table again, sipping at her rum.

They finished their drinks and rose, making their way out of the pub. Amethyst led them, and she couldn't help wondering what the others in the pub would think watching the whole group of them leaving. Again she glanced toward where she'd spied Cadell before and her breath caught in her throat when his dark gaze met hers. He smiled.

She looked away. What was this? Why was she reacting so?

As soon as she was outside of the pub, she breathed in deeply, letting the scent of the sea calm her nerves.

"Ye alright, Cap'n?" Serafin asked.

"Aye. Return to tha ship ahead of me, lads. I'll meet ye there shortly," she said.

"Aye, aye, Cap'n," they said and continued down the beach to the docks.

Amethyst re-entered the pub, moving boldly toward the table with Cadell and the other men. She wondered if they were some of his crewmen.

They looked up as she approached, glancing between her and Cadell.

Once more those dark eyes met her. Those mischievous black depths that somehow caused her breath to come short and yet brought an addicting sort of calm at the same time.

"We never exchanged names," Amethyst said.

"Aye," he nodded, sipping more of his mug.

"I'm Amethyst, Captain of the Gargoyle," she said.

"A pleasure to meet ye, Amethyst. I be Cadell, Captain of the Reaper's Scythe. And these be me men," he paused as he gestured toward each one, "Arlo, Dale, an' Karl." They each nodded at her with grins, echoing the words of greeting.

She nodded, turning away. "A pleasure also," she replied. "Enjoy yer evening." With that, she made her way out of the pub, catching her breath once more.

Maybe she'd done it just to feel that calm that stowed into her heart every time her eyes met his. It was a welcome relief from the otherwise constant torrent of emotions.

Amethyst quickly returned to the *Gargoyle* and they set sail.

"Darien," Amethyst said the next morning over breakfast, "I saw the Reaper's Scythe's captain last night at the pub."

He quirked a brow, and she knew he was waiting for her to continue.

"He intrigues me. When I'm near him, he gives me an incredible sort of calm, and at the same time my heart goes mad. Yet he seems entirely indifferent to whether or not I exist. And not in an infuriating way. More like... I simply don't draw his attention."

"Hmm," Darien responded softly.

"The nightmares didn't come last night," she said after a moment, his gaze meeting hers.

"Perhaps, Captain, your nightmares fading before was in part from your encounter with him?"

She shrugged. "I don't know, Darien. But I'd rather avoid him for now. I'm not sure how to deal with all of it."

"Aye, aye," Darien said, finishing his meal.

The Pirate's Letter

They set course southward once more. Amethyst continued to grow more restless and, as a result, more irritable. The nightmares returned, depriving her of sleep. Several days passed. Amethyst felt her energy draining slowly with each passing day.

The night was particularly dark. Amethyst jerked upward, her breath coming shakily as she reached a hand to wipe sweat from her face. She looked around, slowly taking in her bed and then her dresser on one wall of her cabin and her vanity on the other. The night was calm, the scent of the sea gently fluttering in through her open windows. She breathed in deeply and closed her eyes, opening them again quickly. The nightmares were getting worse. Why?

The images played back in her mind and she fought to subdue them. In her dreams those who had wronged her tormented her, mercilessly grasping her body again and again. It made her blood boil.

Their faces remained prominent. Some of them had already paid a price. But there were others still out there, like her ex-husband. Even with all she had gained on the seas, she prayed she would never again have to face him.

Amethyst glanced at her fingers, forcing her nails to return to their normal size. Perhaps it was a good thing there weren't any others in the cabin with her. In her sleep, she might have torn them to shreds believing them to be someone else.

Or perhaps it was because she was alone that the nightmares were growing.

Creak!

Amethyst gasped and turned sharply to the door as it opened. Darien. She frowned. "You should knock first," she snapped, turning her gaze toward her sheets once more.

"Are you alright, Captain? You were screaming," he said softly, stepping in and closing the door behind him.

She didn't fail to note he ignored her comment.

"I'm fine," she said stubbornly. "Now leave me alone."

Darien hesitated. Her ear twitched as she heard him take another step toward her. "Perhaps you'd like for me to stay with you?"

She huffed, and then shook her head. "No. I'm not going back to sleep anyway. You're dismissed," she said.

As if to emphasize her point, she put her feet on the floor and flung her sheets aside. "I'm going to get some fresh air." With that, she donned her britches and shirt and left.

Part of her felt bad. She knew Darien was only concerned and meant well, but he couldn't help her with this. She had to deal with it on her own somehow. Amethyst made her way toward the quarterdeck where she could lie on the cool wood and stare at the night sky. Maybe it would bring her some comfort. Before long, the lull of the sea and the wind sweeping over her pulled her to sleep.

She followed this pattern for weeks, growing more and more temperamental with each passing day. She had already had to replace her sheets a handful of times from brutally tearing them apart. Perhaps she was growing restless. Amethyst had attempted for a long time now to refrain from senseless slaughter. After all, if she got what she needed, why not spare the others to further spread tales? The thought pleased her.

But the tension from her worsening dreams was causing her muscles to ache and her instincts for bloodthirst were driving her mad. Fae could replenish their energy by drinking human blood. The lack of sleep in combination with her desire not to sleep urged her to give in to bloodlust in order to regain her strength while avoiding the nightmares.

It was mid-day and she stood over her desk in the cabin on the lower deck. She was poring over maps. They hadn't encountered any ships since their last stop at port, though it was in part because they hadn't particularly gone after any.

That was about to change.

Once more, the faces of those who had yet to pay the price for wrongs against her were floating through her mind. A smirk formed on her lips as her finger traced a dotted pattern on one of the maps. She moved around her desk and onto the deck.

"Set course west. We're going hunting," she announced.

Her gaze met Darien's a moment, before he turned to give the instruction to the crewmembers that hadn't heard it.

Amethyst made her way below deck. Perhaps she shouldn't have been surprised as Darien approached her.

"What are we hunting, Captain?" he asked.

"Blood," she said simply, rummaging through one of the barrels for a piece of fruit.

She didn't have to look at his face to know he was frowning. He breathed in and released his breath slowly. "Isn't there much to lose with a blood trail?" he asked softly after a moment.

She knew what he meant. He recognized the thirst for blood that was gripping her and he knew she wouldn't just stop after tasting it once. It was different than her raids and plunders before. As a crewmember aboard other ships, partaking in the plunders and shedding blood had been a part of life. And as a captain, she had hunted down specific ships based on reputation and worthiness. Even when her fears had gripped her and her raids had less reason, she had still maintained control. Now, not only was she shutting him out, but her body was demanding the energy she could gain from drinking blood.

Did he fear she'd go on a rampage? Did he fear that all they had gained would fall apart and her crew would abandon her?

Amethyst found what she desired and pulled a large grapefruit from the barrel, replacing the lid and turning to lean back against it. She peeled the fruit effortlessly with her nails and bit into it.

"Hmm, perhaps." She said no more, but moved past him.

For the next few weeks, Darien left her alone. She wasn't sure if she was glad of it, or worried by it. She didn't want him deterring her from what she had already decided.

It was nightfall, a particularly dark night at that. The lookout shouted as a schooner came into view on the horizon. Amethyst didn't care if it were pirates or merchants that sailed it. Its fate would be the same. Why? Simply the wrong place and time.

She could feel her excitement growing at the prospect of battle.

Soon, they were approaching the other vessel. Shouts could be heard coming from the schooner. Amethyst paid them no mind. Her crew swept the deck like many ships they had plundered in the past, yet rather than draw her blade or use her daggers as in times past, Amethyst merely resorted to slashing with her nails and dodging the sailors. She maneuvered her way in close until she could sink her fangs into the neck of her unfortunate prey.

With each body that fell, her momentum increased. She swept across the deck like some sort of vampire, draining the blood of one and moving on to the next.

Her lips were stained red and her golden eyes were fierce.

Bodies were strewn across the deck and the men barely had a chance to gather loot before Amethyst was shouting. "Set it aflame and let it drift, lads! Return to tha ship!"

Some of the crewmembers exchanged hesitant glances and then did as they had been told.

Amethyst moved toward the galley below deck. She already knew she wouldn't find restful sleep in her cabin, and the blood she had drank would be enough to sustain her for the time being. She retrieved a bottle of rum and made her way toward the main deck, staring off into the sea.

Days later, another ship was in sight and Amethyst demolished it in similar fashion to the schooner.

As she made her way once more to the *Gargoyle*'s galley afterward, her ear twitched as she recognized the voice of one of the crewmembers and Darien in conversation.

"...are ye sure? The cap'n seems as though she's lost her bloody mind!" the crewmember was insisting in a whispered voice.

Darien breathed out slowly. "She won't harm any of her own. She's restless is all, and while it's senseless to us, her bloodthirst can't be helped. It replenishes her strength and without sleep, she keeps the nightmares at bay."

Amethyst gulped at the bottle of rum she had taken. The crew already knew of her night terrors. If nothing else than from the nights when she'd awoken screaming and had to replace her sheets from either sweat or being torn to shreds.

She only hoped Darien could convince them to still have faith in her. She would never betray her own, as Darien had said.

They turned north after that. Their course would pass the Aeidahs island chain between Orlesce and Vorda Isle.

As they sailed past, she peered through her spyglass toward the shore. Docked at port was a fly-boat, a flat-boated simple ship. This one had two masts, as opposed to one, and was square-rigged. It was one she recognized from her days spent on various other pirate ships.

The captain was in for a taste of her wrath.

Her blood urges surged further as she spied the humans on deck.

"Make port," she instructed the crew.

"Aye, aye," they responded, not daring to defy her in such a state. Perhaps despite Darien's assurances, they remained uncertain. It didn't bode well.

Soon, the *Gargoyle* was pulling into the docks alongside the fly-boat. "Keep the sailors at bay," Amethyst told them.

A group of her crew followed her as they made their way aboard the other ship. Immediately, the pirates there sprang into action, swords beginning to clash.

Amethyst cut down anyone that got in her way as she approached the captain's cabin the same way she had her recent blood rampages. She left their bodies slumped and blood stained her lips.

As soon as she reached the captain's cabin, she kicked the door open forcefully.

Inside, he lay back with three wenches about him.

As soon as the sound of the door being forced open resounded, they looked toward her with a start, the blood draining from the wenches' faces.

How disgusting, Amethyst thought.

The captain glowered. "What is this?" he demanded.

She moved forward with her fangs protruding. "Your fate," were the only words she offered in answer as she gripped him and bit into his neck. She sighed deeply as his life slipped away.

The wenches screamed, scrambling out of the cabin.

Amethyst let them go. As long as they weren't on her ship, she didn't care. Part of her wanted to spill their blood, but she pushed it aside. She returned to the *Gargoyle.* "Draw anchor," she commanded. "Resume course north."

The crew only did as she had ordered, leaving the island chain behind.

Their voyage shifted as they sailed from north to northeast and finally south. Perhaps she should consider a stop at Port Mirka to see if she came across anyone familiar.

Several more weeks passed and their only encounter with other ships was more wreckage and debris. Amethyst was hardly concerned by that point; she saw no point in participating in human battles, and she had been causing wreckage of a different sort.

Amethyst resigned herself to her quarters below deck, hoping to distract herself by poring over maps. At least for the time being, her blood lust seemed to have been satiated. She wondered when it would once more rear its head.

Her mind regained some focus, though the clearer it got, the more the nightmares had grown. Would she never be rid of them?

"Captain, do you have a moment?"

Amethyst looked up, recognizing Darien's voice.

"What is it?" she asked, perhaps more sharply than she intended.

He extended his hand forward, a folded parchment in his grasp.

Amethyst moved around the desk and snatched it, turning and opening the letter and quickly reading over the words.

She frowned, turning once more and handing the letter back to Darien. It was a notice of a pirate meeting. A gathering of all the captains for the purposes of making alliances and uniting against a common enemy. The sea was on the brink of war.

"Where and when did you get that?" she demanded.

"It was on the fly-boat." Darien paused. "I felt it was best to give you some time and to see whether you had gained control of yourself before giving it to you."

"And?" she asked.

"I think we should attend, Amethyst." He addressed her as her companion and not her first mate.

"It has nothing to do with me. I can do well enough on my own. If any of those brutes think they can protect me I'll be more than happy to prove them wrong. And I wouldn't trust any of them as far as the horizon," she retorted.

"It would do us some good to see what we're up against and perhaps you might find something that will ease the nightmares," Darien said softly.

She sighed and moved away from him toward the window. She imagined Darien was upset that thus far she had mostly shut him out and he had not been able to help with her nightmares, or her unsettled temperament. Perhaps she could go – even just to put his mind at ease.

"Very well. I will trust you, Darien," she said. "Set course for Orlesce."

He nodded and left.

She glanced outward once more and sucked in her breath as an unexpected though flickered across her mind. Would Cadell be there?

She brushed it aside. What was she thinking? Among the many other captains, Cadell was one of the few who hadn't made advances or specifically expressed interest in her, though she had noted the way she was more at ease when they crossed paths.

She pushed it away from her mind.

Amethyst should mentally prepare herself for dealing with the rest of the pirate dogs that would be there.

Their voyage to Port Drelle, Orlesce, was relatively uneventful. The seas remained calm. She saw other ships in the distance, though assumed many of them were also going to the pirate meeting. She had no interest in interacting with any of them, regardless of if she recognized them or not.

Amethyst resigned herself to lying on her deck to sunbathe and drinking rum, which at least calmed her nerves and relaxed her muscles from her irritation and her lack of sleep.

After several weeks of travel they were nearing Orlesce.

As they were drawing near to the coast, Amethyst looked skyward. Dark clouds billowed and droplets of rain were beginning to fall. For a moment, she debated skipping the meeting. But she had already promised Darien. It was too late to turn back now, and she could only imagine what the other captains would say if she didn't show at this point. She determined she would go in style and demonstrate her dignity. She was better than the whole lot of them, in her mind.

Amethyst had donned her favorite long dark cloak and large scarlet captain's hat. She wore a pale top that stopped just above her midriff and showed off her tanned hardened stomach. Perhaps they'd see she was no mere dainty lass. She had slipped on simple brown pants which she tucked into tall leather boots.

They pulled into the harbor and dropped anchor. The storm was rising and the clouds released their downfall.

Amethyst and Darien were almost immediately soaked through as soon as they stepped foot on the docks.

"Let's get this over with," Amethyst said.

Darien nodded and followed her ashore.

Amethyst glanced around only briefly. The other ships were a mere shadow in the downpour.

They made their way up the docks which opened to a large marketplace. The streets were made of old cobblestone. Amethyst and Darien moved past aged buildings, their footfalls inaudible. It seemed everyone had abandoned the streets for the coming storm.

At last they approached a well-known pub – infamous for its use by pirates. *Skull's Mark.*

Skull's Mark was spacious with several long oval tables in the main room and a stairway along the back wall. The main room was dimly lit from the sunlight filtering in through the windows near the entrance. Beyond the bar were three doors, one of which led to the kitchen. The other two doors hid large rooms featuring long tables at their centers with numerous wooden chairs. The rooms had high ceilings and were dimly lit by lanterns at all times since there weren't any windows. They were used for meetings between pirate captains and sometimes merchants wishing to trade with pirates.

Amethyst and Darien moved toward the large doors and the one they opened creaked as it swung. All eyes turned to them and watched as they crossed the room. Brutes. The lot of them. She'd only come at Darien's request. But she was here now. *'Let the meeting begin...'* she thought.

Glossary

The fae language was invented by myself, K. L. Dimago for the world of Aseath. As such, I've included a glossary of terms for your convenience in translating.

While there are only a few phrases used in *Amethyst: Rise to Piracy,* the fae language is expanded and explored throughout the series. Enjoy!

Mah sieei ueltho – her royal maiden

Iist – lord

Iieta – lady

About the Author

K.L. Dimago is a fantasy author of all kinds. Her passion for writing began at a young age and continued throughout her childhood and into her adult life. She was first inspired by authors Tamora Pierce, C.S. Lewis, and Walter Farley, among others.

She published her first novel in 2015 and went on to publish several more works in the following years including two series, which are still continuing to grow, and a short story published as part of an anthology. She went on to partner with Mostly Imagination to create a new kind of novel experience for readers and continues to pen new ideas regularly. Her favorite thing is to be sitting with a warm cup of coffee or tea and writing.

K.L. Dimago attended Texas Tech University for a B.A. in English and now lives in the heart of Texas with her husband and children. She is always welcome to questions and to connecting with new people, especially fellow writers and readers.

To learn more about Dimago, any of her work or upcoming books, visit kldimago.com.

More by This Author

The Amethyst Saga and Related:

Darien's Tale

Ametrine: Twists of Fate

Iolite: A New Era

Tourmaline: The Pirate's Daughter

The Nefeiah Chronicles:

The City That Fell

The Light That Pierces

The King Who Unites

Aeros: Verses of Oceans:

Verse I: Topaz

Verse II – Coming Soon

Short Stories & Anthologies:

Imprisoned Hearts – Part of Bewitched Love by Kellan Publishing

Thank You!

Thanks so much for reading! I truly hope you loved this first book in *The Amethyst Saga* and that you'll continue Amethyst's journey with me in the next book.

Would you take thirty seconds and leave your honest review on the book page? Even if it's just a sentence! I would *so* appreciate your feedback.

Follow the link below, click on 'Write a Customer Review' near the bottom, and let me know your thoughts:

https://www.amazon.com/dp/B09NXJ7FFC

Thank you more times than I can put on this page!

www.ingramcontent.com/pod-product-compliance
Lightning Source LLC
Chambersburg PA
CBHW021310190726

48288CB00003B/774